The
ERECTION

– Jack Barratt –

Published by Jack Barratt
Publishing partner: Paragon Publishing, Rothersthorpe
First published 2014
© Jack Barratt 2014
All characters and stories created by Jack Barratt

ISBN 978-1-78222-999-5

Book design, layout and production management by Into Print
www.intoprint.net

Printed and bound in UK and USA by Lightning Source

For all the time I wasted not writing my books.
For all the excuses I used not to put pen to paper.
And why I am finally writing them now because
my life has changed forever.

JB

FORTHCOMING TITLES:

The Love Machine
Rise of the Love Machines

www.theerection.co.uk
Email: jackbarratt@outlook.com

LEIGH

My name is Leigh Stratton. I am a senior nurse working in a UK hospital. My story is loosely based on fact and the names that have been used have been changed for obvious reasons.

Within a hospital environment we see some very strange and unusual things; a good deal of what we see is based on people's sexual habits and the end result of some of these acts.

For example, I have seen couples stuck together by a force of vacuum after having had sex in the water, men and women with various food types stuck in their body and many minor and sometimes major injuries after various sex acts going wrong; the worst was a death after hanging, trying to reach a higher sexual stimulation.

Some of these things are funny and some tragically are not.

This story is about one of the longer term patients who was admitted to my hospital.

Found unconscious and left for dead, a single guy – badly injured and obviously someone who had been robbed – was admitted to the hospital after having been found in a street. He was badly bruised, with head injuries and bleeding, and obviously unconscious but still alive. He was taken to the Accident and Emergency department where he was assessed and then admitted into the intensive care unit.

Although it was unclear what had happened, it was quite obvious that this guy was going to be a guest of St Mary's for quite some time. I heard about this man from a friend of mine, her name is Sue Parker and she is the ICU sister in charge.

We had been friends for years from school through to nursing training and beyond, in fact all told we had been pals for more than 22 years, a record by many standards I guess. Anyway, I worked in the maternity department and as a midwife I had seen many births and deaths, but Sue, she saw a different side of nursing and although our jobs were similar, they were very different in many ways.

Quite often we would meet and talk and always the hospital would come into our conversation; it was, after all, a big part of our lives. Sue was recently divorced from Steve which was all amicable, well sort of – no kids, so a clean break. The reason for separating was the fact that they had just grown apart and they wanted different things. In the end, they fought over the dog and the cat. In the end, she got Bimbo the cat and Steve got Zac the Alsatian and that was that as they say.

One night Sue came round for a coffee after work and we chatted as usual. We talked and, as per the norm, the conversation got around to work.

"We had a strange patient admitted last week," said Sue. "It was a guy who had been found unconscious in the street, he was brought to the ICU and there he still is at the moment."

"What is strange about that?" I asked.

"Well," said Sue, " the guy in question has had an erection from the first night he came in and it hasn't gone down since, so what do you think of that Leigh my girl?"

I was a bit taken aback but I took it in my usual stride. My first response was, "Is he good looking?"

"Yes, he is a bit, not a model or anything but he does have a certain rugged charm. I have to say though, for the first few days he looked bad but it is only now he is starting to show signs of what looks like he would appear to be in his former life. The bruising is going down and his cuts are starting to heal, it's the trauma that hasn't started to heal yet and I feel it could be a long haul."

We had sort of moved away from this patient as a topic of conversation when I suddenly asked:

"How big is it?"

"How big is what?" said Sue.

"The *erection*," I said. "The guy's erection, how big is it?"

She looked and laughed and said, "It's a whopper!"

We both laughed out loud, then I said, "Define whopper."

Sue said, "Imagine a large banana, but I mean *large*, and it will give you some idea of the size of the problem."

What else could you say?

We chatted for a while longer, the night got late and Sue went home. I had a quick tidy round, locked all the doors and went to bed. I was very tired and needed to sleep but no sooner had my head hit the pillow than I woke up eyes wide open and all I could think about was this guy and the huge erection that Sue had talked about.

Nevertheless, all night long I slept soundly but when I woke up one thing dominated my thoughts, this guy's erection and had I been dreaming or had Sue really said what I thought she'd said to me?

I had to see it, if for no other reason than to satisfy my curiosity, so next day I called Sue and asked if I could come up to the ICU and see it for myself. Of course she agreed and I arranged to be there for 2.30pm.

As I went into the ICU it was a very strange feeling and I was very curious and very excited at the same time. I didn't know what to expect so I just walked onto the ward and looked for Sue. I could see her talking to another nurse, a girl I also knew but only slightly. Sue saw me and motioned me over and off I went. We walked into a side ward, I stood behind Sue and just looked at him. The first thing I saw was a huge bulge in the centre of the bedclothes and it was obvious what it was.

"Do you want to see underneath?" asked Sue.

I nodded and she went to the bed and lifted the sheets up. Sure enough, there it was – a slightly tanned but very straight erect penis, and it was, as Sue had said, 'a whopper'; I reckon about ten inches.

I had never seen one this big before and it did excite me, the thought of what was in front of me, and I suspect Sue had twinges to. We both just stood and looked and then decency got the better of us and we covered him over again. I know nurses have a bad reputation but we are only human and we intended no harm, it was just an unusual situation and that was that.

We did a quick check on him. He was breathing on his own now and all that remained was the IV drip, other than that he seemed relatively stable and comfortable. His eyes were closed to the world and as we spoke, they did not flicker in the slightest.

Up to this point, no one had come forward to claim this guy and we didn't know where he lived or where he came from, or even if he had family. All they had found originally was an empty leather wallet.

A few days went by and I called into ICU just to see Sue and to see how her patient was doing. I somehow felt the need to go and see him and offer what support I could, all his medical needs were being met and to be honest it wasn't my field of expertise. Nor did I have any interest in intensive care, but I *did* have the need to go and see him and the erection, the fact that it still hadn't gone down and, more to the point, no one knew what to do about it. This situation was no longer embarrassing. It had become the norm to walk into the side ward and see the bed sheets raised in the middle, everyone knew what it was and the nursing staff accepted it.

I had pondered on a number of occasions why this guy could have and indeed *did* have an erection, and how to get rid of it. There was no obvious sexual reason for it, and by that I mean there were no naked women around to excite him. It just seemed a bit strange, maybe not *strange,* but highly unusual.

I had finished shift mid-afternoon and on my way home in the car I suddenly thought of a way to get this guy's erection to go down. What if I were to masturbate it for him, surely that would sort the problem out and maybe give him a bit of peace and dignity back? I waited until I got home and I called Sue. I told her what I had been thinking and at first she was deathly quiet.

"Do you really mean to say that you would do that to a stranger?"

"But he's not a stranger, I've been seeing him for four weeks and I know him well."

We talked a while longer and I asked Sue if she would help me to help him. After a brief pause she said she would assist and we agreed the sooner the better would be the way forward. It would be tomorrow night and we both discussed our plans.

The next day I was to work night shift so it would be easy to slip away and go to intensive care and carry out my plan. Sue was also on nights, so we were in a good position to work this situation out together.

I had a break about 10.30pm when I told the girls in maternity I would be upstairs if they needed me, and off I went. I arrived at the ICU and there were two nurses present. Kath was one, I knew her, and of course Sue. I walked in and nodded to Kath and, as I headed to this guy's side ward, Sue followed. I asked Sue about Kath and she said, "Kath knows and she is going to keep an eye out and stay out of the way."

We both walked into the side ward and as I approached the doorway all was still and quiet; the lights were low and the room was warm.

I paused briefly then pulled the sheets back and there it was, as large as life. It was an impressive sight. His erection was laid straight and immense, it had a large girth and it was very tight and very big indeed. The erect penis was lying on his tummy and as I watched it I could see the vein throb. My heart was pounding. I thought for a moment that this may be wrong and then I thought of why I was doing this and that made it feel right, I had to go on.

I turned to look at Sue and she said, "I have to go, I feel this is a personal thing and the world and his brother don't need to see it."

I smiled gently at her and she left. It was just me and this stranger. I had brought with me a small pot of massage oil in case his skin was dry; I took out the oil and started to apply it gently. I took hold of the shaft and it was hard and solid. My heart was in my mouth. I applied the oil the length of the whole erection and then I pulled the foreskin back and covered the end of his penis in scented oil too. As I slid my hand back and forth I could see the erect penis shine and glisten in the dim light of the room – it was amazing. I looked at this guy's face as I took a firm grip of his erection and I started to pull my hand up and down his manhood. At first I moved slowly and then I gradually began to get quicker and quicker,

I watched him and his expression did not change. As I masturbated him I could feel his penis throb and I could see his testicles move and something was definitely happening. I suddenly stopped. What if he comes and it goes everywhere? I looked around and I saw a small disposable bag on the side of his bedside unit. I quickly put it over his erection and I continued to bring him off. By now I was going quickly and I watched his testicles move as I felt the sperm coming up the shaft. I pulled my hand as fast as I could and there it came, gushing forward like a fountain, it seemed like there were gallons of the stuff, thick and white and creamy and very hot. I moved my hand up and down the shaft to help clear the sperm from within. I took off the bag and wrapped it in tissue and then I put it in my pocket. I got some cleansing tissues and wiped the full penis down, pulled the foreskin back over the end and made sure there was no evidence or telltale signs.

By chance I turned to the door and both Sue and Kath were there watching. They did nothing and I said nothing, when suddenly Sue pointed to this guy laid in the hospital bed and he looked peaceful; after he had come the erection had lain down and relaxed, so I had *thought*. However, to my surprise and to my shock, it was starting to grow again. Within a few moments it had straightened back up again in defiance of the act we had just committed.

This huge cock was back to where we had started: erect, solid and pulsing once again as if nothing had happened.

I covered him over, I kissed him on the cheek and I left his room. I was shaking with all of the emotion of the last few minutes. The girls had only watched briefly, but they made no comment and nor did I. I went back downstairs to maternity and completed my night shift, but what a night.

I had thought I had found a solution to this poor guy's problem and the very fact that I had made him come seemed to me to be very straightforward. However, it had created another problem – and that problem was *me*.

The first time Sue had spoken about her patient I had felt a little curious. However, after I had met him I felt drawn to him, even attracted in a strange detached way. I felt guilt too, mainly because he could have a family and they could be worried about him, or that he could in some subconscious way be missing them, and that made it even worse. I pondered long and hard all that had happened, but what was worse was the fact that I felt more was going to happen. I began to feel strange desires; this situation had raised feelings in me that I had not felt for a long time. What was I going to do?

Sue and I met very often, either at work or at our homes, and more and more I felt myself talking about *him*. I had on many occasions found myself going up to the ICU and standing at the door just looking at him, and on a few occasions I had gone inside and held his hand or stroked his forehead and sadly, I have to say, I had put my hand under the sheets and had held that powerful erect penis.

Each time I did this I felt the heat and the pulsing and it felt like it was a separate entity alive and breathing, and this thing in my hand called to me. It made me ache, God did it make me ache!

For some time now I had felt the maternal instinct, the need of a woman to have a child, although the urge was strong, the need for a husband was not. I had seen how Sue's life had been and it was a situation I felt I did not want to get into. Life with children would be what I wanted, but the burden of a husband was a thing I could do without.

I was talking to Sue not long after I made *him* come, when we fell on the need to call this guy by a name something other than *him*, or the patient or even 'that guy'. Sue said one of the male orderlies had said to her "How is Hugh today?" and Sue had responded "Who is Hugh?" "Hugh G," said the orderly. Sue replied again, "Hugh G who?" The orderly said, "Hugh- G- Erection" and everyone had started to laugh at the HUGE ERECTION. Sue had been a little angry at being the butt of someone's humour and also at the implications and lack of compassion for the guy who was in a hospital bed and in a very serious situation.

After Sue had explained what had taken place, I said to her, "Let's call him Hugh. It's not a bad name and it does bring a sense of civility to the poor guy's predicament and if nothing else, I think it suits him and I like it."

Sue pondered for a moment and said, "Yes, I agree. Let's call him Hugh." At that point we both smiled and went to see Hugh to tell him the news.

It may sound strange to say but we both felt it was important to talk to Hugh, as he was now to be known, and to tell him things as if he could hear and communicate with us. Any form of stimulation is very important for any coma patient's recovery and because of the obvious trauma Hugh had suffered, it was a vital part of his healing progress that we offer this therapy of at least speaking to him in the hope he could or indeed would respond back in some way: a focus we had to keep in our minds.

Hugh was released out of the intensive care unit and he was a more stable patient apart from the fact he was in a deep coma. His heart rate was always slightly elevated because of his erection. He didn't seem affected by it, but it was clear it could not and should not remain erect forever.

Apart from Hugh's nurses, I was his only visitor. By now I was there every day and it became part of my life. I felt responsible for his well-being and I felt he needed someone to care, other than those doing so in a professional capacity; in short, he needed a friend and that friend was me. I saw myself as a self-appointed saviour. I firmly believed that if anyone was to wake him, it would be *me*.

Around this time the thought of children seemed to occupy my thoughts a great deal, that and Hugh of course. The trouble was that, as a midwife, I saw babies on a daily basis and it gradually made me feel worse than it ever had before, so much so in fact that I began to hate going to work just because I knew I would have to deal with pregnant women and newborn babies. It got to the stage it made me sick; the only saving grace was I would see Hugh and that made all the difference to me.

While sat at home one Thursday evening I was having a quiet moment and thinking about babies and the thought of a husband when I had an insane but erotic thought. What if I were to make love to Hugh and get pregnant by him? I hadn't used contraception for a long time and there was no reason to suppose it wouldn't work, after all, who would it affect? The more I thought about it the more I seized on the idea. After a while I was convinced that was what I was going to do – Hugh was to be mine and I wanted his baby.

I went to bed and in the cold light of the next day once again I felt guilty about my thoughts, but this time I quickly wiped them away because the feelings I had gone through the night before were still in me and by now I really did want to make love with him; to me it would be the perfect situation – the passion, the child and no commitment. It was a win on win situation. At this point I was totally convinced this is what I wanted and no one and nothing was to get in my way.

I had decided to tell no one, not even Sue with all her good intentions. I felt it would be impossible to get her involved; it would certainly compromise her position in the hospital and I felt would change our relationship as well. I did not want that to happen, so from that moment on I was on my own.

The plan was made for the following week. I was on night shift which meant the hospital would be quiet and there would be less chance of being caught, so next Tuesday it was to be. I counted down each day. As the moment drew near, and with each day passing, the anticipation got worse and the erotic notions got stronger. I wanted to mount him like a woman possessed. What a dirty bitch I felt, but I loved every thought I had. This was going to be some moment in my life and I was going to enjoy every second of the encounter.

THE FIRST TIME

I left home at my usual time but I seemed to fly on the way to work; where my journey was boring and mundane, that was not the case tonight. I was on wings and going like a bat out of hell, I could even hear Meatloaf singing the song in my head. Before I left home I had spent extra time getting ready as if I was going out on a date. Crazy I know, but that's how it felt.

When I got to the hospital I bounced up the steps and I had to physically calm myself down, I was on a natural high it was fantastic. I was on a 10 o'clock start; we had the usual handover and then I did my duties as expected, trying hard not to think of what I was about to do. I had to choose my time very carefully and not change too much from my usual routine. Everybody knew I visited Hugh, so that was not going to be an issue, but what might be a problem was the time it would take me, I did not want to rush what I was about to do so time was of the essence.

I decided to take a break at 2.30am, this would be the quietest time. So that was it. I watched the clock and as the moment approached I calmly said, "I'm on a break girls, see you later." A wave of hands and I was on my way.

I got onto Hugh's ward and it was very quiet. Karen was on duty and I approached her. She smiled and said, "Going to see Hughie?" I replied, "Yes". She just motioned for me to go in and away I went.

I opened the door to Hugh's side ward and I was shaking. I looked at him and I almost could not breathe, the anticipation was electric. I stood for a moment and watched him. Strange as it seems, I had never heard this man speak and I had never seen him open his eyes, yet I was about to make love to a stranger and yet he was not a stranger, such a mixture of emotions, all of which fired me up even more. I was burning with a desire I had never felt in my life before.

I approached him and ran my hand over the top of the sheets. I felt all of the contours of his body and, of course, his erection.

My heart was pounding and I ached to get into bed with him. I had gone to work wearing no pants, I needed no obstacles or impediments. I had also brought with me a scented oil to lubricate myself, but I didn't need it. My feminine area was flowing and the juices were rich and warm. I looked outside the door, Karen was sat at her station and all was quiet.

I went back to the bedside and pulled back the sheets. Hugh's erection lay back slightly, facing up towards his head, it was pulsing and strong and huge. I took hold of it in my hand as I had done before when I made him come and I was excited. My body was pounding and I wanted him.

I put my fingers between my legs and moistened them with my juices and then gently pulled his foreskin back and rubbed my wet fingers all over the end of his penis; it shone in the dim light and looked superb. I leaned forward and, with the skin pulled back hard making the end bulge with a strong purple colour surrounding the entire head of his cock, I put the full head of his erection in my mouth.

I sucked and licked and I tasted all of the pleasure of that moment, I looked at him as my head went up and down and I watched to see if he responded, but he did not.

I spent several minutes enjoying his erection deep inside my mouth when I felt it was time to mount him. I stood up and climbed onto the bed. I eased myself above him and guided his erection into position below me and I slid down onto him. At first I eased him into me a little way; I did not want to hurt him or me. This was a huge tool and had to be treated with respect. I then gradually pushed down hard. It was clear to me from the start that I couldn't take it all the way; never before had I had a man this big inside of me. As I sat astride him I could feel his pounding penis erect and straight and very hot inside of me. I just sat there and enjoyed the moment.

As I paused I felt the sensation that only a woman can feel and I knew it was time to ride him, and ride him I did. Slowly but surely I moved up and down the shaft of his cock and as I did I tingled and burned for the feeling of ecstasy. For several minutes I pounded his body tightly squeezing my vaginal muscles to feel the full strength of his rod.

As I had expected, I started to feel an orgasm strong and powerful and deep within. I started to shake as within my body I felt a feeling that I had never felt before. *Jesus Christ*, with an explosion of passion there it was, an orgasm of epic proportion; I thought I was going to pass out. The moment lingered and, as I started to settle down, something else began to surge in me again, a second or maybe a third orgasm. Shit, it was a multiple orgasm, something I had never felt before.

I started to pound Hugh up and down, harder and harder and on the final last thrust down onto him I took the full length of his cock deep into me and at that moment I exploded into the biggest climax my body had ever experienced. "Fuck, Fuck, Fuck!" I cried as I slumped down onto him, exhausted but satisfied. I had done it.

I sat up. I could feel that Hugh's erection had gone down; I lifted myself up and got off the bed. I cleaned him with wipes and myself also. As I was about to cover him over I looked at his face and there was no expression and as I pulled up the sheets to cover him I watched his penis grow back to full size once again. I was amazed.

As I turned to walk out I looked towards the door to find Karen looking straight back at me. My first thought was 'my job has just been lost', then I thought of Hugh and what I had done to him and then I thought of Karen and what she was going to do.

I took one last look at Hugh and thought it might be my last, then I moved towards the door and prepared myself for what was about to happen. I went through the door and stood and looked at Karen. As I did so I sensed something other than I had anticipated.

Her first words were: "That was the most erotic thing I have ever seen in my life. I have watched porn movies at home but I have never seen anything like that, you were amazing girl." I was both shocked and pleased and then flattered. Karen said, "You could make a living doing that if you ever got sick of nursing."

I smiled at her and then put my head down. Embarrassment hit me. I was not a public person and my sex life, in whatever form it takes, has to be hidden from the world.

Karen looked at me, put her hand on my shoulder and said, "Your secret is safe with me Leigh, I won't tell anyone, not even Sue. I know you feel something special for Hugh and I know it's easy to fall for a patient, but I think this is different for you and it is for you to sort out and deal with in your own way. Time will help you to deal with things, but be assured, my word is my bond. Only you, me and Hugh will know about this."

As I looked at her I had tears in my eyes. I put my arms around her and thanked her, and as I turned to walk away she said, "Come back anytime. If it helps I will give you my shift rota, that way you will know when it is safe." I smiled and nodded in acknowledgement and also with gratitude. By the way, she said, "Sorry for watching but it was a hell of a show." I walked out of the ward and back to work in maternity.

I got back onto the ward a little late and the girls just looked at me. They could see I was upset and they all assumed it was about Hugh and nothing else, a gentle pat on the back in a supportive way and that was that. I completed my shift, but as the night went on my only thought was Hugh and our encounter. I did not know what the hell to do but from that moment on whatever choices I made I had to plan with a bit more care. That last situation could have been the ruin of me and I did not want to ever put myself in that position again.

*

A few days later I arrived at work. Everything was calm and all was well. I had completed the usual handover when I found an envelope at the nurses' station and it had my name on it. I opened it and inside was the rota sheet Karen had promised. It gave me the shift pattern for the next three weeks. She had also put her mobile phone number on there 'just if you need me' it said. She had been true to her word and it made me feel a lot more settled inside. It also gave me a huge feeling of relief – people can say one thing and do something else, so her action had eased those fears.

She was on night shift in two days' time. I, however, was not. I quickly checked our rota system to see who would be on nights in maternity that night and asked for a swap.

I approached Helen, the girl who would be on the same shift as Karen, and asked if she would like to swap shifts. She said yes straight away, as I knew she would, no one liked nights, so that was the easy bit done. I gave Karen a call and said thanks and I also said, "See you on Wednesday night if that's OK."

"No problems," she said. "See you then."

I put the phone down and I felt great. I really felt happy, something sadly I had not felt for a long time; this was the start of something good!

Two nights later at 2.30 in the morning I went to see Hugh. I walked onto the ward and looked at Karen, I smiled at her and she smiled back. She then put her head down and continued to read her book. We didn't say a word.

I went to Hugh. I took off my nurse's uniform and stood before him naked and bare, I needed to do this as a gesture to him. Although he did not see, I felt it important that I did this.

I have a good figure, so I am told. I am tanned and firm and I do get the occasional whistle from the boys, even the younger ones, but this was for Hugh and for me this was an important moment and I was making a powerful statement. I stood before him and my body shook. I needed him, but this time I would make love to him and I would be part of him.

I pulled back the sheets and there was my prize, it was the erection of dreams and I was going to mount him like a beast impaled on a spike. I pulled back the foreskin and licked and sucked the huge purple end of his throbbing cock. I rammed that enormous rod into my throat almost stopping me breathe. I felt like Linda Lovelace in deep throat. I withdrew the erect penis from my mouth, I climbed above him and paused for a second, then I took the cock in hand, opened the lips of my vagina and impaled myself on him. Within 30 seconds I came and then I came again and again this cock was going to be the death of me. I thrust him up and down, up and down and I came again. Within the span of about eight minutes the man had me exhausted and all he had done was lie there. Imagine what he could do to me if he was awake. With that thought I thrust again and one more orgasm for the road and I was fucked to the point of exhaustion.

I got ready and went to leave the room with a gentle kiss on Hugh's cheek, I left him and I walked past Karen. She didn't even look up this time; I quietly went back to work to finish my night shift, tired but satisfied.

*

My visits to see Hugh were regular and part of my normal routine. No one was bothered in the least about my turning up unannounced, it was just as if I was a relative visiting a sick patient, all very normal and uncomplicated. Throughout the hospital Hugh had become a joke, although it is sad to say the constant erection had been used for many jokes and it made me and a few other medical staff a little sad. Yes, it was curious, but also it was obviously not a normal situation.

I was in the hospital one day when Sue came looking for me, she seemed a little excited. She came over to me and said, "Doctor Reece thinks he knows what is wrong with Hugh."

"Tell me more!" I said.

"Dr Reece believes it is A.G.A."

"What is that?" I asked.

"It is Acute Genital Arousal syndrome. It basically means that he has a hard-on most of the time.

I listened and then said to Sue, "Yes, but he has a hard-on *all* of the time."

"Reece believes it is the coma that may be causing the problem. Usually this syndrome is controlled with drugs or therapy or sometimes just left alone as it does not seem to affect the patient, it just means he is horny most of the time. Strangely enough this syndrome can affect both men and women, so watch out Leigh, it may be contagious."

We both laughed. "I guess most men would like this syndrome too." We laughed again and I thanked Sue for letting me know what had been discussed. I now had an idea what Hugh's problem was and it helped to understand a little more about what was affecting him.

Hugh had been in the hospital about ten weeks now and for six of those weeks I had been having sex and making love to him, and to me this was now a normal event too.

I woke up one morning and felt very sick, so much so that I could not go to work. I was sick several times and for me this is not a normal thing, I am usually fit healthy and very seldom am I ill for any reason. The sickness passed and I assumed it was something that I had eaten, although I could not for the life of me think what it might have been.

I got up for work the next morning, got dressed and set off as usual when on the way in I felt this sickness again and I felt awful. I walked into the maternity unit and one of the girls saw me and said, "Leigh you look terrible!" That made me feel even worse and off to the toilet I went to be sick once again.

After 10 or 15 minutes I returned to the ward to start work when a colleague, Kathy, walked over to me and said something very strange: "Are you pregnant?"

This question stopped me in my tracks. The thought had never occurred to me, but I suddenly realised that I could be having a baby and the only reason was HUGH!

I was suddenly hit with a mass of emotions and I was in a real state of shock. My condition must have been visible to all around me as I began to feel faint. The girls quickly helped me to a chair and I was offered a glass of water. For a few moments I sat still, then I said, "I need to go home now please."

Sally, one of the nurses, called over a porter to drive me home in my car, the hospital would send a taxi to pick him up, I heard someone say.

Before long I was in the car and the next thing, I was at home. Alex the porter helped me into the house and sat me down. "Is there anything you need?" I politely said no, and once he was sure I was OK he went outside to wait for the taxi to take him back to work.

It had never dawned on me that I was pregnant. It had taken a midwife at work to see what I had not, and it had taken her just seconds to diagnose. I felt bloody stupid; I also knew I needed a pregnancy test ASAP.

I realised that I had been naïve. I reflected on all that I had done and I was both shocked and ashamed of myself; with all my experience I had both diminished my position and abused a patient that I had befriended. I was lost in a storm of confusion. I was desperately alone in all that I had done and all the issues that I had caused. I was afraid.

If I was pregnant and the test was positive it was going to have a massive change on my life forever.

The next day after I felt a little better, I went to the local chemist and bought a pregnancy test kit. I went back home and took the test. Within half an hour I knew the answer was positive and I was having a baby. It was official, I was having Hugh's baby.

What the hell had I done? I was the only one to blame and it felt wrong, or was it? I am full of confusion but yet I still feel good inside. What the hell was going on with me? I am a single woman with a good career and I have gotten myself pregnant to a man in a coma in the hospital where I work and I still feel OK with things. I must push on with my plan and my life, I *will* have this baby and I *will* be OK. If and when the time comes I will deal with any problems that have come from my relationship with Hugh and I *will* be able to cope with the fallout.

I have decided to take a few days off work to sort out things in my mind, at least it will help me to get my head around things and decide which is the best way to move forward. I think I need to tell Sue. She needs to know and to be honest I want her support at this time, she is my best friend and I need a good friend right now.

I decided to call her and invite her round for a glass of wine that night, I phoned her and asked her to come over. Of course she agreed and the time was set for seven that night.

As usual she was prompt and once she came in and settled down I knew that she knew that there was something wrong. I said to her, "Brace yourself, I have some news that might shock you."

Sue put down her glass of red wine and sat up in the armchair. "Go on then," she said, "spill the beans. What's wrong?"

"I'm pregnant." There, I'd said it.

Sue looked on in a state of shock. "Who is the father?" said Sue.

"Is he a one night stand or have you been seeing someone on the quiet?"

"It's Hugh," I said. "It's Hugh."

I burst into tears and my emotions were out of control, I just let it all come flooding out into the open.

Sue's jaw hit the floor. "I don't believe it, how can it be Hugh?"

"It must be obvious to you," I said. "I didn't use protection and I have been having regular sex with him. "In fact I planned it and I hoped it would happen, but to be honest I had forgotten about it because nothing had happened. It has caught me unawares. It was only when I started to get sick in the morning that I realised and when I went to work one morning the girls spotted it straight away, it was only me that couldn't see it and I felt bloody stupid, but that's just the way it is. What do you think Sue, have I done wrong, do you hate me?"

"Of course I don't hate you, I am having difficulty understanding what you have done, but you obviously have your own reasons or needs to do this but no matter what, we're still friends and I'm here for you. If you need it and I can help you it will be done. I promise Leigh, I am always your friend."

We had a little more wine, we chatted and we laughed and didn't talk much about my pregnancy or the problems that were going to come from it, but what the hell, tonight I relax and have a good time with my best friend and I did enjoy myself even though it was short lived.

It was quite clear I needed to make changes in my life and indeed my routine things would need to reflect that I was now having a baby. People at work were going to ask questions and I can deal with that. I had also agreed with Sue to keep things under wraps until I could create a good cover story to divert any attention away from my intimacy with Hugh. I need to make sure everything is believable and that I can continue to work for as long as I can without any more difficulties in my life.

I returned to work and the questions came flooding forward. In the end I said it was an old flame that had come back into my life, we had a fling and I ended up pregnant. He has gone his way and I have continued on my path with an amicable agreement being reached – it was as simple as that. The story held and the questions stopped, and that seemed to be that.

I continued to work and, as per my usual rota at work, I was taking my turn in the fertility clinic. This was a sad place to be; there were so many women and men hoping for children and for one reason or another it was difficult if not impossible for some of them to conceive naturally or otherwise. You do see the same faces and it is inevitable that you become friends with the people that you see.

It happened that I had got close to a girl called Julia. For two years she and her husband had tried for children and it had not happened for them.

JULIA

On my second day of rotation in the clinic Julia arrived for further examinations and tests to see what could be done to help her. As usual, once she was booked in we sat and talked and she confided in me it was clear that things at home were getting difficult with her husband Mike, they were both under pressure and it showed in her face every time I saw her at the clinic.

I had been hoping that the doctors would be able to help her and that by some miracle she would find a way to conceive and put her life back on track.

It had been six months since she started coming in to the clinic and it had been confirmed that the problem was definitely with her husband Mike and not with her. Because of this Mike had taken it badly and the tensions at home were at a high explosive point making life very difficult for both of them.

I wished there was some way I could help them both. I had thought of talking to Mike but I felt that may have made things worse mainly because I was a stranger and the fact that other people knew their personal details, even though I was working at the clinic, I don't think would have helped. Julia knew I was pregnant and she also had heard from members of the nursing staff that it had happened accidentally. She was told the story that I had planted and she only knew what she thought was correct as far as she had heard it.

I could not tell her that I had planned this pregnancy with a man who was in a coma.

I felt guilty for Julia's situation more so because I had fallen pregnant so easily and she could not. I spoke at length with her this day and the test results had clearly shown that Mike could not have children; nothing short of a miracle would be the only way that they would have a family. As I absorbed the information from Mike and Julia's results I was inspired by an idea that hit me like a bolt of lightning. I had a solution for her, the only question is how can I tell her what was on my mind?

I left the clinic that day and returned for the next seven days as part of my rotation. Every day I turned up to work my mind went straight back to Julia and the desperation I saw on her face. I knew I could help her and I felt that I had to try, so I *will* help her! My mind is made up and my determination is strong. I will tell her what is on my mind and if she agrees then maybe she can become pregnant. I logged on to the computer and retrieved Julia's personal details, including her telephone number. I will call her tonight and arrange to meet with her. It is then I will tell her my thoughts and see what she has to say to me. I am going to introduce her to HUGH!

I called Julia at 5.15 that afternoon. I finished work and went home, made myself a cup of coffee and dialled the number. The phone rang and someone picked up.

"Hi, is that Julia?"

"Yes," was the reply.

"Hello, this is Leigh from the fertility clinic, I think we need to talk. I want to help you and what's more, I think I can!"

We had a brief conversation and arranged to meet at my home at 7.30 later that night.

Julia arrived promptly. She knocked on the door, I answered it, invited her in and offered her a glass of my usual red wine, the cure for all ills. She took off her coat and sat down. I was not sure of what to say or indeed how to say it, but after a few brief moments I braced myself and said:

"I know how to get you pregnant, it is unusual but I think it will work!"

Julia looked at me, eyes wide open, and leaning slightly forward in the armchair, she said, "Tell me, please tell me."

I began by explaining about Hugh, who he was and how I became friends with him. I explained very gently how I had become pregnant and why I had done things as I did. Julia listened and did not speak. At times her eyes rose up slightly in surprise at what I was saying. I spent some time talking calmly and quietly to give a clear picture about my situation and then I said, "I feel that you can follow my lead and do the same as me."

"What do you mean?" was her reply.

"I want you to consider going with Hugh to get pregnant."

Everything went quiet. She looked at me in total shock, dropped her head down and then lifted it up again to look me square in the face. She paused and said, "I have already thought of this, but not in the way you have said."

I asked her what she meant.

"Some time ago I thought of having a one-night stand to see if I would fall pregnant, I was going to look for someone like Mike and go through with it, my only concern was if he found out and that future blood tests would show the baby was not his."

We talked a while longer and we covered every angle, the whys and the wherefores, and we had a little more wine. Mike knew Julia was with me, he thought it was for a girly chat and he felt Julia needed the break as well.

"It would make sense to ask Mike about this," I said. "What would his views be?"

Julia paused and said, "I honestly don't know. I suppose me going with another man will not be on the top of his life-pleasing experiences list but as for his point of view I don't know what he would say or do."

I had already thought of how we could go through with this and I was sure I would be able to get away with it; the only questions now were, could Julia go through with it and would Mike support her? There were some tough choices to be made and some really harsh discussions ahead but I felt that some real headway had been made and I believed that I was doing the right thing in telling her.

It was around 10.30 and Julia said it was time to go home. "I'm not sure how to tell Mike, or indeed, *if* I should tell him. Anyway, tonight is not the best time. If I do say something it will be tomorrow in the cold light of day."

As Julia left she embraced me and said, "Thank you for caring and whichever way it goes thank you for trying. We have had little or no hope over recent times and at least you are trying to offer us both a choice, and for that I am grateful." Julia gave me a kiss on the cheek and left.

I cleaned the room, tidied round and went to bed, I was actually very tired. I think the emotional pressure had taken its toll on me and with everything else around me all I wanted to do was sleep, and sleep I did!

I awoke next morning to the sound of the phone ringing. I sat up with a start, pulled myself together and grabbed the phone.

"Leigh?"

"Yes," I said.

"It's Julia, we need to talk *now*!"

I was surprised. Julia sounded aggressive.

"Sure," I said. "When?"

"Half an hour, at your place please."

"Of course," was my reply. "I will see you soon."

"Thanks, bye." And she was gone.

Jesus Christ, that's all I bloody need, a fight on my hands! What the hell is going on?

A knock at the door. I opened it and there she was. "Come in," I said, but Julia was halfway in anyhow. "What's wrong?"

"Mike said *yes*."

"He said *what*?" I responded.

"He said *yes*. I could not wait to talk this morning so I told him last night. We talked the whole night through. We talked and talked and talked and we both agreed that your idea could be the solution we need to help us get our life back on track.

Mike and I are both clearly aware it's not a perfect solution, but it is something we can explore as a means to an end, that end being that we start our own family. To us it makes more sense because this Hugh guy is in a coma. He won't know anything and he won't have any claims on the baby, and you can give us medical details such as blood type and stuff that we can have for the future. It's a real chance for us and we are going to go for it."

I was very shocked and surprised and to be honest I didn't know what to do next. Julia and I chatted. We had several cups of coffee and we even found time to have a laugh and a joke, but once we came to grips with the initial euphoria we began to take a more serious view of the situation at hand. Julia was afraid of what was going to happen. Mike had been her only partner in life, and that included sex, and she did not know what she would have to do. But what was more important to her was to be in control of what she did.

I told her of how I had conceived with Hugh. I did not go into the sexual heights I had reached, but I told of my excitement and need for the connection that Hugh and I had. I assured Julia to be herself and that she would not have to encourage Hugh to be sexually aroused because his erection is always there, so there is no need to have any foreplay only direct contact and the rest would happen on its own.

Although still full of anticipation, Julia was coming to terms with what needed to be done and with the full support of her husband she was confident all would go well.

Two days further on and I was still trying to get things clear in my mind, I was going to need help and I need to be sure that no one finds out. It is a serious thing I was about to do and it was absolutely vital things were planned correctly down to the last detail.

I called Karen the night shift nurse who had helped when I first made love to Hugh. I asked if we could meet to have a chat. I explained that there was an important matter I needed to discuss with her and it was a conversation no one else should hear. Karen was on night shift tomorrow, and I was too, so we agreed to meet at break time the following night. My big concern was that I may overstep the bounds of friendship by asking for her help with Julia. Although the situation is slightly different, it was still a big ask of anybody, especially in a public place.

We met on Hugh's ward at 1.30 in the morning.

I walked into the ward. It is electronically coded so I knocked gently on the door and Karen saw it was me, pressed the release button and the door lock allowed me access. I walked over to the nurses' station and gave Karen a hug.

"You needing some time with Hugh?" and she laughed.

"Yes and no," was my reply. "I need a big favour and I hope you can help me."

Karen could see that I was uptight.

"Tell me what you need girl and we will see what we can do."

With the comfort in her voice I felt more relaxed and more able to explain my situation and what I wanted her to help me to do. I told Karen of Julia and her husband Mike. I explained how they could not conceive and the problems that had been found stemmed from Mike and his inability to produce the sperm needed for conception.

"I get the picture," said Karen, "you want to use Hugh's sperm."

"Wrong," I said. "I want to use Hugh!"

Karen looked at me for a long time. "Have you told this Julia what you intend to do?"

"Yes, I have, and she has also told her husband and they are both in full agreement about doing this. The only problem now is how we do it and that is where you come in Karen."

"What do you have in mind?" said Karen.

"Well, my plan is to bring Julia in one night as a visitor, then when the bell rings for the public to leave, she can stay behind and both you and I will help her to do what has to be done."

"Sounds simple enough, but if I am to get involved in this act I need some form of compensation."

"What do you mean?" I said.

"I want a cash payment to smooth things over."

I was visibly shaken by what Karen had said.

"It's alright helping you a friend and colleague," said Karen, "but not a stranger. Anything could go wrong and that puts me at risk. I will help, but for a price. I am not greedy, but I am not stupid either. Let's see what they can pay me and if I like the sound of it we will have a deal."

"How much do you want to ask them for?"

Karen's response was, "A £1000 cash and you have my support, my help and more important, my silence. See what they say and get back to me. If it is a 'yes', she can be here tomorrow, it's as simple as that."

I must admit I felt upset but I could also see the logic and the practicality of what she was saying. Karen was taking a risk and needed something for her involvement and I could not argue with that type of reasoning. I stood up, thanked Karen and touched her lightly on the top of her head in acknowledgement of our conversation. "I will get back to you with an answer as soon as I can."

"Thanks," said Karen. "Please don't be angry with me, I will do what needs to be done. Just consider my position."

"I *am* considering your position. I said leave it with me and let's see what happens."

I went back to work downstairs with a little sadness in my heart but at the same time a relieved feeling inside that my plans may yet still go ahead, albeit not exactly as I had expected. Tomorrow was another day, I hope it is a good one.

I finished my shift that night in maternity and my head was full of concerns for everything going on. I just hope Julia and Mike have the money, and although I had reservations about asking them, I had to try.

After arriving home, a restless seven hours sleep and I was up and out of bed, a shower and a cup of coffee set me up for the phone call I was about to make to Julia. I made the call and she answered. I told her of my meeting with Karen and what we discussed and the end result. Without a falter in her voice she said, "OK, I will tell Mike but it shouldn't be a problem. We have some money put aside for IVF and that will cost far more than a £1000. Give me half an hour and I will call you back."

Sure enough, 30 minutes later the phone rang and Julia was on the other end of the line.

"Hi Leigh, I spoke to Mike, he is at work but he agreed to a £1000 cash and the money will be available tomorrow after 1pm."

"I am shocked and surprised," I said, "but happy. I will call Karen to tell her and get back to you with details and times. When will you be able to come with me to see Hugh?"

"Whenever you like," said Julia, "any time at all. If you arrange it I will be ready when you are, the sooner the better."

I called Karen the next day and told her the news. I also said that the money was available and that I would bring it with me the night I introduced Julia to Hugh. Karen seemed a little upset as it appeared that she may be having doubts about the money. However, I reassured her that her requests were proper and right and that Julia, Mike and I were happy with the arrangement. She sounded a little better after our conversation and I felt good about things, too.

From the first time Sue had mentioned Hugh to me my life had changed, although you can never plan what will happen to you on life's journey, all in all my situation was not too bad. For the first time in a long time I felt as if I knew where I was going with things. Although it was a bit of a bumpy road I could still see clearly ahead of myself and the future looked good and that made me feel better about the path of life I was on and the choices I was making, and that had to be a good thing.

I was full of contemplation when suddenly the silence was broken by the sound of my mobile phone ringing. I saw the caller I.D. said Karen. I answered and I heard a positive "Hi Leigh, how are you?"

I spoke clearly back, "Fine, how are you?"

"Good," was her reply. "I want to suggest tomorrow night for Julia, tomorrow being Friday."

I asked, "Why Friday?" and Karen said it was the quietest night for her department, with fewer people around because of the weekend starting and because there would only be a few patients on the ward at that time.

"So now is a very good time for our trial run."

"Trial run," I said. "What do you mean?"

"Isn't it obvious? What if Julia does not conceive on the first go? She may need to come back for a few more times until it happens."

"Jesus Christ!" I said. I had never thought of that and neither, I suspect, had Julia and Mike. In my mind I had only thought about it being a one-time deal and this may affect things slightly as I can't imagine Mike being happy with multiple visits to the hospital for his wife, especially with what was going to happen there.

I agreed on Julia's behalf, thanked Karen, said bye and hung up. I immediately called Julia to tell her of the plan and I also told her of the potential to go for more than one visit. As I spoke to her she hesitated and said, "I have already thought about this and I am prepared to do it, even though I have not spoken to Mike about the potential of this.

Let's just see what happens and go from there." With a confident tone in her voice we decided for Julia to arrive at the hospital at seven the next evening, Friday the 26th, where I would meet her in the waiting area of Hugh's ward and take her in. She could sit at the nurses' station as if she were a friend of Karen's and mine and we would take things from there.

Friday evening came around very quickly and, as expected, Julia was in the waiting room escorted by Mike. I must have looked surprised at the sight of him being there and I quickly said, "You can't be here as well, it won't work."

Mike put his finger to his lips to sshhhhh me and said, "I know that, I am just dropping her off and supporting her. I'll be gone in a minute, don't worry."

"We are not bloody stupid you know," said Julia. "This is hard enough for the both of us without her having a pep talk."

I went silent and immediately Julia apologised to me.

"It's alright," I said. "I understand."

I was both relieved and grateful, but I also can understand why the man was there. I should have been a little bit more sensitive, their situation was different to mine and I suppose I had not realised this until now. I wondered if I had been a little bit callous towards Mike and Julia but the look on his face brought me back to earth with a heavy bump, I would need to tread a little more carefully from here on in.

Mike kissed his wife on the cheek then turned and walked away. He did not look back and Julia did not look at him, it was a very difficult thing to watch and I could see how hard things were for the both of them.

Karen was stood near the nurses' station. Julia and I walked over to her and she smiled politely. I introduced them both to each other and they shook hands. It was a strange meeting, almost surreal, if I'm honest a very calm and almost passive connection. We chatted for a while in an ice-breaking sort of way of doing things and all seemed good, well, as good as it could be under the circumstances.

It was about 7.50pm and nearly time for the end of visiting bell to ring. There were only a few people around and as Karen had said to me, only a handful of patients on the ward, some with no visitors and a couple with visitors. Julia drew no attention and as 8pm came around the bell automatically rang and people got up, said their goodbyes and began to leave. By 8.15 the ward was clear of visitors and only staff and patients remained.

I was surprised to see another nurse on the ward, I did not know her and I was concerned and I said so to Karen.

"Don't worry," she said. "Alison will be on break when we need her to be, I have told her Julia is a colleague from the local befriending society and she thinks Julia is here to spend time after hours with Hugh. Don't panic, things are under control I promise," said Karen. I believed her. If nothing else, she was an organised and pragmatic lady. I was happy with how she was managing the situation and I was not concerned at all.

While all of the hospital stuff was going on both Karen and I had neglected Julia. I turned to look for her and she was stood outside the door of Hugh's private room. Julia knew where he was because as we had entered the ward earlier I had simply pointed in the direction of where Hugh's room was, just so she knew where we were going to go.

Alison said, "Would everyone like a tea or coffee?" We all nodded. "Won't be a moment," she said, and off she went.

I looked at Julia and said, "Do you want to meet him?"

"Yes," she said.

Karen turned and walked over to the nurse's station and said nothing. We both walked towards Hugh's door, I turned the handle and we walked in.

Hugh was asleep as usual. He had never opened his eyes in the whole time he had been in St Mary's and he was still, as far as the doctors could tell, in a deep coma-like state. Julia looked at him and I left her a short while and then I said, "Julia meet Hugh, and Hugh this is my friend Julia. She needs your help. I hope you don't mind but she has arrived here tonight because you are her only hope and both you and I are going to try to put her life back on the rails and send her in the right direction. Please don't be angry or upset with me my prince, but God has sent you to me and I hope you will understand."

Julia looked at me and nodded gently towards me, then she put her hand on the bottom of the bed to touch Hugh's left foot, at the same time she stared at the bulge under the bed sheets. For the first time she looked at what she was here for, his *erection*!

"Can I touch it?" she said.

I nodded and motioned her to do so. She ran her hand from Hugh's foot all the way up to the bulge. She touched it, then passed her hand over it several times and then she stepped back and just stared at Hugh's face.

"It's alright Julia, he is in a coma. If he is aware of anything, I have never seen him show it or give any response at all. I made love to him on a number of occasions and I was vigorous to the point of sexual stimulation. I climaxed passionately and he did not respond in any way whatsoever. I am sure you are safe in what you are about to do with him."

A noise behind us at the door, it was Alison. "Tea is up," she said. Julia and I turned away from Hugh and walked out of his side room to the nurse's station for a cuppa and a biscuit. We had to act as normally as possible, we did not want to draw any attention to ourselves in any way so the conversation with Alison was fake but factual about the reasons behind Julia visiting Hugh. Between Karen, Julia and myself we painted a picture of a care society with only a couple of friends who visit the long-term sick to offer comfort and friendship for those alone. Alison accepted the description of Julia's need to be here and the conversation changed to other things.

Break time for Alison had been set for 9.30ish so we knew when to be ready to proceed with Hugh. Julia and I returned to Hugh's room after our coffee and tea and we sat discussing the preparation needed to do what had to be done.

"What do I need to do?" said Julia.

"Just be yourself and do what you would do with Mike," I said. "If it's any help think of Mike, just make it work and make it happen."

"What do I need to do for Hugh?"

"Nothing," I said, "he is all ready to do what you need." And at that I pulled back the sheets to reveal the huge, erect penis. Julia's eyes shot wide open.

"My god!" she said. "It's huge, much bigger than Mike's. I don't know if I can take that inside me!"

"Yes you can. At first I thought the same thing but I managed. If I can do it then you can do it, you *have* to do it. Take hold of his erection, Julia," I said. "Feel it, hold it, make friends with it, it won't hurt you and Hugh won't respond to you I promise."

Julia's hand reached out towards Hugh's huge cock. She gently put her hand around it and held it firmly in her left hand. The erect penis was burning hot as usual and the blood was pulsing through the whole length of the shaft. Julia gently moved her hand up and down the erection in a very gentle wanking motion.

"Will he come if I do this?"

"Only if you make him," I said. "It's just like any other sex act, you have to be physical to get the end result and believe me, when you start you will get a result you will not forget."

As we spoke I started to feel aroused myself and I could feel the emotions and the passion that I had previously felt when I had sat astride Hugh myself. I was getting horny! I had to clear my mind of what was in front of me, this time was for Julia and her needs and not mine. I was going through my thought process when I was aware of Julia watching me; she knew what I was thinking.

"Are you jealous of me?" she said.

I put my head down and said, "Yes, a little."

"Do you want me to stop?"

"NO!" I said emphatically. "This is *your* time, not mine. We are here for a different reason and that reason is for you to try to get pregnant, it's not about sex or jealousy."

I had quickly put Julia on the right track and reinforced why we were here.

"This is the second man's penis I have held in my life, the first was Mike and now Hugh. I feel very strange about the whole thing."

I'm not sure if Julia was focused on the work she had to do but it was clear that Hugh's cock was having an effect on her and it showed you see by the colour of her face and the way she moved. She was having a reaction to the situation and I was not sure what to do. Throughout all of this I was keeping an eye on the time and it was getting near to Alison's break time. For some minutes Julia continued to rub Hugh's erection as if she was bonding with it, it was not masturbation but it was a sort of affection or something like that.

It was 9.35pm, Alison had gone on her break and it was time to get things underway. I looked outside the door to Hugh's room and looked at Karen. She gave me the thumbs up and that was the signal for Julia to go with Hugh. I stepped back into the room and pulled the curtain across the window of the door. I then realised what I was doing and turned to go out when Julia said, "Stay! Please stay."

I was a bit taken aback. "Why do you want me to stay?" I said.

"To help me," she said. "I can't do this alone, I need your help to do it."

I looked at Julia and smiled. "I will do all I can for you, just tell me what you need."

She smiled and stood back from the edge of the bed where she had been standing near to Hugh. She straightened up and lifted off her flowered dress, she pulled it over her head to reveal a very attractive sexy body. I had never noticed before how well her figure looked, but then again why should I? She put the dress on the back of her chair, she then reached into her bag to bring out a tube of lubricant which she was going to use before mounting Hugh. She pressed the top of the tube and a gel-like fluid oozed out. She caught it on the fingers of her right hand and gently rubbed between her legs to moisten the area. Julia did not look at me or Hugh but after she had lubricated her vagina she climbed onto the bed and sat astride Hugh, her hands were still covered in the lubricant and she rubbed the rest on Hugh's erect penis. Once she had done this she raised up to insert the shaft inside her when she said, "Leigh, grab his cock and put it in me please."

I just stared at her in pure shock.

"He is your man, you have to do this for me to make things feel right. Please do it," Julia said to me.

Without a second thought I walked to the side of Hugh's bed and took hold of the erection. It was burning hot. I held it for a moment and then put my hand on Julia's backside and pushed her forward to line up her vagina right over Hugh's cock. I could feel the hairs of her pussy on my hand. I whispered gently, "Down now". Julia eased herself onto Hugh's shaft and went all the way down in one go, something I had not done the first moment I sat astride him. Her pussy sat on my hand and squashed it down onto Hugh in a deliberate motion. Julia's fanny was also burning hot and she was soaking wet but not, I feel, from the lubricant she had just applied. I pulled my hand away and stepped back to watch.

Julia sat astride Hugh for a few moments, then she started to ride up and down the length of his shaft, at first she was slow and deliberate then she began to ride him a little harder. Julia looked straight forward and did not look at Hugh at all. However, she said to me, "Grab my tits and play with my nipples now!"

I did not know what to do. I had never touched a woman in that way before and I was unsure and uncertain what to do at her request. Nevertheless, I moved close to the bed again and took hold of Julia's nipples. Her tit ends were standing out firm and proud and they were huge, dark brown and slightly pointing upwards. I squeezed her tits the only way I knew how; I could only try to do it for her as I had done it for myself during my own masturbations and self stimulation.

As I squeezed Julia's nipples I felt a sensation of excitement. I was not a lesbian, nor did I fancy women, but the feeling of Julia's nipples between my fingertips did give me a certain thrill and by the way she was responding, she too was getting some benefit from this connection between the two, sorry three, of us!

Julia was now riding Hugh in a strange way, it was as if she was not there and by that I mean she was staring into space but still having the sex that you would expect her to have. For a good ten minutes she fucked Hugh until she came to a positively erotic climax supported by her body tensing up and a sigh of contentment as she flopped on to Hugh's chest. She lifted off him and there were signs of sperm oozing from within her. Julia seemed a little irate at this.

"Don't worry," I said. "It has reached the right part of your body. If you're going to get pregnant *that* will be the cock that will do it."

Julia looked at me and didn't speak. She quickly climbed off Hugh and away from his bed; she put on her dress with speed and tidied herself up.

"Do I look OK?" said Julia.

"Fine," I said, "let's go now please."

I cleaned Hugh's penis and wiped it with tissues and wet wipes and covered him back up.

His erection had gone down for a while and as I moved away I saw the bed sheets move slightly. I went back to his bed, lifted the sheets and watched the erection rise up again. It is a magnificent cock and I love it, I thought to myself.

By now Julia was out of Hugh's side ward and talking to Karen. I saw her pass over an envelope, the money I thought. I had forgotten about that part of the deal. Karen smiled, Julia nodded and she was gone. Julia didn't say goodbye, she just left. I looked at Karen then went to her and gave her a hug and I said, "Thank you."

"You are welcome," she said, "anytime. And if Julia needs to come back just let me know."

I smiled and left.

Three weeks goes by and not a word from Julia, when out of the blue I get a text message on my phone. Julia's name flashed on the screen as I opened the message it said: *Hi Leigh, just to let you know Mike and I are pregnant, it worked thank you, call me when you can. Thanks again Julia & Mike.*

I couldn't believe it – Julia was having a baby. I couldn't call her while I was at work, it would need to be later once I had finished my shift, I don't want anyone at work to hear my conversation with her.

I finished work at 15.30 and was gone like a shot. I went home as fast as I could, I opened the front door to my house, breezed in, put the kettle on, made some tea and called Julia. I was very excited and I was overjoyed when she answered my call.

"Hiya, it's Leigh."

"I know," said Julia. "I saw your name on the caller I.D."

"How are you?" I said.

"Fantastic," was Julia's reply. "Mike and I are both feeling fantastic thanks to you."

"Well, it's not just me, but thanks for the credit. How did you find out?" I asked.

"We got a home test kit yesterday and tried it last night. It showed up as positive straight away, we are over the moon and couldn't be happier."

"I am happy for the both of you but I think you need to go to the clinic to get confirmation just to be on the safe side."

Julia agreed and said she would make an appointment with her GP or the clinic direct. We talked for a little while and the feeling between us was fantastic. We had a pause in our conversation when I said to Julia, "Could we meet at my place, I have something I want to ask you and it's personal?"

Julia said, "Of course, anything you need ask away. Is tonight good for you?"

"Yes, definitely."

"What time?" she said. "Around 8ish? Sounds good. See you then." And with the press of the button on my phone the call was ended.

Julia arrived punctual as ever and she looked radiant. Mike dropped her off at the door and gave me a big wave from the car and blew me a big kiss as a thank you. I felt really good at seeing the both of them happy, it made all the efforts and risk seem worthwhile. Julia hugged me and kissed me on the cheek and in she walked, bouncing along like a child, it was fantastic to see her like this and I felt great too. Julia sat down on the armchair and stared straight at me. "What is it I can do for you?" she said.

"Well," I said, "this is a little bit tricky but here I go. When you were on top of Hugh you asked me to help you sexually and I did it for you. I did not really understand it but the contact with your vagina and the need for you to have me hold your nipples during the sex act had an effect on me. I am not sure what to make of things. I'm not gay, or at least I don't think I am, but it was also not an unpleasant experience either."

Julia smiled and said, "Well Leigh, I will let you into a little secret. I used to go with girls before I met Mike, he was my first real male relationship and we did fall in love. I wasn't expecting it, but life deals you some strange cards and that was one of them. You may have noticed that my reaction to Hugh may have been a little different than the one you may have had, but this was because men other than Mike don't really do anything for me, so I needed a little female help from you and it worked."

I was shocked and surprised but not unhappy or angry at what she had said to me either. "Do you find me attractive?" I said to Julia.

"Yes I do – very," she said.

I was very surprised to hear this but again, not shocked.

"I noticed you the first time I came to the clinic," said Julia. "Let's say you are very easy on the eyes."

This made me blush and she just laughed at me. The mood between us was relaxed and friendly and not sexual at all, just two friends having a coffee and a chat and, by the way, both pregnant to the same man – now that *is* bizarre!

LISA

I was at work three weeks after Julia's encounter with Hugh when in the middle of my shift I got a message from the main reception asking me to come through, a girl was there wanting to talk to me. I went through to see who it was and as I walked through the door I could see a woman around 30 years of age standing at the reception desk. As our eyes met she looked vaguely familiar and as I got nearer to her she said, "Hello Leigh, how are you?"

It took me a few moments to realise this was Lisa Hunt, she had been a patient at the fertility clinic a couple of years earlier. She and her husband had tried hard to have a family but sadly without any success. As memory served me Lisa's husband had a very low sperm count and I think that had been the problem. After their initial consultations I never saw either of them again until Lisa turned up here and now. Lisa was smiling at me and approached to give me a hug as two old friends would normally do after not seeing each other for some time. We went to sit down in my office and I made us two coffees. We chatted for a while and I asked about her husband Scott. Lisa looked at me and her eyes filled with tears when she told me he had died.

"I am so sorry," I said. "What happened?"

Lisa said that she had received a phone call from the company he worked for. While at work he had had a massive heart attack and died, he was 33 years of age. I walked round to her and put my arms around her and held her tight, she held me too and I could feel the pain and loss that she was suffering. I felt very bad for her, very bad indeed. A few moments went by and she seemed to calm down and she talked some more about the loss of Scott and how things were at the present time. She talked a little more and then she said, "I have a question, in fact it is to ask a favour."

"Ask away," I said. "If I can help you I will."

"I want a baby," Lisa said.

I was a little taken aback and asked her why.

For some time Lisa and Scott had tried to have children without success and after Scott's death she hit a low point, so low she wanted to die and had even contemplated suicide. Sometime after the funeral Lisa was sitting one day when she thought she could feel Scott's spirit around her. Lisa also believed it was a sign to go on and fulfil her dream of having children, the only problem for Lisa was she still loved her husband very much and she did not want to marry anyone else. These emotions Lisa had about her husband ran very deep inside her and they went on for quite a while. Before Lisa came to see me, in fact a week or so earlier, she was talking with a girl who used to go to the same clinic. It turns out the girl she was talking to was Julia.

Lisa and Julia had met at the fertility clinic a few years before and although they weren't good friends they did keep in touch mainly because of the common bond they shared, that of both being women who could not conceive children. Lisa had called Julia just for a little support. Julia did not know that Scott had died, so it was a big shock to her. After a brief and emotional telephone call between them they arranged to meet for lunch.

"This we did and after I'd poured my heart out, Julia suggested that I speak with you. Julia said that you would understand and that you may be able to help in some way. Julia was a bit vague but she said speak with Leigh please, she can offer you something special which may be the answer to my dilemma. I was not sure what to make of Julia's statement but she was strong in her belief that you could help me in some way. I sat with the idea of contacting you and after a few days of thought I decided to come back here to see you, and here I am. My biggest question at this moment Leigh is what can you do for me? And my second question is – *what* was Julia talking about?"

I looked straight at Lisa and said, "This is not the time or the place to discuss such things. Here is my phone number, give me a call tonight and we can meet up for a chat."

Lisa could see this was a difficult situation. She quickly took the piece of paper out of my hand, nodded her head at me and said, "I will call you tonight. Thanks, Leigh." And at that she was gone.

I was shaking. I was not expecting anyone to put me in this position and I felt vulnerable, very vulnerable indeed.

I finished work a little later than usual, drove home and went into the house and started to make myself something to eat. After about half an hour I had a knock at the front door. I opened the door and there was Lisa. She stood looking at me with a strained face and she was obviously in distress.

"You had better come in," I said to her.

Lisa sat down and I offered her a cup of tea or coffee. She took the coffee option. I made us both a cup and sat down in front of her.

"My first question is how do you know where I live?"

"Julia told me," she said. I was desperate, so she told me your phone number and your address."

"But I gave you my number today at the hospital."

"Sorry," said Lisa, "I know. I just did not want to say anything in case I upset you."

"Why be afraid you may upset me?" I said.

"In case you would not help me," was her reply.

Lisa definitely had something on her mind so I simply said, "Tell me what it is you want and I will see if I can help you."

"Oh, you can help me," she said. "I just don't know if you *will* help me."

I was now more curious. "Tell me," I said in a stern voice.

"I want sex with Hugh as soon as possible." Her eyes were bulging and her face bright red and she spoke with a tone in her voice of pure determination:

"I need to have a baby with him and I NEED IT NOW!"

"Wow," I said, "you are a determined lady."

"Yes I am," she said, "but to do it I need your help and support please. *Please.*"

The situation was a little tense but not too bad. We began to talk and I listened very carefully to what she had to say. Lisa was a very sad lady indeed but she had a plan that she believed would help her to solve most of her problems and to also help her move on in her life. I hoped what she wanted would also help her as well. After we talked I knew what she wanted and I also was very aware of the part I had to play in this situation. I said I would help her but I did need time to think about this. Lisa stood up, held me and then thanked me, and I could really feel the relief in our embrace.

Lisa had gone to Julia for comfort and support after the death of her husband, and during that time Julia had told her about Hugh. She even went further and told her almost everything that had happened with both herself and with me. Once the idea had entered Lisa's head she quickly decided that she could also do the same thing and get pregnant by him. It was at this point that Julia had told Lisa to come and speak with me to see if I would arrange this for her. I had reluctantly agreed to help her, and I say reluctantly because I knew there was a big risk, but I also understood how she was feeling. So with that in mind I said, "Yes, I will help you in any way I can."

I arranged to meet Lisa a few days later to explain to her what we would need to do; this would also give me time to put things in place in the hospital and to speak with Karen. I would need to see when Karen was on night shift and also to see how much money she would want. I hoped she would do this for free, but I do not think she will agree to any help if there is no money. Karen was very clear last time that she was not going to put herself at risk without some form of cash payment. To be truly honest I don't really blame her, after all it is a big thing that I was asking of her, friend or no friend!

I had checked on Karen's shift rota and found her night time working pattern, then I called her. When she picked up the phone and heard my voice she knew almost immediately what I wanted.

After a brief hello I said I needed a favour and she simply said to me yes and asked when I wanted it. I was a little taken aback but I told her Thursday night around 9pm.

"No problem," she said. "Same arrangement as before?"

"I suppose so," I said.

"If there is a problem I will call you back."

I thanked Karen and put the phone down. It was all organised and ready to go.

I contacted Lisa and told her the plan. She seemed very calm and happy about the process. I explained where and when and then I said, "I have one small problem. The girl who will help us needs a £1000 to go through with it."

To my surprise Lisa said, "That's fine. When do you want the money?" I told her to just bring it with her on the Thursday night.

"OK," was her reply, "see you Thursday. Thanks for your help Leigh. See you soon. Bye," and she closed the call.

I felt strange about this situation. When Lisa first came to me I felt really sorry for her with the loss of her husband and not having a baby with him. She was lost and very alone, but right now it felt like I had just closed a business deal. My feelings were a little different now it appeared that Lisa had changed and in a very short space of time. I was not sure what it was, but there was a change in her attitude and I could not fathom out why.

Although I had not realised it, I had not seen Hugh for over a week. In fact a week past Tuesday things had been very hectic and with all that was happening I had simply just forgotten to go. I had thought about him a great deal but I had not visited him for a while and I did feel guilty about it. However, I would soon see him again, in fact tomorrow night when I take Lisa.

Thursday evening came around very quickly and sure enough at the appointed time of 7pm Lisa knocked on my front door. I opened the door and invited her in. She said "hello", walked into the living room and sat down.

I offered her a coffee and we sat together on my blue 3-seater settee. Lisa picked up her handbag and put her hand inside and pulled out two packages, a small one and a larger one. Lisa gave me the small package and said, "Here is the money for Karen."

I looked inside and there appeared to be more money than I expected. I asked Lisa, "Is this a £1000?"

"No, it's £2000, I want to be sure I get her discretion as well as her help tonight."

"With two grand you will surely get it."

Lisa smiled. She then gave me the other larger package and said, "Here Leigh."

"What's this?"

"A gift. Have a look."

I opened the light brown bag she had given me and inside was money, quite a lot by what I could see. I looked at her and said, "How much is here?" "£10,000," was her answer. My jaw dropped.

"I can't accept this," I said to her.

"Yes you can," she said, "and you will! If you don't take it, the deal is *off!*" and she emphasised the word 'off'.

"Look Leigh," Lisa said firmly, "before Scott died we had a little money, but when he died his company had him insured and we also have, sorry I mean *had*, life insurance on both of us. When it paid out it was a lot of money. I can afford this, and more if need be, so don't bother yourself. I am grateful and I am showing it, and besides, you have a baby on the way and I think you could use the extra cash I would imagine."

I briefly, and I mean briefly, pondered on the idea and then I simply said, "Thank you, I am grateful Lisa", and at that she put her hand on my shoulder and said, "You are doing a wonderful thing for me, this is my way of saying thank you Leigh."

There was not much more to say other than "Let's go". Time was moving on and we needed to be at the hospital. I wanted to slip in with Lisa before the visitors left; it would look less obvious so we needed to be there as soon as possible before 8pm.

We set off for the hospital and arrived about 7.50pm just as some of the hospital visitors were starting to leave. Visiting time finished around 8pm and we needed to be in place at Hugh's ward before then. We arrived at the nurse's station and I could see Karen busy with a patient on the ward. She saw Lisa and I stood at the counter at the nurse's station and she gave a gentle wave of the hand and a smile aimed at both of us.

Her acknowledgement was a good thing, it made me feel more relaxed. I had not thought that I was uptight, but obviously I had some tension inside of me. I just hoped it did not come out in front of Lisa, especially knowing what she was about to do and also the awareness I had of what she was going to do with Hugh. It was going to be a very emotional and painful experience for her. I believe that the memory of Scott was haunting her and I felt that she also believed that she was betraying his memory and the vows that she had shared with him at their marriage ceremony.

Before we walked into Hugh's room I looked at Lisa and said, "Are you sure about this?" she looked back, smiled and said, "I am positive about this."

I took hold of Lisa's hand and led her into Hugh's room.

Once inside I closed the door behind us. Karen had stayed away from us this time, she just went about her business. All the visitors had left and she was just settling people down for the night. It was about 8.30. By now most of the patients in this ward were unable to move around or get out of bed, so they should not be a problem. As I stood with Lisa I watched to see what she would do next.

Lisa stood for a while and looked at Hugh. She moved her eyes up and down his bed and then she stepped forward and pulled back the sheets to reveal the giant cock that lay there. She was about to touch him when I stopped her and said, "Hello Hugh, this is Lisa. She needs your help as did I and also Julia, please don't be angry with us and if you can hear me please forgive us for using you this way."

Lisa looked at me but she did not react in any way at all, she just stepped back from the bed and lifted off the flowery white dress that she was wearing. She pulled it up over her head and revealed a beautiful satin white skin, her body was smooth with no blemishes or marks. She was toned and very firm with very unusual nipples that stuck out, but in a sexy pert way. She was a very attractive woman in every way possible. My first thought was that if Hugh was in a bar he would try to pick Lisa up; she had the look of a woman men would want and right now Hugh was getting her for free without any courtship or bull shit just getting her easy and without any hassle or complications. For some men that would be a gift from heaven.

As usual, Hugh made no sounds or responses to any of the things going on around him.

As Lisa stood there naked before Hugh and myself I quickly went into my bag and took out some lubricant. I squeezed it onto my hand

and rubbed it up and down the length of Hugh's massive cock ready for Lisa to mount him. She watched but did not speak. I stepped back and just waited. While travelling to the hospital in my car Lisa had told me that she wanted me to stay with her during the act, so I already knew not to leave her alone with Hugh.

Lisa climbed onto the bed, straightened Hugh's cock upright and then eased herself onto his erection.

Even still, the sight of his cock was as an amazing thing to me, and to see yet another beautiful woman ride him turned me on like you would not believe. Lisa was gorgeous and to watch her on top of this man was an erotic sight.

Lisa was still for a moment and then she started to move slowly at first, up and down, taking his full huge knob in her she took it all and she worked herself up and down and then up and down again and as she did this I watched her. I saw the shaft of his massive cock show itself and then disappear time and time again as she worked herself into a beautiful but sensuous orgasm. She sighed and moaned and as she came she flopped on to Hugh and said, "Thank you Scott my darling husband, thank you."

I had noticed a strange look on Lisa's face when she mounted Hugh. At first I was not sure what it was but at the end of her experience I realised she had conditioned herself to believe the man under her was her dead husband Scott. It was a clever thing if you can do that with your mind and Lisa obviously could do this. It had been her way of dealing with a powerful situation where emotions would always run very high. She coped with it and dealt with it very well indeed.

"I take my hat off to you Lisa," I said. "That was a truly beautiful and emotional thing you just did. I hope it gives you both the baby and the peace that you need."

Lisa climbed off the bed and Hugh was lying there apparently none the wiser for the experience. Lisa quickly cleaned herself and got dressed and I gently cleaned Hugh and pulled up his foreskin to stop any discomfort. Lisa was ready to go and we were about to go out of the room when I asked her if I could spend a few moments together. Lisa nodded to me and walked outside the door and closed it behind her. I turned to look at Hugh and as I did so I saw the bed sheets move as his erection started to come back. 'Fuck me,' I thought to myself, 'the bloody thing won't stay down.' I put my hand under the sheet and got hold of his enormous cock and felt it grow back to full size in my hand. My grip was tight, my heart started to pound and my fanny ached for his cock in me. Immediately, I took off my skirt, ripped off my panties and jumped on him.

I needed no lubricant as my cunt was flowing fast. I raised myself up and impaled myself on this magnificent cock and rode him hard, well, as hard as I could. I did not want to damage the baby but I still wanted a good fucking, and by Christ I got it. I came fast and hard, just as well as time was against me. I felt an enormous final orgasm and a few smaller ones and fell on Hugh's chest. I raised my head and looked at him face to face. His eyes were shut and he remained in a deep sleep.

I pulled his limp cock out of me quickly, cleaned both Hugh and me, and then I quickly jumped off the bed, got dressed and went out of the side room, closing the door behind me.

Lisa was about six feet away from the door to Hugh's room. I looked at her, she looked at me and she said, "You must love him."

I hesitated and said, "You saw me?"

"I saw you," she said. "Thank you again, Leigh, thank you."

Karen was by now at the nurses' station. She looked up and said, "All done?"

Lisa frowned a little at the comment that was made but reached into her bag and pulled out the cash for Karen. Lisa passed the bag across the desk and Karen took it, no words were spoken. We both walked away from the ward and we did not turn back to look.

I could hear the rustling of paper as Karen obviously opened the package to check inside. Next thing, I heard a chair being moved and footsteps behind us. As we got to the elevator Karen caught up with us and said we had given her too much. Lisa looked at her and said, "Let's just say it's a bonus and leave it at that, shall we?" Karen replied "Thank you", turned on her heels and walked back to the ward.

I drove back to my place. Lisa and I got out of the car, stood and talked for a few moments and Lisa shed a tear or two. We embraced gently, and a kiss on the cheek was her way of saying thanks and good bye. I told her if she doesn't fall pregnant first time to let me know and we would work something out again. Lisa got into her car and drove away.

Three weeks later a text message came through: *Just to let you know Leigh I'm pregnant. I owe you the world. Thank you my friend forever, Lisa.*

I was now four months down the pregnancy road and of course my body was changing rapidly; my breasts had grown, my tummy had grown and I felt out of sorts, just the usual pregnant woman thing. Although my sex drive had dropped quite a lot, I still enjoyed going to see Hugh for a visit. I would sit with him, talk with him and from time to time I would pull back the sheets and suck his cock or wank him off. I still got great pleasure in doing this and I still loved to watch his cock grow after every time he shot his massive load, and sometimes I would sit on him and bring him off in my hand and get the hot spunk to shoot onto my tummy and his baby inside me. I enjoyed this very much indeed and deep down I hoped Hugh did too, it was my only way to be close to him. I also knew that I loved him and even though I told him every time I saw him, it would be nice to say it to him if he were conscious and able to respond to me – if he wanted to respond that is. One day it may happen and if it does, I hope what I want does come true and Hugh or whatever his real name is loves me back as well.

Since the first night Sue told me about Hugh my life had definitely changed and for the better certainly, and as well as my life being touched by him, he had also changed other people's lives too. His presence was almost like it was meant to be and although his situation had tragic overtones, the end result of him being here in this hospital at this particular time is very prominent for the difference he has made to our lives.

Sue Needs Help

I had not seen Sue for some time, either at work or for a drink. This did happen from time to time so it was not unusual; her shifts and my shifts sometimes clashed and that was usually the reason. I got a call one day from her and she rang just to see how I was doing. We chatted for a while and I asked her round for a drink that night. Sue agreed and we arranged for 7pm. As usual Sue was prompt. I heard a taxi pull up outside and a knock on my door and there she was with a bottle of wine and a package under her arm.

She came in, we hugged, she took off her coat and sat down.

"This is for you," Sue said. "It's for the baby."

I opened it and there was a shawl inside, it was white and very pretty.

"I bought white to stay neutral in case it's one or the other."

We both laughed and I thanked her, it was a lovely gift. I poured the wine and we began our usual girly chatter. I could, however, sense a little tension in her voice and as the conversation went on curiosity got the better of me and I said, "Sue, what is wrong?" She stopped talking and looked at me.

"I'm in trouble," she said, "big trouble. Since the divorce, money has been tight and as time's moved on it's gotten worse."

"How much worse?" I asked her.

"I owe out around £35000 on credit cards and to the bank and each month the mortgage, the bills and the other outgoings are bleeding me dry. I've asked for extensions on the mortgage and I have tried to get other loans to help catch up but it hasn't happened. I've been turned down every time now and I am near losing the house. I don't know what to do and I have no one else to turn to, just you Leigh."

I looked at her for a while.

"Something is in your head," she said. "What are you thinking?"

"Give me a moment," I said, "I need to chew something over in my mind."

Sue looked at for what seemed like a long time when I said to her that I may have a solution.

"I don't want to say too much yet, just give me a while to get my head around my idea and let me see what I can do. Meanwhile I will go to the bank tomorrow and pull out £5000 cash for you, will that help?"

"Christ almighty Leigh, that will save me right now!"

"Good," I said. "Spend it wisely and also contact all the companies begging for money and tell them you should have cash coming in soon and that you will be able to meet all of your obligations very soon."

"All my obligations?" Sue said.

"All of them," was my reply. "Now Leigh, don't ask any questions please, not yet. I will explain things once I know what is what and how I am going to get things to work."

Sue had a taxi booked for 11pm. A horn sounded outside and that was the taxi waiting for her leave. I told Sue to be patient and stay strong. "I think I may have a solution, just leave me to sort things out and to deal with. When I have some news I will call you, Sue."

"Thanks old friend, for everything."

"No problem," I replied. "Just wait for my call, it may take a little time but it won't be long."

Sue left the house, got into the taxi and drove off.

The minute she left my home my mind started to turn over. Not a few weeks earlier I had made a great deal of money from a woman who wanted a baby in an uncomplicated way. Although there was risk involved, the basic plans were already in place. Hugh G, as I now called him, was a baby-making machine. Each time I had used his erection it had produced the desired effect in more ways than one. If it worked then, it will work now, I just need to get things clear in my mind and have a word with Karen and see what I could do to help my old friend Sue out of her difficulties.

I went to work the next day and I pulled out files of women who had been to the clinic over the past few years and I tried to recall those that had been unsuccessful in having a baby. I needed to find the desperate and moreover, those with money to get my plan to work. I spent a good part of my day searching through patient files until I arrived at around 25 names of potential customers, or potential sources of cash. I took all the information home of all the ladies whose names I had collected, my intention was to call as many as I could to arrange separate meetings with each and every one of them. I wanted to try to recruit as many of these childless women as possible and then to weed out those that I thought would not go for my plan to get them pregnant, and then focus on those ladies desperate to go for my proposals.

Since my first encounter with Hugh G I had been driven by passion, lust and even love crept into the equation. I had become pregnant by him and allowed two other women to be impregnated by him and both successfully had fallen pregnant, but throughout all of this at no time was I driven by money. This time, however, it was all about money because my best friend, my lifelong friend, needed help – and I was in a position to help her out.

I sifted through the list of names that I had taken home and put them in some sort of order, choosing the ones that I could remember clearly and those which I thought were more open-minded and who would accept my idea more easily; the rest I would take pot luck with.

I planned to call them on the following Friday night with a hope to meet them sometime on Saturday. I wanted to set a schedule of around half an hour to forty-five minutes each. I had a few people to see and not much time to do it in.

I started making the calls on Wednesday evening. For various reasons some people were not interested any more in proceeding with any form of fertility treatment, other phone numbers were no longer available and the rest just declined politely. The phone calls had been easier than I had thought and not as painful as I had expected, and in the end I arrived with nine women who were very responsive to my suggestions. In all my calls I gave no indication as to what my plan would be, I only hinted a high chance of success of becoming pregnant and that was all I said to each and every one of these women.

As I had gone through my checking process I had also been careful to screen women whose husbands had the fertility problem, giving a much better success rate because the wife was more likely to be the fertile one. This had been a big part of my plan too.

Saturday morning arrived. I got up early, prepared myself for the tasks ahead and set off from home for the first meeting at 9am at the LIDO coffee bar in town. My first meeting was with Anne. She was in her late 30s and had been a patient at the clinic about 18 months earlier. She was a pretty women, but very ordinary. Although she had a nice figure, she dressed in very old style clothes and it made her look older than her years.

When I arrived she was sat in the window. She was alone and she had already bought a cup of coffee. I recognised her straight away and when she saw me she also new me immediately. I said "hello", she replied with the same response. We shook hands and sat together in the same spot she had been when I saw her. I ordered a coffee and began talking to Anne. We talked pleasantries – how are you? where are you living? things like this. I have to say, sitting there things felt very intense; we were both a little nervous, me because I didn't know what to say, and Anne because she wasn't sure why she was there.

I opened my approach by simply asking, "Do you still want a baby?"

Anne looked at me and said, "I have adopted a child."

"When?" I asked her.

"February last year," she replied. "My husband Mick and I decided that we had been through enough, what with tests and probing and what we felt was a great deal of personal humiliation, and so we hit a point where enough was indeed enough and so we adopted a nine-year old little boy called James."

I thought at this point I had lost before I had begun, her response seemed to be terminal in that she had decided to give up her quest for a child of her own and that she had settled for an adopted son. I was about to end the conversation when Anne said, "What do you have in mind?"

I looked at her and said bluntly, "I have a male coma patient who can probably make you pregnant."

"How can a man in a coma possibly do that?" she asked.

"Because he has a permanent erect penis and a sperm count which is off the charts by normal standards," I replied.

"So what are you proposing?" Anne said.

"I am offering you the chance to come to the hospital and use his body to get you pregnant. I know it sounds bizarre, but it has worked three times now and I can't see any reason why it won't work again. I have chosen a number of women to do this because I feel it will work, and as all of the people I have contacted have basically the same problem, I think there should be a high chance of success."

As I sat in the cafe Anne just looked at me. She did not speak, she just looked at me, her eyes pierced me deep inside. I had to ask her what was wrong.

"I am thinking about what you have just said to me and I am wondering if I can do it."

"You mean you still want a baby?"

"Yes," she said. "Yes I do. I have never stopped wanting a baby and to be honest I thought my chances were over. You have just started a flood of emotions inside of me, I want to laugh, cry, or scream and I want to say 'yes', I just don't know what to do about it all."

"One thing I have to tell you, firstly, what I am doing is against all the ethics I believe in. It is also against hospital policies and it is probably illegal too, so we need to keep this secret."

Anne agreed to this.

"One final thing, I need to pay people to help us achieve this objective, so it will cost about £8,000. Can you manage this?"

"Yes, I think so," said Anne. "I need to talk it over with my husband to see if he agrees. I have your phone number saved on my mobile, let me have a little time to see what I can do."

I smiled at her and said, "Take all the time you need."

Anne stood up shook my hand, thanked me and left the LIDO coffee shop.

That's the first one done. I felt relieved, but I was also exhausted. I could not believe that a 20-minute conversation would use so much energy and I wondered if I could manage another eight women sat in front of me going through the same discussion time and time again. I spent a little more time considering my options when I suddenly had a change of plan. I would call them all up and arrange to meet at my home later in the day, with all of them in the same place at the same time.

I made the calls to all of them and everyone agreed. I set a time of 2pm that day, I gave them all the address and that was it. I suppose I would now go home, sit and wait to see who, if anyone, turned up.

The first knock on the door was around 1.40 pm. I opened the lock and invited in three ladies. They walked in and sat down, I asked their names and they replied Linda, Shola and Julie. I asked them to make themselves comfortable. I had put on tea, coffee, biscuits and some fruit juices. The conversation was very general when Julie said, "What's this meeting all about?" I told her I would explain things when the others arrived and she seemed happy with this. Linda asked how many people were coming and I replied I hoped eight in total. I said I had spoken to one lady already, so there would have been nine in total. More chat and a few biscuits and others started to arrive gradually and surely. Seven ladies arrived a little late but nevertheless they were here.

It was about 2.30 when there was another knock at the door. I opened it to find three women stood there, one of the faces I recognised but the other two I did not. The girl I knew was Helen. Before I could ask about the other two, Helen said, "These are two friends of mine and they want the same thing as me. If it is alright I would like them to be included in the proposals, whatever they are, please."

I said no more and ushered them in, asked them to find a seat where they could and to please all make themselves comfortable. After my meeting with Anne earlier I felt that I could not beat about the bush with these ladies and I simply said, "I am going to cut to the chase, but before I do I want a solemn promise that whatever we say here today remains here, a lot of people will put themselves in a position of great risk to help you ladies, so this information has to remain confidential, whether you accept the offer or not. Do we all agree on this?"

Everyone looked around at each other and everybody said "Yes".

The response was said in a positive way which was very encouraging for me to hear. I had to trust these people because I was breaking some very ethical rules to help them but also to try to help Sue, after all I was in this position because of her and she was the very reason why we were all here today. At this point I asked everyone to introduce themselves, so I went around the room and one by one I heard "*My name is ...*" Linda, Shola, Julie, Beth, Helen, Christine, Grace, Ruth, and the two girls I did not know were Alison and Jade.

I told them that there was another member of the group and that I had spoken to her earlier that day, her name was Anne and she was now considering what I had told her. "There are eleven of you in this chosen group and you will all meet each other at some point just so you know who is who. Right ladies," I said, "you were contacted because of your desire to have children. Apart from two of you the rest have all been patients at the hospital clinic for couples struggling to have children. For whatever reasons you no longer attend the clinic but because of your presence here I assume you still want children. Am I correct?" I asked.

A few of them said yes and a nodding of heads confirmed what I expected to see and hear from them.

"I have a patient at the hospital, a man who is in a coma. We have called him Hugh G because he has a constant and very large erection."

A few ladies laughed, some smiled and a couple frowned, a mixed response shall we say.

"My proposal is to let each of you go with him and use him to fertilise you the natural way if you wish, or for you to extract sperm from him manually and then inseminate yourselves to get pregnant. The reason why I am doing this is that I have tried this 'process', for want of a better word, and it worked for me and I am now pregnant. It has also worked for two other ladies and they are also pregnant. It has worked three times in a row and so now you may get your chance at having a child if you take up the offer.

There are a number of conditions. One, there is a charge per person of £8,000 and two, the risk is very high. People who are involved in this situation are putting their careers on the line so they need to be compensated. When, or if, you pay the fee you take your chances – no baby, then sadly no refund."

I asked the girls if they wanted to chat for a while and they agreed to that. I sat around and listened to the conversation. Some of them asked a few questions, while others just sat and listened. The obvious questions arose such as *is he an attractive man*? and I of course said yes, although I did not express my own feelings for him to them, and the next questions which were bound to be asked were *how big is the erection*? and *why does it stay up?* I did laugh at that point, and so did most of the rest of the women sat there.

"I don't know why it 'stays up' as you put it, but it is *big*." I tried to describe it but then I said they really needed to see it for themselves. Beth suddenly spoke up and said, "I think it is immoral using a man like that and I think it is wrong what you are doing." She spoke in a stern schoolmistress-like tone and I think it spooked a couple of those sat there.

I looked straight at Beth and said, "Of course it's not right and of course it maybe is not the ideal situation, but I feel that in this room there is a great deal of misery and unhappiness for all of you. I also feel that you don't often get a chance to change your lives like this. I saw an opportunity and took it and it worked for me. If it will not work for you then leave now and enjoy the rest of your life. For those who stay it may change your lives for the better forever. Please consider this before you make your decision."

Beth put her head down as I continued to say, "Please do not condemn those who feel this might work for them. We make choices in life and I believe that this may be the start of something good for all of you, this is a life choice not a compulsory thing and you and you alone will make the choice with or without your partner's input."

Voices mumbled around the room again and Beth was silent. However, one of the ladies who had turned up whom I did not know put her arms around Beth's shoulders and Beth began to cry. I realised once again how much of an emotional pressure these ladies were under and of course how much it was affecting and indeed is still affecting their lives.

I made more coffee and then, as I started to pour some of it out to those who wanted it, my mobile phone rang. I was going to ignore it but I saw it was Anne. I picked up the call by pressing answer, she spoke and said simply, "I am in."

My reply was, "Are you sure? Are you absolutely sure?"

"Yes," she said emphatically. "YES!"

"Thanks Anne," I said. "I will be in touch shortly."

She said "Bye" and then she was gone.

I looked at the group in front of me and I said in a firm but confident voice, "That telephone call is the first member of the chosen group of ladies to say 'yes' to the proposition. WHO IS NEXT?"

There was a feeling of confidence and optimism in my voice and I sensed the women sat in front of me felt it too. At the beginning, when I first looked and researched the names in the hospital to see who might be potential candidates, I have to admit I was very sceptical about the outcome of my idea but after getting the call from Anne, and my own experiences with Julia and Lisa, my confidence suddenly grew to a massive high point. I felt that even if some of them said no it did not matter in the slightest. I spoke to the group again and I said:

"Look ladies, this is a big decision for anyone and God knows I had to make the same decision too. You all need time to think about what I have said and you need to think long and hard about the consequences as well for both you and your husband or partner.

Please all go home and take the idea with you and when you have made a decision either way, yes or no, then give me a call. I won't judge you. If my proposal is good for you fine, if not then we will part on good terms and I will wish you each and everyone a happy life."

A couple of the ladies spoke out in agreement and that was where the meeting ended. One by one they put on their coats, finished the tea or coffee I had given them and they left. I shook hands with some and received a gentle hug from others.

I had closed the door when I noticed two of the ladies were still sitting there. They were the two who had come with Helen. I looked at them and asked if there was a problem. "Well yes and no," said one of them.

When they had come into my home earlier I did not remember if they had introduced themselves or not. I said, "Sorry girls, but I can't remember your names." The first girl said, "I am Grace" and the other responded with "And I am Jean."

"OK," I said, "now we know who we are what is the problem?"

The two girls looked at each other and Jean said, "We are a gay couple and we have been together for about two years. We have decided to have a baby. Will this be a problem?" I responded no, I didn't think it would be a problem at all.

I looked at them when Grace said, "But really we want two babies because I want one as well."

This was a bit of a turn up for the books and in my mind I was going through the information they had just given me, when they then both said, at almost the same time, "We will pay twice, one payment from each of us, is that alright with you?"

I looked back at them both, I smiled and said, "Yes of course, it will be fine." These gay ladies were looking for some form of confirmation and I gave it to them both with a positive yes.

There was a look of joy and relief on their faces and for me a feeling of great satisfaction as I had earned £24,000 that day for Sue and the money pot was starting to build up. They waited a few moments longer and left and went on their way.

By now everyone had left and I was on my own. It had been a busy day, but very productive. Although I had been apprehensive in the beginning I was now feeling much better about everything and also confident that I could achieve all of my goals and targets. Over the next two days I started to receive calls from the girls and most of them came back positively with a resounding yes. However, the call from Beth was not so good.

Beth called me on Monday evening. When the phone rang I looked at the display and caller I.D. and I knew who it was so I pressed the answer button.

"Hello, it's Beth," said a harsh voice.

"Hello," I replied, "how are you?"

"Not very happy," she replied. "I have battled all weekend with my conscience and I need to say some things to you."

"Carry on," I said.

"Well," she started. "I think what you are doing is immoral, it is an ill-conceived plan which breaks every rule of decency and humanity and what you will do and what you have already done is evil and dirty. You are going against God's will ..." Beth went on and on.

I listened as she said a few more unpleasant things and I did not interrupt. I simply waited for a break in her ramblings and then I said, "If it was God's will, you would all have children and this situation would not be here. In my heart it hurts me and it pains me to do the things I have had to do but I also know there is a painful need for these women to have children and if nature had worked correctly this situation would never have arisen. I can only say this to you Beth, that if you believe in God then God may also have sent this man Hugh to all of us as a solution to the problem of childless couples and women. Please consider that God may also have done this too."

I went on to say that I fight with my conscience every day and I still feel pain in what I am doing but I also know that if I can improve people's lives and give them the chance of a child that is so badly needed then I have to give it a try.

Beth was silent and I went on to say, "If my proposal is not for you that is fine, I do not expect all of you to take up the offer, but if you do not want to be part of this then please don't spoil it for anyone else. I also need to say to you Beth that I remember when you came to the clinic you were desperate for a baby and although the hospital and doctors could not help you I found a potential way in which I could help you. Before you make any decisions please remember why you came to my clinic and remember why I have brought you here. I am sorry Beth but I need to go now as I feel terribly upset at your harsh words. If you need me to talk to about anything that is hurting you then please get in touch and I will be here, but only call me if you need something, do *not* call me to hurt me or the ladies I am trying to help. This is hard enough for me to do without any more pressure, especially from people like yourself who should know better.

Finally, from this conversation I will assume that you will not be part of this situation and I will scrub your name off the list. I am sorry this hurts you, but I have other people to consider and I must move forward for them. Take care Beth and I wish you all the very best for the future, goodbye and good luck." And with that I ended the call.

I called Sue on the Wednesday and updated her on all the news. She sounded shocked and surprised, but also very happy at the expected outcome. I knew also that she was not totally happy with what I was doing but I also knew for certain that she was extremely grateful too. I had received a call from all but two of the ladies that I had contacted, one of them was obviously Beth and the other girl was Christine. I had no intention of calling Beth, as I think that there was no point going down that avenue again. As far as I could see she had made up her mind and nothing was going to change her opinion. I did not expect a 100 percent conversion but I had been fairly certain that Christine would be a strong candidate. However, that said, I was going to give her more time to go over things in her own mind before she made any decision of this magnitude.

While all of this was going on I still had to work and I still had to go through my normal routines, nothing must change and I had to be sure everything around me appeared as it should. One other thing I needed to be sure of was Karen. I had neglected to involve her in my plans and without her nothing could take place so I needed to see her as soon as possible to make sure she was onside with all of this. I had all of Karen's shift rotas for quite a while ahead so I knew in advance when she would be at work and of course when she would not. I gave her a call on the Friday after the meeting with the girls and said we needed to talk. She said this was fine and I suggested she come to my house the next day, which was Saturday. We agreed lunch time was a good time and that we would see each other then.

One thing Karen said to me was that she needed a favour from me and that she would discuss it when we saw each other.

"No problem," I said, "see you tomorrow and I will do what I can for you. After all," I said, "I owe you big time. If I can do it then it will be done."

Karen laughed out loud and I laughed too. We both said goodbye, see you tomorrow, and I ended the call.

The next day and right on time a knock at the front door and Karen was here. It was her first time to visit me at my home. Really speaking we were not friends at the hospital before Hugh G so there had never been a need for us to meet socially, so this in fact was the first time.

"Coffee?" I asked her.

"Beer would be better," she said.

"I can manage a beer for you. I'm sure there is a can or two somewhere in the fridge."

When I checked in the kitchen it was lager not beer. I shouted to Karen "It's lager".

"That will do," she said.

I walked back into the living room, gave her the can of Heineken and a glass. I poured myself a glass of wine. It was a little early in the day but we were off work so what the hell! We sat opposite each other and we did not say much at all. I did sense a little apprehension but nothing bad, just a bit of uncertainty between us. I looked at Karen and said the reason I wanted to see her was about Hugh G.

"I thought it might be about him."

"It's complicated."

"Tell me," Karen replied.

"Well," I started to say, "I have a number of ladies who want to use Hugh G's services."

"His *cock* you mean," said Karen.

I was a little shocked at how she said that word and also using the word 'cock' as well. I somehow did not imagine she would speak this way. I replied, "Yes, his cock."

Karen laughed at me and I suppose because I was sensitive about him and very defensive it must have showed on my face. I relaxed a little and laughed too, after all I could see the funny side of this I suppose.

"I have possibly ten ladies."

"Fuck me!" Karen replied. "Ten?"

Her response this time did shock me. I had never heard Karen speak this way before and it made me sit up and pay a bit more attention to her. Karen laughed again and took a drink from her glass of lager and just sat in her chair looking back at me. Karen had an intense look about her, something which I had never noticed before. It was as if she was looking into my mind and I could actually feel her thoughts probing mine. I said, "What are you thinking Karen?" and she replied back to me, "No Leigh, what are *you* thinking?"

I responded with, "When do we start our project?"

Karen smiled and said, "As soon as we can. I also presume I get the usual financial kickback from this little venture?"

"But of course," I replied. "I would not have it any other way."

At this point I did not want to mention the charges that I was making as I believed it may cloud Karen's judgement in this matter. If she thought she was getting what she asked for, to me that would be enough. If I gave her £2000 a time, that's twenty thousand pounds – not bad for turning a blind eye, very easy money indeed!

Girls' night Out

We sat for a while longer and we chatted about many things when Karen suddenly said, "Let's call this little adventure *Operation Girls' Night Out*."

"Why would we do that?" I said.

"It's a code name silly," she said. "If you need to discuss something in public it is a safe way of talking about it without drawing attention to what we are doing."

This idea actually made sense so I agreed I would also tell the girls the same thing and although they knew to keep things quiet it may be necessary to use a code name for whatever reason, so that was agreed.

We sat and talked some more when I suddenly remembered that Karen had mentioned that she wanted a favour from me, so I asked her about this: "What favour were you going to ask for, you have not yet mentioned it and I think we need to talk about it?"

Karen's eyes widened and she said to me, "Do you really want to know Leigh?"

"Well, yes of course. If I am to help you with it I need to know what it is, don't I?"

"OK," said Karen, "I want to make you climax."

"WHAT!" I said out loud. I nearly choked on my glass of wine.

"That's right," she said, "I want to make you climax."

I was shocked and surprised and I really did not know how to respond.

"What on earth makes you want to do that?" I said to her.

"I have felt this way for many years. I like men and women but I really enjoy making women climax, it gives me a really big sexual high and I am very good at it. I also think you will enjoy it too."

I didn't know what to say, but I could tell that now it had been mentioned Karen's mood had changed and I felt then that she was starting to get aroused and I could feel the atmosphere change to.

"I don't know what to say or do and I can't tell if I'm flattered or not."

Karen looked at me with a deep and penetrating stare and I was almost hypnotised by the way she looked at me, it was as if I were paralysed, I simply could not move.

Karen spoke and said, "I have watched you with Hugh many times and seeing you with him has made me so horny that I could have burst into the room when you were with him and dragged you off him and taken you for myself. When you fucked Hugh you became a dirty, filthy bitch and I wanted some of what you were giving him and I want some of that right here and right NOW!"

Karen's tone was determined and powerful and as she spoke I still could not move a bloody muscle. I was in a state of shock but I have to say I was not afraid or unhappy at what she was saying to me, in actual fact I felt horny too! Karen moved forward and put her hand on my left breast. "Is this alright?" she said.

I just nodded back to her mainly because I could not speak. I was wearing a light pink cardigan with about six pearl-type buttons on the front. Karen started from the top and opened every one of them, she twisted me around slightly and very gently then eased the cardigan off from behind me and put it on the back of my chair.

Next she put her hands around my waist and pulled up my white T-shirt and pulled it up over my head and took it off completely. My breasts were bigger now than they had ever been because of the baby and my nipples were huge, right now they were massive and stuck out like two doorstops and boy were they feeling sensitive. Karen rubbed her hands over the outside of my bra and made my nipples tingle with excitement and I felt good and I really enjoyed the way she touched me. Without a word she unclipped my bra and she let it fall on to my lap. She brought her hands to the front of me and cupped my tits in her hands, she put my nipples firmly in her finger tips and started to pull them and rub them and Jesus Christ I nearly came then.

Karen stood up and said, "Wait here a minute, I need to go to my car for a moment." She went outside and a short while later I heard the clunk of a car door and she returned into my house with a medium sized box in her hands. I looked at her and asked what was inside. "Wait and see," she said, "wait and see."

Karen stood straight in front of me and started to pull off her own top, she lifted it up over her head and dropped it on the floor behind her. I had not noticed before but she was not wearing a bra and when she revealed her breasts and they were beautiful they looked firm with unusual pointy nipples which faced upwards and her tits were very shiny and nicely tanned, as was her whole upper body. Karen put the box on the floor in front of me and kneeled down at my feet. She started to take off my sandals, then she moved upward towards my skirt. With both hands she raised my skirt upward towards my waist. I eased my bottom off the chair to help her. Once my skirt was raised high up she put her hands into the top of my small panties and pulled them down very slowly and very provocatively. She removed my pants to reveal my pussy. My fanny is shaved very neat and tidy and trimmed so no hairs everywhere. Karen opened the box she had placed on the floor and took out a gel lubricant. She popped back the top and squeezed some of it onto her fingers; it smelled sweet, almost good enough to eat.

She put her fingers into my fanny and applied the gel to my vagina inside and out, her touch was gentle and tender and she felt good, really good. She rubbed my pussy lips for a while as I started to lie back and respond to her touch; I wanted to scream but I remained quiet.

Karen looked back to the box and she put her hand inside and pulled out a vibrator with three heads on it. This unusual dildo looked wrong, it seemed as if it were not the right tool for the job but how wrong I was. Karen pushed the vibrator into me and up me and once in place Karen squeezed more gel onto her fingers. She slid her hand underneath me and applied lube to my arse. Karen pushed her fingers inside my hole and around the outside and probed me deep inside, she then positioned one of the other heads of the dildo and pushed it into my arse. At first it was a little uncomfortable and I winced, but Karen said "Easy girl, it will be OK."

I just looked at her and said, "Keep on going" and she did just that.

The third head was in the front of my vagina and it sat just into the clitoris. With a bit more lube applied around that area, Karen switched on the monster machine.

It started to hum and it started to vibrate in all three places and each place had a different feeling. "Turn the power down," I asked.

"It is down," said Karen. "It's on the lowest setting, let it work, you will get used to it."

Within moments I started to respond to the vibrating machine and *Oh my god* did I respond. Karen kept hold of the outside of the machine to stop it coming out of me. I was squeezing it so hard with my fanny muscles I thought it might break, but of course it would not.

Karen gently moved the vibrator to help stimulate me and then she said "Hold on" and before I knew it she turned the power up to another level.

"Fucking hell!" I screamed, as the machine turned my arse and my cunt into two completely different pleasure zones. I did not think it were possible to orgasm in the anal area but it felt like I was about to do so but as this feeling hit me my fanny started to get a feeling I had never had before and I came. *OH fuck me* did I come and at the same time my arse seemed to climax as well, not the same but *by Christ* not bad, not bad at all. I had a final burst with a couple of short orgasms supported by me writhing around and a powerful ecstatic scream as I flopped into the chair. Karen put her hands on my face, put her lips to mine and kissed me in a way I had never felt before, it was unbelievable and amazing.

I lay still with my eyes closed and I felt totally fulfilled and invigorated, what an experience I was thinking to myself when suddenly I opened my eyes to see Karen removing her tight jeans. She was nearly naked apart from her skimpy panties. I looked at her as she pulled the pants down to her ankles and as she did so she kicked them off and away behind my three-seater settee. She was totally naked and the first thing that caught my eyes was a big black bushy fanny, it was as black as coal, well trimmed and very tidy, but strangely attractive.

"Come on then," she said, "it's my turn."

"My turn what?" I said.

"Frig me off with your fingers, your tongue or the dildo." I looked at Karen's wanting eyes and I had never thought that as she brought me to full orgasm that I would have to do the same back to her.

The realisation that this is what she wanted was a huge shock to me and I did not know how to respond. "Don't be shy Leigh, you know what to do and now is the chance for you to do it to me!"

I looked at Karen and I was speechless not knowing what to do or say to her. However, I pushed Karen down on the floor and picked up the dildo in the hope I could give Karen what she wanted. I bent down between her legs and before I could do anything she said, "Take all your clothes off for me Leigh."

"Why?" I asked.

"Because I want you naked when you make me climax.

"I am self-conscious about my baby bumps," I said to her.

"Well don't be," she replied, "just do it for me, it's what I want and I want to see it now, RIGHT NOW!"

There was that tone again, the one she used earlier to emphasize what she wanted. I decided to throw caution to the wind and I took all of my clothes off and stood before Karen naked and vulnerable. She just smiled at me and said, "Bring me off Leigh and make me orgasm now!"

I looked down at her fanny and pushed her back down onto the floor, I parted her legs, squeezed lube on my fingers and pushed them deep into her bushy black cunt. I have to say it felt fantastic and I felt excited again. I had never touched a woman's pussy before so this was a first time experience and I was really enjoying it and I wanted more and more from this experience. I rubbed her cunt deep inside and it wasn't long before she started to moan and groan and she was obviously enjoying what I was doing as she responded more and more to my feminine touches. For ten minutes I kept on working my fingers deep up her vaginal pathway and I tried to touch her in the same places I enjoyed being touched, and whatever I did she seemed to enjoy and that meant everything that I did to her.

Inevitably I had to reach for the vibro machine; I picked it up and looked at it closely. Not 20 minutes earlier this machine had brought me to an amazing climax and now I was going to do the same thing to another woman and yes, I was excited more than I would have expected.

I switched it on. It had five settings so I started at one. I put the biggest tip on the outside of Karen's vagina and held it there, for a moment or two I did nothing else. Karen spoke and said "Turn it up to three", and I obliged. I turned the button to three and the change of power was immense. I placed it gently against Karen's vaginal lips once again, pushed it hard against Karen's pussy and what a difference it made to her response. I applied a little more lubricant to make things smoother and Karen started to show signs of a full-on orgasm. I put some more lube on my fingers and put my hand under her bottom and probed her arse hole. I found the centre and pushed my fingers inside I slid them inside and out up and down and Karen loved it. I withdrew my fingers from her arse hole and placed the vibrator in the same position as my fingers had been and I pushed the second big vibrator head up her arse.

What a response I got from her and fuck did it turn me on, I could clearly see the speed setting so I turned the button to 5 and fucking hell, Karen went crazy.

My nose was itchy so I rubbed it with my free hand and I could smell the shit from Karen's arse and you know what, it did not bother me at all. I started to get myself aroused again and started to finger my cunt while at the same time I brought Karen off to a powerful climax, and as she came she screamed, *"Fuck me, fuck me, oh fucking work my fanny Leigh, work my fanny!"*

I was in a daze, my senses were all over and I could not think clearly, so many things were happening to me that I seemed very lost in my feelings and emotions and everything started to become a blur as if I was in some sort of dream state. I almost felt as if I had been drugged, this feeling I was experiencing was something that I had never felt before and I was not sure if I enjoyed it or if I was afraid of it because I was feeling a loss of control over myself.

I was going through a thought process when I looked down to see Karen absolutely exhausted laid in front of me on the floor. She was soaking wet with sweat, her body was shining and even though I was not gay she looked fantastic with a beautiful body and fantastic breasts and I suddenly realised that I had just brought this woman to a full and erotic climax and I felt exhilarated by what we had just done.

I sat back on the floor in front of Karen. I had been sitting a little uncomfortably because of the baby, but at the time of the excitement I had not felt any discomfort, but I was feeling it now. I realised I still felt horny and I had not finished what I started with my fingers on my fanny a moment or two earlier. Once again I started to rub my pussy when I heard Karen say "Don't waste it Leigh, we have more to do together."

I looked at Karen and said "What more is there?"

"Let me show you," she said. She went back into the box that she had brought with her and took out a long sausage-type device. It looked like it had a cock head on each end. It was about a foot long and it was shiny black, it looked like it was made from a rubber or latex type construction, it was flexible and yet firm at the same time.

Karen also took out a different tube of lubricant which smelled like almonds. She covered this new device with this new lube and said to me, "Sit back Leigh and open your legs."

I did as I was told without question. When I was more comfortable Karen pushed one of the cock ends into my fanny very gently but quite a way up inside me. Karen moved closer and pushed the other end up into her fanny as well and it went a long way up her, much further I think than it did in mine. I lay back on the floor but I had to pack some cushions around me to support myself and my baby bump. I got myself in a comfortable position and waited for Karen, I was not sure what to do so I waited for Karen to start to do something as she seemed to know all the moves and I obviously did not.

Sure enough Karen leaned forward and grabbed hold of the double dildo as I called it and she pressed it. Immediately it sprung into life with a very powerful and strong vibration. This vibration seemed to start in the middle and travel towards the ends and we could both feel its power and *Jesus Christ* was it good. I watched Karen as she started to writhe about the floor, she looked amazing and she could really respond to the way the double-headed vibrator stimulated her pussy.

I too was feeling a totally new experience and it was mind blowing, it must have been some sight if anyone could have seen the two of us on the floor enjoying the double dildo experience together. Karen was ramming her cunt hard towards me and each time she did I felt like I was being fucked really hard, but it was a fantastic feeling.

Karen sat up, grabbed the dildo again and seemed to press it again, and a different action came from the dildo. It started to pulse, sending a shockwave along the length of itself and fuck me, it blew my brains out. I thought Karen was about to climax when all of a sudden I exploded inside my fanny and boy did I come, it was a fucking orgasm to beat any I had felt before.

As my cunt exploded Karen showed me the sign of a woman in ecstasy as she too climaxed, and as she came to full orgasm she let out a mighty scream and she was there. As she settled down she had two or three shudders as the orgasm faded away and we were both well and truly done.

We both lay still for a while just letting the moment pass and eventually Karen spoke, you could tell she was out of breath but to be honest so was I, partly because of the experience I had just gone through and also because of how I saw Karen perform, it was quite an unbelievable thing to be part of. Karen ushered me back and she withdrew this mighty dildo first from my fanny, then she pulled it out of her own. By now it was turned off and it was now asleep and at rest. I looked at Karen and said "I have to get myself one of those."

"Keep that one," she said, "a gift from me to you."

I smiled at her and said "Thanks, I will take you up on the offer."

"It's yours," she said, and with that I stood up with Karen and we embraced. We held each other in our arms and Karen kissed me with a passion I had seldom felt before.

"That was a beautiful thing," she said to me and I said to her it was also a fantastic fuck.

We started to get cleaned up and dressed. I cleaned my new dildo with some wet wipes and I placed it in a drawer out of sight but not, I might say, out of mind. After we were through I hit an awkward point, I was not sure what to say or do and I think Karen could sense this.

"Did you have a good time?" she said to me and I replied, "Yes Karen, yes I really did."

She put her arms around me and hugged me, and I hugged her back. I kissed her on the cheek and with that she said, "I will call you to sort everything out", and then she left.

I'm not sure what I was feeling, everything around me was a bit unclear and I think for me I didn't quite grasp the things that were happening around me. There was so much activity in my life right now that I simply could not see where I was going. I felt very alone and a little afraid.

I was having a baby without the support of a father, I was organising something involving the use of a patient that once upon a time I would never have done, and ethically, I did feel very bad and if that wasn't enough, I had just had sex with another woman which is a thing that I had never ever contemplated before.

I spent the rest of the day relaxing, drinking coffee, eating chocolate (which by the way I was eating a lot of!) and I tried to clear my mind and start again. I had so many things to put in place and so many risks to take that I needed to be clear in thought.

My previous encounters with Hugh G had worked relatively well and because of Karen's help things had gone without a hitch. However, with a change in how many ladies were going to use his erection meant I had to plan the process much more precisely, like a military operation.

I did not return to work until the following Tuesday, so at least I had a few days to myself and boy did I need them. Over the weekend I wrote down notes and I tried to formulate a good plan that was timed to make sure that I achieved my objective which was to get every lady to have sex with Hugh G at least once.

'Have sex', that sounds strange because really that is not strictly true, you see I keep forgetting that Hugh G is not a willing participant. If he were a conscious patient he may want to enjoy what was being offered to him as any normal man might, but I also think that if he were in a non-coma state his erection may be normal and he would respond in a normal human way.

I was starting to think about things too deeply and I was creating a debate in my mind and the more I thought about things the more I battled with ethics, guilt, doubt, sadness and confusion. STOP Leigh now, I said to myself. Get focused girl and get with the programme and remember *why* you are doing this. Somewhere along the way I had forgotten about Sue and her money problem and the whole reason for the childless women being called together was because of her. I needed to re-think what I needed to do and I had to make sure plans were put in place to protect everyone, including me.

Since I had begun planning how I would execute this operation I had covered many different ideas on how to get these women onto the ward where Hugh G was and of course, how to get them out again. When visitors were there it was easier because people just blend in but after visiting hours are over it becomes much more of an issue and the risk obviously increases.

In the early plans I was thinking of one woman at a time spread over a number of nights but I was now more inclined to send in two at a time or maybe even three, it may sound crazy but I had seen the amount of sperm Hugh produced and I was of the opinion that he could deliver three times in one night. My idea to send in two or three ladies at a time means that the overall timescale is reduced and in my mind the risk aspect would also be much better, although I would be taking in more than one lady at a time it will in my eyes cut the timescales down to a more manageable level.

I put together a timetable based on Karen's shift pattern which she had already given me and I put the names together in four groups of who will go with whom and when. I had now acquired ten ladies who would be involved, although there had been originally eleven including Beth, but now she was out of the game and with the additional two gay girls who joined the group I was at a combined number of ten people.

The groups were Jade and Alison the gay partners; group two Linda, Shola and Julie; group three were Helen, Christine and Grace and finally Anne and Ruth who were last but not least. I checked and re-checked to satisfy myself that I had thought this through. I will contact Karen to get some input from her and once we both agree I will call the girls and tell them the plan.

I felt a little bit surer about what I wanted to do so it eased some of the stresses I was feeling. In my mind I felt that I have everything in hand, all seemed reasonable and with the support of Karen things felt good; at this point I think I am ready to go for it and set things into motion. Throughout the whole process I had not discussed any of my plans with Sue as I felt it would compromise her should anything go wrong, so she had no involvement at all. I firmly believed this was the best way to go and also the safest option for her too, in the words of the politician 'plausible deniability' – what you don't know should not be able to hurt you!

I called Karen on the Monday and discussed everything with her, she seemed comfortable with the plans and the ideas that I had put in place, so with her backing and her blessings we decided that the first group of ladies would be with Hugh G on Thursday of this week. However, I wanted a final meeting with everyone on Wednesday evening to make sure all participants were clear on what was to take place, what they had to do and how I intended to move forward with the plans.

I called all of the ladies and requested them to be at my house for 7pm Wednesday and I also asked each and every one of them to bring the payments as we had agreed.

I needed this to be done so that there was no misunderstanding about our intentions as we moved forward. After each and every call I ticked one more name off the list as confirmation of their attendance and acceptance of the meeting and the payments which were due.

As usual time moves on and Wednesday came around quickly, by 7.25 on Wednesday night all the girls were assembled at my home, all the money was paid and the plans were discussed. The money was passed over by each woman, some of it in large envelopes, some of it openly and in sight for all to view. I put the money in a box behind a chair. I would deal with it all later when everyone went home. At least I had achieved one part of my plan and that was to help Sue out of her financial problems and that had just been achieved very easily. It was a lighthearted evening with a few bottles of wine and a few nibbles to eat, it almost felt like a girls' night in and although there was a serious element to the meeting it was actually a pleasant evening.

At around 8pm I had a knock at the door. I opened the door to see Karen standing there, I had invited her to meet the girls and to make sure everyone was clear who was who and also what we all needed to do and the parts people would play in this operation. I had never done anything like this before and although the cause was a good one for all concerned I was still not totally comfortable with how I was using Hugh G. I knew what I was doing was ethically wrong but I also knew that a lot of people were depending on me to deliver on promises made, so I felt that this was the most important thing right now and any morality or any ethics would have to stay at the back of my mind for now.

As the night rolled on all of us were in a sort of party mood and it was actually nice to see people enjoying themselves, the reality was that some of these ladies may fall pregnant and some may not. Although their medical histories were similar regarding the conception issues, it was still a 'take your chance' scenario and that was one of my concerns. I really wanted everyone to be successful and achieve pregnancy, I was praying for this to happen.

Right now at this time in my home we were all full of hope but like any challenge you face in life a challenge can quite easily turn you from hope to despair. Already these ladies had felt and were feeling despair at not being able to have children in a natural manner. It must be a painful experience not to be able to conceive with their chosen partners with the exception of the gay girls who had different challenges from the rest of the group.

When Karen arrived I introduced her to the team so to speak and they all accepted her very quickly, some even hugged her and thanked her for what she was doing for them, it was a comforting feeling watching the acceptance and integration of everyone. It did have a strong family feel about the whole evening and that made me smile, it also helped me to be invigorated and re-energised as I had been feeling a little low recently.

This low feeling may have been partly due to the hormone changes within me because of the baby and also I think because of the pressure of all that was happening too. We eventually got down to business and I told the girls of the plans I had made and I also told everyone that I had discussed them with Karen and we felt good with all that was to be done.

I told the girls of the groupings and sequences and why I had done it this way. Once I had said that people were going in groups there was obviously something that a few of the ladies did not like and there was an obvious change in the atmosphere. "Spit it out ladies," I barked. "Who is not happy? Just spit it out."

They all looked at each other and Anne said, "I think I speak for a few of us when I say that I am not happy about going with a man before or directly after another woman. It has a dirty feel to me and also it may reduce the chances of conception if his sperm delivery gets less for the next customer so to speak."

One or two ladies laughed but the rest had serious looks on their faces.

I fired back quickly and sternly to all of them, "Look girls, I have seen how this man's erection and sperm delivery is and I can tell you that from the first to the last you will not lose out. However, in the likelihood that it is not exactly as you need we can do it again until you give up or you fall pregnant. As for the queuing system, Karen and I are taking a major risk and we have to balance this against everything else. I hear your concerns Anne, but hear mine too. If we get caught people will lose jobs or may even go to prison for this, I believe this could be deemed as a criminal act. Let us not play down the facts here, this is a big thing that we are undertaking and I have to make it as safe and as sensible as I possibly can. There needs to be a compromise and this will be part of that compromise so sorry ladies, it's this way or no way."

Everyone looked at me and I expected resistance but there was none that was made obvious, a few of the girls nodded in approval and the rest just sat there in a sort of accepting way. It made no difference to me they were in or they were out, at this stage of the game I can't afford to take chances or more risks than we currently were taking.

I changed the mood by suggesting a toast. "Charge your glasses ladies," I said. The wine bottles on the coffee table were picked up and wine was poured. Once all the glasses had been topped up I said out loud, "To good fortune and providence, may our endeavours bring forth healthy and happy rewards for each and every one of us. CHEERS LADIES!"

And "Cheers!" was the reply back from all of them.

By 10.30 all of the ladies were gone and only Karen remained. We sat talking for a while and of course apart from the main topic of discussion for the evening *Operation Girls' Night Out* which was the code name we had given to our project, we discussed our sexual liaison which we had together a few days before. I was a little uncomfortable talking about it because to be honest I was a little ashamed of myself and I wasn't sure how to deal with it and especially talking about it this way it just seemed odd. We were both a little tipsy but definitely not drunk, so we both knew what we were doing and what we were saying to each other.

Karen started by saying "Any regrets about the other day?"

I hesitated and said, "No, not regrets as such, just a little uncertain about things. I did not expect what happened between us so I was shocked and, to be honest, once the shock was over I really enjoyed myself. One thing I kept asking myself *is am I gay?* and I know that the answer is definitely *not*."

Karen spoke out and said to me, "You do not need to be gay to enjoy a sexual encounter with another woman and as you rightly admit you *did* enjoy it."

"Yes, I did enjoy it but it still raises concerns and doubts in my mind and I can't help that."

"I understand," said Karen, "but I also know that if something like that feels so good then don't fight it, just enjoy it for what it is. If you want to try it again we can but next time we will plan it so we can make it a more balanced experience, what do you say?"

I paused for a moment and said to her, "After all of this other business is over then we can have a look at things and see where we go from there."

Karen smiled at me and said, "That sounds like a good plan."

I felt OK with this as it gives me time to think things through and to help me decide what I want to do or if I want to do anything with Karen at all. For me the experience with her was a good one but I also had reservations about any more sexual contact with her. I had to be sure before I said yes again.

Since I first heard about Hugh G and indeed from the first time we met I had gone through some life-changing experiences, my world had turned upside down and it all stemmed from the first night Sue told me about him. From the very thought of talking to Sue that first night when she had said about this patient with a huge erection to now my life was on a completely different pathway.

From that time I have met new people and made some new friends, I was pregnant to a stranger whose real name I don't know and I was potentially about to break the law or at the very least break all of my ethical codes. My bloody head was full of everything and nothing and inside me I was back to a mix of emotions and pain, it was a nightmare and yet it still felt like the right thing to do. 'Go to bed Leigh,' I said to myself, I need to sleep and clear my thoughts as tomorrow was to be the first of my girls' night out sessions and I wanted to be on top form for this first stage of the girls' night out plan.

I did not sleep as well as I wanted but it was alright, I tossed and turned throughout the whole of the night but I did manage some sleep. I woke up on the Thursday morning and started the day with a good cup of coffee. I reviewed in my mind the events to follow that evening and I thought about the first set of girls to go with Hugh G.

Jade and Alison were to be the first tonight. I had already arranged with them to be at my home for around 6.30, today was a day off work for me and it was just as well as I felt a bit queasy with the baby and to be honest I could not have gone to work anyway. I spent the day doing a little cleaning; I didn't do much as my house is usually clean anyway. That said I dusted and hoovered and also went and did some shopping. All in all it was a quiet pleasant day. I got back home and watched a TV movie which was on about a child and a dog lost in a forest. It was quite a good film based on a true story and Dean Caine starred in it. He was the guy who played Superman in the TV series some time ago.

I tried to clear my mind but I still felt anxious and uptight and sick inside too. The day moved on I had a little snack for tea, I could not eat much at all or else I would have been sick, it was that sort of feeling inside of me.

I had occupied myself all day quite well and I tried not to think of the forthcoming events although from time to time I did ponder about what was going to happen and how things were going to work out. My biggest hope was that all the women in the group fell pregnant but sadly and realistically I felt that this would not be the case, a percentage like everything else in life was sure to fail and that was one of the hardest things for me to deal with.

One of the things which struck me in all of this was that none of the ladies in our group had mentioned their husbands or partners and this surprised me. Usually at the clinic most women brought their husbands or boyfriends with them, it was usually part of the process for checking who the problem lay with based on the couple not being able to conceive a child. That was a normal part of the process but throughout all of my talks with the girls none of them had mentioned partners except for the two gay girls of course, which was quite obvious. It was just an observation, but it was something that really hit home to me.

Around 6.30 and there was a knock at the door. I opened it to find Jade and Alison standing there. I greeted them both and in they walked, they sat down together on the two-seater settee and they held each other's hands very tightly. I looked at them both and I could see the tension on their faces. "It will be OK ladies," I said to them, but it did not seem to make much of an impression. I asked them if they wanted a drink and both declined, there was obviously something wrong so I asked outright, "What is the problem as there is obviously something not quite right here?"

Jade looked at Alison and then looked at me and she said, "I have never slept with a man before and I am terrified. Alison is bisexual but I am not so tonight is difficult for me in many ways. Alison has had many relationships with men and I have never known that feeling of either emotional or sexual contact and it is having a big effect on how I feel tonight."

Jade went on to say that they had both talked about this situation but no matter how much they discussed it she felt strange about it all.

"Will this be a problem?" I asked.

"NO," she replied, "not at all. We are both in this to the end!"

At first when Jade had spoken I thought there may be a problem but her confident and decisive answer was enough to reassure me that things would be OK I had initially felt a little tension between them but Alison and Jade held hands tightly and I could see how strong they looked together. Of course everyone involved in this situation will be uptight but I still had to be sure of things, after all there was a great deal at stake here for a lot of people and I had full responsibility for a good outcome for everyone and I mean everyone involved. I looked at the digital clock on the wall and it was time to go, it was nearly 7pm and it was around a 20-minute drive to the hospital. I ushered the girls outside and into my car.

I had decided to use my car because I could use the staff car park and my pass was cleared so it would draw no attention and also I wanted to reduce the chance of any of the girls' cars being spotted on CCTV should anything go wrong.

We drove to the hospital and arrived about 7.25. The public car park was full and the staff car park was definitely the right choice. I drove up to the electronic barrier, put in my key card and the barrier raised. I drove straight in and found a parking space.

I quickly moved the girls inside to blend in with the other members of the public who were visiting patients within the hospital. I proceeded to go to the main ward were Hugh G was, and as I entered I saw Karen about halfway down the ward. She was stood near some people but not talking to them, it was as if she knew we would be there and was discretely ready for our arrival. I looked at her and she nodded gently to me and smiled lightly at me. I walked towards her with Jade and Alison, nobody paid any attention to us. We moved swiftly into the side ward where Hugh G was lying in his bed.

The girls got the first glimpse of him still in a deep sleep as he lay silently in his bed. I did my usual and introduced everyone to each other, this was now almost a ritual and I still felt that it was important in some strange but courteous way.

The girls both looked at him and then looked at each other, there was an eerie silence and a strange feeling. I asked them if they were both alright and they both replied, "Yes thanks, we are fine." I looked at Jade and she seemed to have an intense stare looking deeply at Hugh G and not looking anywhere else.

"Are you *sure* you are OK Jade?" I asked.

"YES," she snapped. "Sorry," she said. "I don't mean to be snappy, I am just getting my head around what I have to do, it's not your fault. I just need a moment to think that's all."

I acknowledged her difficulty and simply stood back out of her way and I allowed them both some time to get prepared for the task ahead of them. I went back onto the main ward and went to speak with Karen and make sure all was well. The time was approaching 8 o'clock and visiting time was nearly over. A few of the visitors had by now started to leave and the ward was getting quite empty.

At the end of visiting time there are a few jobs that need to be done for the patients on the ward and because of this nurses from other less busy wards usually come to help those nurses on more hectic wards to clear up the workload. It was at this point two other junior nurses came in to Karen's ward to give her a hand. Karen went to the two girls and gave them instructions where to go and who needed assistance. Karen was a highly skilled senior nurse and the two junior nurses quickly responded to Karen's instructions and there were no problems or issues. It was at this time I decided to go back into Hugh G's side ward to see how the girls were doing. I opened the door to find Alison on top of Hugh G and she was riding him like a crazy woman; she clearly had his cock inside her and she was sweating heavily as she sat on top of him.

Jade was also sat on top of Hugh G but she was only watching her partner have vigorous sex. Jade was watching closely as her female lover climaxed. She was about to shout out as she came and I quickly stepped forward to cover Alison's mouth with my hand to keep her quiet. I was fully aware of who was outside Hugh G's side ward door and this would have been a major problem if Alison had screamed when she climaxed with the two other nurses outside the door – the whole operation would have been ruined.

Alison turned and looked at me with an evil angry glare. I held her mouth tight and then looked towards the door and nodded my head several times. Alison looked at the doorway then she looked back at me and she must have realised there was a problem.

Alison stopped resisting my hand over her mouth and she relaxed. I moved away from the three of them on the bed and went towards the door. I opened the door slightly to see Karen and the other two nurses working around the ward dealing with the handful of patients who were there. Karen caught a glimpse of my face and she could see I was looking distressed. Within a matter of minutes her work was complete and the two nurses were ushered away out of the ward and the coast was clear. I opened the door and entered the main ward and I walked quickly towards Karen.

"What's wrong?" Karen asked in a nervous voice.

"The stupid bitch in there started to bang Hugh G and I had not told her to start anything until the coast was clear, sadly she did not listen and she started to fuck Hugh while I was here with you and the other two nurses. That was a bloody close call, I don't know what she was playing at but that was a near miss and almost the end of the venture before it started. I am going to have a word or two with her. That was foolish to say the least."

"Keep calm Leigh," said Karen. "You know this is a highly charged environment right now and we don't want to be hasty, so stay cool girl, stay very cool."

I looked at Karen and told her I would keep my cool but I was very angry inside and very upset; all of this was inside of me and in my mind as I reached Hugh G's side ward doorway. I stepped in and started to speak to Alison.

Jade and Alison were still on the bed and I was trying to contain my emotions as I said to the pair of them, "What the hell were you playing at? I have told you time and time again that we are all at risk doing this thing and you pull a bloody stunt like that! What did you think you were doing Alison?"

Alison spoke to me and said, "I am sorry, I thought that when you left the room we could get started. I tried to get Jade to go first but she was having difficulty and so to help her I showed her what to do. It isn't that she does not know what to do it's just a difficulty in actually having sex with a man that is the problem, so I thought that if I could lead the way she would find it easier to follow me. It's not just the fact that we have both paid cash to do this, we really need these babies and we are both hoping that one of us falls pregnant, but if both of us can do it we will be very happy indeed.

This is for both of us a life-changing commitment and we really need one of us to have a child. One other thing you should really be aware of is that I enjoy sex with men and women and this is also a big problem for Jade. We are both fighting many issues here and this is the first time in two years I have been with a man. For Jade this is like a betrayal and although it is not we both are still having difficulty with what we are doing here tonight."

I could hear in Alison's voice both the sincerity and the desperation and I realised that they were devoted and determined to make a life together. Alison and Jade both apologised and then they started to climb down off the bed when I stopped them both.

By now Alison was off Hugh G and I could see his erection was down which suggested he had ejaculated. I got closer to Alison and told her to lie back alongside Hugh G and open her legs I wanted to see if there were any sperm signs in her, or if he had come after she climaxed. She did not question me but instantly lay back down and opened her legs.

I looked closely and gently parted her vaginal lips to see around the edge of her inner pussy, there were signs of sperm. I leaned forward to smell her vagina and I could smell the sperm around her opening.

Everyone, including Karen, was looking intensely at me. I moved back and then looked at Hugh G's cock, it was just starting to come back up but it was quite obvious that his sperm was not all over the bed or all over him so the conclusion was that Alison had taken his full load up her and that her fuck with Hugh G had been a success. I told her to climb off Hugh and lie on the floor for a few minutes to help the sperm travel to where it needs to be. Alison did not speak, I simply put out my hand to help her down from the bed and she lay on the floor next to the wall at the righthand side of Hugh G's bed.

"Right Jade," I said in a positive voice, "you are next and we are going to help you achieve this task and by *we* I mean both Karen and myself."

Alison looked at me and said, "What are you going to do to Jade?"

"Trust me," I said to her. "Please trust me. We don't have time to waste here, so let me try something. If it works, fine, if it does not, we can try something else."

Jade was very uptight and so far she had said very little. I understood her situation and I believed that it was possible to help her get through this difficulty with a little help from Karen and me.

THE HYPNOTIC APPROACH

A few years earlier I had attended a seminar on hypnotherapy, although I had no interest in the subject I went along for the day to see what it was all about. As the day unfolded I became very interested in the contents of this programme, the idea was that the participants on this one day course were to then move on to a three-month training schedule whereby at the end you would be a qualified hypnotherapist. Anyway, to cut a long story short I enrolled for the course and passed it with a high percentage and became a qualified practitioner. From that day to now I had never found a reason to use my new found skills or to even practise on anyone until now.

It was quite clear to me that I needed to do something and at this point it was the only thing I could think of. Both Karen and Alison had no idea what I was going to do so they just watched and looked on so to speak.

"Alright, Jade," I said, "please listen to everything I tell you and please do what I ask of you. I need you to follow my instructions to the letter and hopefully we can get you through this difficult process. Are you ready?"

Jade smiled gently at me and I smiled and nodded back to her. I took hold of her hand and squeezed it gently and said to her, "Here we go. I want you to close your eyes and I want you to keep your body upright and reasonably straight, keep your knees apart and move forward until you can feel the middle area of Hugh's body under you."

Without hesitation she moved up the bed towards Hugh and positioned herself over his middle area as instructed.

"I need you to relax as much as you can Jade, and as you do all I want from you is to listen to my voice and respond to my words, do you understand?" I said to her.

She replied to me, "Yes!".

I spoke to Jade and I said, "Start to breathe for me counting in your mind, one is in through your nose and two is out through your mouth." I said it again, "One is in through your nose and two is out through your mouth." I repeated this three or four times more to help her get a rhythm in her mind and then I let her do it herself until I could see the response I was looking for.

I watched Jade's expression on her face and gradually I saw her muscles around her cheek relax, I watched her shoulders relax and I could see by the way that she was now sitting that the relaxation process was starting to work on her. I moved closer to her and started to talk softly in her direction and as I did I gave her instructions which took her to a safe and relaxing place. I talked briefly about her life and I asked her to remember good things in her life and these things allow the body and mind to follow a route which will make it easier to achieve the next level that I was aiming for. As I talked she became fully engrossed in the situation and circumstances in which I was placing her and gradually, and as I had hoped, she reached the place in her mind where I wanted her to be.

I now began to start my direct suggestion process and I took hold of Jade's mind and began to walk her to the areas of passion that I wanted her to feel.

"Jade," I said, "please look out in front of you and I want you to see the person you most want to spend the rest of your life with. I want you to imagine that this person has agreed to all your needs and desires, and the person you see has unconditionally agreed to service all the pleasures you ever wanted and hoped for. At this moment in time you can explore everything sexually that you never thought that you could. Right now this is the most exciting feeling you have ever experienced and that right here and right now you can express yourself and feel all the things that you ever wanted to feel, in short you are going to have the best orgasm of your life."

I concentrated closely on Jade and I gave her my fullest attention. My voice was soft, my instructions clear and my resolve was absolute, and in my mind I believed I now had her where she could overcome her problem and mount Hugh G's massive cock and ride him just as Alison had done a few minutes earlier. Jade was now in a very deep hypnotic state. I had placed her exactly where I wanted her to be and now she was ready to be guided to the point where she could fuck Hugh G and enjoy the experience without fear or regret.

I looked at Hugh and I could see his cock was now back to full size and ready to be used. I paused a moment to look at him and I have to say I was feeling jealous and although he was not my man, I did feel as if I had ownership of him to a certain extent. This connection between him and me was being damaged somehow and I could feel a real difficulty inside of me both physically and mentally. However, I had to overcome these feelings otherwise I would not be able to go through with the rest of my plans. I started to re-focus my mind and concentrate on what needed to be done.

I looked at Jade and said, "Reach forward and slightly down and you will feel a man's cock. You already know this is your first time but you really want to have the experience of a penis inside of you. Your desire at this moment and at this time is to fuck a man and to take this enormous cock deep inside of you and climax and orgasm to the fullest. I want you to feel the power of the strongest vibrator you have ever used and imagine it working in you as you fuck the man below you. I want you to gradually build up from a slow and gentle riding up and down motion to a full on hard fuck. I want you to tighten your cunt so that it squeezes the cock inside of you and I want you to drive yourself down on this fantastic cock end until you feel it push up hard against the inside of your pulsing fanny."

As I was talking to Jade I was using images of me and Karen and of Hugh and I to give me a sense of the feelings that I wanted to transmit to Jade. As I looked at her I could clearly see that the efforts were starting to pay off. Jade was now beginning to move up and down and up and down. I suddenly realised that Hugh G's cock was not in her and that she was moving as I asked, but not with Hugh up her.

I moved closer and took hold of Hugh's erection in my hand, stood it upright and waited for Jade a moment. I asked Jade to stop moving for a second, which she did for me. I then gently said to her to lift up a little higher so we can put the cock in her cunt. Jade responded and lifted up a little higher and it was just enough to get Hugh's cock in place below her opening. I put my fingers on either side of her fanny lips and parted them easily. Her pussy was soaking wet and there was no need for any form of lubrication whatsoever.

I spoke to Jade and said, "Be ready girl, you are going to have the climax of your life now." I asked Jade then to slide down real slow and take the full length of his erection deep inside her. My hand was still in place and as I watched them both I could feel and see Hugh G's massive cock disappearing deep inside Jade's fanny. At this point I was turned on myself and I mean *really* turned on. I could actually feel my own fanny juices running and I felt the quiver of a quick and gentle climax.

I held my hand in place to feel Jade fuck Hugh and as my hand felt the cock and the cunt bang together I shivered and orgasmed in response to the sexual act that these two were involved in. My hand was now wet with Jade's love juices, as was my pussy with my own inner fluids, in fact I was soaking wet. I stepped back to watch my work in motion, it was a marvellous thing to see. I continued to talk to Jade and to encourage her to fuck the man below her. She was in full flow with all the passions of a natural male female relationship. I gave her one final and positive instruction which was *"fuck him girl, fuck like you never fucked before"* and she did exactly what she was told, she fucked Hugh and she fucked him HARD!

As I went through the hypnotic process I did not pay any attention to Karen or Alison, my focus had been on Jade and the need for her to overcome the problem she was facing, which was to have sex with a man. I had been concentrating very hard on her and, to be honest, I was totally zoned out from everything else in the room.

I watched Jade for a moment or two when I decided to look at Karen and Alison. When I had started to put Jade into a hypnotic state Karen had been stood to my left side and Alison had been on the floor to my right side, but both of them were behind me. I turned to my left to face both of the ladies and I looked at them, first Karen then Alison, and to my horror they were both in some sort of daze. I briefly looked back at Jade and she was still riding up and down on Hugh G's cock, no problem there, but the other two were well and truly gone!

As I looked at Karen she was moving her body up and down in almost a squatting motion and she was rubbing between her legs with her hand up inside of her nurse's uniform and it was obvious she was masturbating herself vigorously and I would say passionately too.

I went over to Karen and I spoke to her softly and she was well under the hypnotic spell. I asked her to sit on the floor and she did as she was told. I was afraid she might fall down and that would be all I needed – an unconscious bloody nurse, if that happened who could I have called? Anyway, I got her on the floor and once she was safe on the ground I looked over to Alison for a little help. I glanced her way to find her laid on her back fingers up her fanny in a full flow of bringing herself off to a full orgasm.

My bloody head was about to explode.

As she started to climax she screamed. I quickly said to her, "Orgasm quietly, you must not scream, Alison hear me, you must *not* scream." All I could think of was the room filled with medical staff or patients rushing into Hugh G's ward to find us all there. Alison did respond and she stopped her screaming but she still carried on to complete a full orgasm and it was a powerful climax believe me!

I stood up and looked through the glass in the door to see if anyone had heard Alison but it looked clear and no one was there apart from the patients, who should be there. As I looked at them there were a couple wearing headphones and watching TV, and the other two were asleep.

I turned to look at Jade as I heard a couple of gentle sighs, and as I looked at her she had a final thrust or two as she climaxed on top of Hugh. Jade immediately lay down on top of the man below her and put her arms on either side of him in almost a very natural end to a very passionate sexual act. Karen too had now climaxed, or at least I think she had, because I missed the end of that one.

I quickly had a thought. I took out my phone and took a picture of all three of them. I needed a record or proof as I felt that they may not believe me, and to be totally honest I don't believe it myself. I knew that I had spent a good deal of time and concentrated effort into inducing a hypnotic trance for Jade, but I did not think that I was affecting the other two women in the room.

It had been said during the hypnosis training to be very careful of this phenomenon. However, I had either forgotten this or ignored the idea of this ever happening. I was indeed shocked at how easy it had been and how very powerful the suggestion had been. One of the features of hypnosis is to use the name of the subject you are dealing with and the target information or instructions you give to the subject. I had used Jade's name all the time, but somewhere in the instructions and guidance I was giving her both Karen and Alison had picked up the thread of what I was saying to Jade and they had taken hold of the idea and accepted the information as if it had been intended for them. I did not realise how powerful a tool hypnosis really was and now I know for sure that it really works and it gives a very good positive outcome if used correctly. It was quite obvious to me that I had used it correctly and that it had worked and worked very well indeed.

I looked now at all three ladies in the room with me, and all of them had achieved orgasm and all three were now soundly asleep. My only fear was that I could not wake them up.

I looked first to Karen as I needed her to be awake first. I was about to try to talk her out of hypnosis when I suddenly realised if I had put them all in a trance together I should be able to bring them all out together, it had to be worth a shot. I stood at the back of the small ward and in a position where all three of them should be able to hear me clearly (I did not want to speak loudly for obvious reasons) I felt I was in the best position for all of them to hear my instructions to them.

I spoke to them and said, "Karen, Alison and Jade you can all hear me clearly, you are all in a deep sleep, I want to bring you back to a waking state so please listen to my voice, listen to my voice, listen to my voice. I will count from ten down to one and as I do I will instruct you to come back to the here and now and be with me in the present time." I paused for a moment and said, "**Ten** you are about to wake up, **Nine** you can feel yourselves waking, **Eight** you are starting to feel fresh, **Seven** my voice is getting louder to you, **Six** you are starting to wake up, **Five** you are beginning to be aware of your surroundings, **Four** start to wake, **Three** you are waking up, **Two** you are nearly there, **ONE** you are awake, wake up **NOW**! You are all back with me here and now."

I was looking at all three of them and as I had spoken to them I watched each and every one of them respond to my words and sure enough all three of them came back to a waking state seemingly as easy as they had gone under. I was very happy with what I had just achieved, very happy indeed.

I spoke first to Jade and asked, "Are you alright?" She was a little sleepy-eyed but she responded with a "yes, I am fine thank you". Next Alison, same question "how do you feel?" she replied, "I am good but what happened?" "We will talk in a moment," I said to her. "It will take a little explaining", and I smiled at her.

I now turned my attention to Karen. I looked directly at her and watched her for a moment. She looked directly back at me and shook her head as if to clear her thoughts. I asked Karen the same question, "Are you alright?" She put her left hand on her forehead and said, "I feel like I have been asleep for hours, what happened to me?"

"Listen to me all of you," I said. "We can discuss this all later, right now we need to get things straightened up here and get away as soon as we can."

I stood looking around the small side ward looking at two naked women who both had just had sex with a male patient who was in a passive coma-like state with an erection that just would not quit, and a dazed nurse who is supposed to be in charge of patients. We had to get back on track and sort ourselves out now!

Jade stepped down from the bed and as she did so we could now see Hugh's erect penis once again back to full size and looking as hard as a rock and as usual it looked fantastic. I still marvelled at how good it looks and each time I see his cock it drives me wild inside but sadly here I could not show any emotion, or indeed do anything about how I feel. The four of us need to get sorted and fast, no time for day dreaming. "Come on ladies," I said to them, "let's get going."

Alison was now on her feet and Karen too was stood up and starting to pull herself together. Within a matter of a few moments we were all ready to leave the room. Jade and Alison went beside Hugh G's bed, one on either side of him. They both took hold of his hands and both Alison and Jade kissed him on the cheek and said, "Thank you", this was a very touching thing to see, it was a mark of respect to the man and although he was not a willing participant he may have changed these ladies' lives forever and I hoped in my heart he was going to give them both what they wanted, I really did.

Jade and Alison stepped back as Karen stepped forward to check that Hugh was alright. She also put his bedding straight, put her hand on his forehead and she said, "See you later Mr Hugh G". I moved closer too and said, "Sleep well my good friend, see you soon, good night", and at that we all turned away and left the ward. We left a small side light turned on at the side of Hugh's bed and as I left I shut the door behind me. I turned back to look through the glass window in the door and I felt a pain in the pit of my stomach. What the hell was I doing with this poor man? And as this thought and feeling flowed over me I felt so guilty that I could have slit my throat.

For a moment or two I thought I had lost control and then, as it had done before, I got a grip of my emotions and stood strong again as I remembered why I was doing this – it was for my good friend Sue and these desperate women who need to have babies. That's why I'm here and that is why I am going to get all of us through this right to the very end.

We were all on the main ward now and it was emotional. Two of the male patients on the ward were still awake and watching TV, they had headphones on and clearly saw the four of us. The way things looked I think these people thought we were upset because of a family member in the side ward and so it was not such a big issue showing some emotion in this place. Because of the nature in the hospital crying was something that was seen all of the time, so it was something that happened every day and both patients and nursing staff see it all on a regular basis. We all gave Karen a hug, including me, and we left. As I walked away I said to her, "I will talk to you later, Jade." Alison and I left the ward and quickly exited the hospital as calmly as we could.

We did not say a great deal in the car although Alison asked about the hypnosis and I said when my head was clear I would call her and we would go over things. Alison accepted that we had been through an emotional event tonight and all the three of us wanted to do was go home. We arrived back at my place and got out of the car. I embraced the girls, said goodbye and went into my house. They went their own way too.

I got inside, put on the light, went upstairs, took off all my clothes, threw on my dressing gown and lay on the bed. I went through the night's events in my mind and I could see everything that had happened. I closed my eyes and I was seeing in my mind a video of the night as if I was re-living it again, and as I looked around in my mind I could see Karen in a hypnotic trance, Alison sat on the floor in a hypnotic trance and Jade sat on top of Hugh G in a hypnotic trance, and all of this made me start to laugh.

I could see it all and I laughed even more, I laughed so much I started to cry it was so funny. I started to double over as the laughter began to hurt me and then I stopped laughing because I was crying and sobbing for real.

The laughter was an emotional release because I saw the humorous side of the night's events but I have also just felt once again the pain of the process I was going through as well and laughter easily did go to tears and I was now crying harder than I had done for a long time. I need to go to bed and sleep and sleep I bloody well will. This has been an emotionally draining experience and I need to sleep and get the best rest I can for me and the baby.

I went to bed and I did feel as if I fell into a deep sleep and although I was sleeping my mind did not rest at all throughout the night; I was dreaming of diving under the water. It was a strange sensation but that is what I did. The dream lasted all night and it did not change at all. It was constantly about diving and learning to be a professional diver. I feel that the dream was giving me a greater meaning and I was trying to interpret what this meaning might be.

I met some people in the dream that I didn't know and they had a deep well in their home which was 199 feet deep and I had to dive to the bottom to achieve something special. There was also a house opposite their home and it was a large house which had been abandoned, someone had removed the double glazing from all of the windows and the house appeared to have water pouring from every opening, including windows and doorways too. It looked as if everything was being washed clean and as I looked at this cleansing process I then was about to make the dive alone into this water, when someone, in fact a group of military people, came to see me attempt the dive. It was a really strange feeling because one of the young men in the dream said, "If she goes", meaning me, "then I go", meaning he would follow me.

I presumed this young guy was saying we dive together. Anyway, as far as I could remember we went to start the dive in this deep well and I woke up.

It was a strange feeling because the dream had some other symbolic meaning but also it was as if I had taken a journey that night and some of the dream did make sense but the rest of it I needed to spend more time on it, thinking about what message was being sent to me.

I am a great believer in intuition or psychic things so because of my beliefs I always pay attention to dreams or feelings I may have and I use them to help guide me through life. There have been times when I have had a dream or a premonition and I have found it to be something that has come true in my life or very close to coming true. To be honest it could be just a dream and a trick of the mind, but the feeling was so strong that I did believe there was something deeper in the translation. I just needed to figure it out, if I could that is!

I was by now up, washed and ready. I was supposed to go to work but I could not make it today, I felt out of sorts and all I wanted to do was take things easy. I called in to the hospital sick line and Jacky took the call. I knew her very well, she was the senior HR manager and she was a good person. I simply told her I did not feel too good. She said to me, "Is it the baby?" "No," was my reply, "just one of those days and I feel a little bit under the weather." I said to Jacky I would be back in the following day, it was just a 24-hour thing and nothing to worry about. Jacky said, "OK, take care, see you around work." I said "bye", she said "bye" and the call was ended.

I felt relieved that I was not going to work, I needed time to think about the rest of the girls and what was to be done, and I wanted some more time to think about this dream; it was starting to bug me and I wanted to be quiet and undisturbed to think about it.

I was going over things in my mind and I seemed to hop from one thing to another – the girls, the dream, my baby, my work and, strangely enough, my future. After all, I was going to be a single mother and that thought was never far away from my mind even without everything else going on.

This dream was playing on my mind and I started to analyse it. The biggest thing was the diving under water, I am not a lover of the sea and yet my mind seems hell bent on pulling my thoughts that way. The thing that hit me the most was 199 feet deep; that part of the dream kept coming back to me. My only thought was that I may be in too deep, but I wasn't sure if that was it, the windows on the house opposite the house in the dream were being removed. What did this mean? The military personnel, why were they there? So many things to think about.

My other main thoughts were centred around the next girls to go with Hugh G. Although the first night with Jade and Alison was a bit of a shock and a catastrophe, we got away with it, but what about the next group and the ones after that? I was not sure of what was to happen because in my mind now there were, and indeed are, too many variables which can lead to many problems just like last night.

That said I was in it now so I had to focus yet again and start to organise myself and to call Karen and talk with her. It is probably too early in the morning, she will still be in bed from the night shift and I do not want to disturb her until mid-afternoon; she needs her rest time and to sleep.

I did call Karen around 3pm and she answered the phone. "I was hoping you would call me," she said. "I want, no I *need* to talk with you as soon as we can get together."

I told Karen to come round now I was at home and not really busy. 40 minutes later a knock at the door and Karen was at my home, I opened the door and she came straight into the house. "I need to know what happened last night," she said to me.

I smiled at her and said, "Sit down and I will tell you."

I told Karen first of my training in hypnotherapy and then I gradually told her what had happened to her and Alison and how they had been drawn into the hypnotic process. Karen could not believe what I was saying but after a little persuasion and explanation she got the message and realised that what I was telling her was absolutely true. Karen had clear and precise memories of the events when she was hypnotised but her strongest feeling was the orgasm she had. She told me that everything she saw and everything she felt was real and the memories were so vivid that she could actually remember being where I put her and experiencing the feelings that I suggested to her.

Karen looked at me and said, "I want to do it again please."

I started to laugh.

"What is so funny?" she said.

I replied to her, "I never thought I would ever use this training and the first time I apply it to one person three people get hypnotised and after all of that one of those people, namely you, wants to try it again. It just seems funny, but in answer to your request, yes I will do it again for you. No problem."

I changed the subject and turned back to the main business at hand.

"We need to get back to discussing the next ladies to go to the hospital of course," said Karen. "We do need to focus on this absolutely."

I went through the names of the girls left to go in the group and I just numbered them: "Linda and Shola are one and two, next Julie is number three, and Helen and Christine are four and five, Grace and Ruth are six and seven, and finally Anne will be number eight. I don't know if I should make the last group a three and try that by adding Grace, Ruth and Anne together. I am not sure if that will work," I said to Karen.

"I am not sure either," she replied, "but it is worth considering the possibility. It is something we could discuss with them and we need to do it sooner rather than later."

Anyway the numbers basically made sense and between Karen and I we worked out the dates of the night shifts she was on and that seemed all a well defined plan and the best way to move forward. It was around tea-time and once again this dream came into my head. I started to talk to Karen about it, I gave her a brief outline and I chatted about it with her for a while when she suddenly said to me, "I feel horny, do you want to fuck me again?"

I was taken aback by her statement, it came right out of the blue and I wasn't ready for what she said. I looked at her and she was already taking off her blouse revealing a pink bra, and within seconds she was removing that too. Karen pulled off her blue skirt and her pants were off in a jiffy.

She stood in front of me and said, "Well, do you want this or do I put my clothes back on?"

I was not used to people being this blunt with me but I have to admit it was something of a turn on. I slipped off my clothes to reveal myself to her. I was conscious about the baby bump but she did not seem to care. Karen took my hand and helped me to the floor and no sooner was I sat down she pushed me back gently and put her head between my legs and started to lick my fanny.

Karen started with a very gentle motion then suddenly she went crazy and within no time I was having a great orgasm. I thought I was done when she sat up and put her finger in my cunt. Karen has long fingers and she reached inside of me and up on the inner side of my fanny wall, it was a place I had never been touched before, and she put her finger on something and she rubbed and she rubbed.

I started to get a sensation that was out of this world and I started to come again but *fucking hell* what a feeling! Karen kept on using her finger in this one place and she got it just right and fuck did I come and fuck me did I scream.

Karen kept fingering this place until I eased back down on the floor. As I had come I arched my back high and rode the orgasm to the end. I went down to rest as although it was a very short time and a quick double orgasm I was very tired indeed. "Now me," she said. "Come on."

I did not get time to take a breath when Karen fell back on the floor with her feet under her backside and legs spread wide, it gave me clear access to her cunt. I kneeled forward and tried to do to her what she had just done to me. I put my face right into her fanny and pushed the vagina lips apart with my tongue, there was a salty sweet taste which was sort of nice. I licked as hard as I could and it seemed to do the trick for her.

Karen took longer to orgasm than I did, but not much. She came with a little whimper and said, "Now the finger, come on get it up there in the same place I touched you."

I used the middle finger on my right hand and pushed it in her, I fumbled for a while trying to find the spot she found in me and a few times Karen said left a bit, up a bit, until I found it.

The place I felt was a little bumpy to my touch and as I pushed my finger up and down I could feel ripples like those on a beach as the tide goes out. I gradually picked up the pace making my finger go faster as Karen had done to me. She responded very well and I could both see and feel the effect it was having on her and me too.

"Fucking hell Leigh, rub my cunt faster, *faster*, harder, bring me off!" she shouted. "Bring it now! Ohhhh *fuck me!*" she cried as she came to a powerful and very expressive orgasm and she shook all over her body, and I mean *really* shook as the full extent of that climax travelled from the top of her head to the bottom of her toes. This woman really knew how to climax and it showed both audibly and visually and it was really nice to see and watch too.

Karen calmed down and relaxed. She gave herself a moment or two and then moved closer towards me. We were both naked and we had also shared another wonderful sexual experience together, and for the second time I was still shocked and amazed that I was doing this.

Both Karen and I chatted a while about nothing in particular really but it was nice to sit there and just talk. Karen then said that she needed to go, she was on nights again that night and she needed to get ready for work. We had already arranged for the next two girls to go to see Hugh G and I also needed to call them. It was a bit short notice but that was the only way I could do things. The planning and timing was always going to be an issue and I had discussed this with the girls on previous meetings so they were already prepared for a phone call at short notice.

I called Linda and Shola shortly after Karen had left and I explained what was going to happen. I also told them that we had a few issues the night before but things still went alright. I asked the girls to be at my place around 6.45 and they had both said that it was OK and that they would be here. I had a shower and had a quick tidy round. There wasn't much to tidy as my house is usually clean anyway.

Linda and Shola arrived about five minutes apart, Linda was first and then a knock at the door and there was Shola. This situation was a bit unusual because Shola was a very beautiful black woman.

Shola was born in the UK but her parents had arrived from Africa in the late 70s. Her father came to the UK to work in banking and his life changed so much that he and his wife decided to stay here. Shola was born in 1980, she was now 30 years of age. Shola had married an older white man and that is why it was important that she go with Hugh so the child would resemble a baby from a mixed race background. I have to say Shola was stunning in every way and I do mean every way possible.

Shola's husband was a wealthy businessman and he was unable to give her the baby she wanted. Her man was an older guy apparently, and by what she said he kept her as a trophy wife on display to the world. Shola's husband was a high flyer and very successful. He had been married before but now divorced. Her husband had seen her at some posh function and said 'I want her' and the rest, as they say, is history. He wined her and dined her, and then married her.

Whoever sees Shola knows she is a prize that many men would want. It was a strange situation because Shola had been to my clinic a year earlier and I was a little surprised as, to be honest, she could have gone to a private clinic but she chose my place of work. I never asked her why she did this but her choice in medical care brought her to be here with me now. Shola was sultry and elegant but also a very quiet woman too, she had a sort of mystery about her and it was a haunting feeling that you got from her. She looked like the woman in the film with Michael Caine, Ashanti, and the more I looked at Shola, the more I saw the resemblance.

It was a strong choice Shola must have made to come to a general clinic rather than go private. Apparently it had been her choice because her husband could and would buy her whatever she wanted.

All of that said it was also a nice feeling, comfortable and peaceful in a strange sort of way, to see such a wealthy and attractive woman choose a more basic approach in the pursuit of trying to have a baby.

It was later now and we were ready to go to the hospital once again. We left my home just after seven o'clock and set off. As we got into my car I saw a Jaguar XKR outside with a private registration plate: S H O 1 A (Shola) T. That was an expensive car and a very expensive private registration plate too; Shola had money and that was a fact of life. We did not say much on the way to the hospital, the mood was a little sombre and after my last experience here I was more than a little apprehensive about the night's forthcoming events.

For me this situation was almost a routine event, the whole thing was about a routine and within that routine was caution and observation. One thing to be careful about is knowing who to look out for and what to do. The hospital works on rota systems and shift patterns so the same people would not be working all the time, which is a good thing, however because of my regular visits I saw the people working here more often than not. This regularity was a bit of a concern as I tried hard to be as invisible as I possibly could, very difficult in a place where everybody knows you.

The three of us went inside and straight to Hugh G's ward I walked the girls directly to him. I saw Karen but did not acknowledge her at all. We went to the side ward, I opened the door and walked in. Shola and Linda followed behind me, I let them pass me and I turned and closed the door behind them. For a moment or two I held the door handle tightly as if I was stopping someone else entering after us. I felt a bit foolish but it was tension that was causing this feeling inside of me and also a little paranoia too.

As usual I introduced Hugh G to Linda and Shola and I then allowed them a few moments to see him and to hold his hands. After the introduction nobody spoke, it was a very eerie silence, a much different situation to previous times.

I turned back to look through the window in the door of the side ward, nearly all of the visitors were gone. I could only see two patients on the main ward tonight so that makes things a bit safer and indeed a bit easier for all of us involved here tonight. I became a little more relaxed as people left the main ward and I was also less apprehensive about things tonight and I also felt a little bit more hopeful of things both now and in the near future. I checked through the window of the door again and everyone was gone except for Karen and another nurse. This was normal as the second nurse helps to bed everyone down for the night and then she usually has other duties to perform elsewhere. Sure enough, after around ten minutes she left the main ward and as I watched her leave Karen looked over and gave me a thumbs up sign to say we were good to go.

While I was waiting for Karen to do this Linda and Shola were at Hugh G's bedside. Shola had been rubbing her hand over the top of the bed sheets and feeling the contours of Hugh's body, Linda on the other hand, was just stood looking at him and occasionally she touched his face and his forehead. I was not sure what was going through her mind because these two women were reacting in two separate and completely different ways and yet they were both here seemingly for the same reasons. Occasionally Linda said 'you poor man, how could this have happened to you?', while Shola on the other hand said nothing at all, she just continued to rub her hands up and down Hugh's body. As she did this every time she slid her hand along the length of his erection.

I said, "Alright ladies, we need to make a start." I looked at Linda and said to her, "You can go first."

She turned to look back at me and said nothing. I moved forward to uncover Hugh and pull the white linen sheet down him and off him to reveal his fully naked form and, of course, that huge erect penis. I once again said to Linda, "Come on please, we need to be moving along as time is always against us."

Linda took off her jacket and shoes and she then loosened her skirt and let it slip to the floor. She removed her panties, placed them on top of her skirt, which was now lying on the floor, and climbed onto the bed. She positioned herself above Hugh's cock, took it in her hand and started to cry. "I can't do this," she said. "I simply can't do this. I have been married to Pete for over ten years and I love him, I cannot and I will not do this. I have never been with another man at all and this is not worth damaging my relationship for. I want a baby for sure but I love my husband and I won't break my vows to him. I will not take another penis inside me and potentially ruin my marriage to my lovely man."

With that statement she climbed off the bed and proceeded to get dressed.

"Thanks for your help ladies," she said to us all, "but I am out of here. Please give me the car keys Leigh, and I will wait downstairs. There is no problem at all here. I have made a great decision and I feel proud of what I am doing, this is the right choice for me and the right choice for my marriage. Pete has always supported and loved me in everything I do or anything I want, I am doing this for him and I love him and I feel very happy with what I am doing now but more importantly what I have *not* done with Hugh. Thanks ladies, see you downstairs." And with that she left the side ward and walked straight out of the main ward. Linda walked past Karen, briefly touched her on the shoulder as an acknowledgement of thanks, and she was gone.

I saw Karen's face and all she did was shrug her shoulders at me as much as to say 'what is happening?'. All I did in response was to just give her a thumbs up sign, it seemed to be the only thing to do.

I turned round and I now looked at Shola to see what she was going to do. She looked straight back at me and said, "Can we go on with this girls' night out please?"

I replied, "Yes of course." Shola used the code name we had agreed on and it was strange to hear this come from her lips, but it was also very unusual in the way she said it too.

As I said earlier, Shola was a beautiful black woman. She was slim and elegant and very different from the rest of the group. Shola had a way about her, she stood upright and straight, not unlike a model. She also walked with confidence and a certain pride and, of course, she had a fantastic figure as well. Shola just looked at me and said, "Can I get started?"

I said, "Yes of course."

Shola was wearing a red dress which fitted all of her curves; it was an obviously expensive piece of clothing but not over the top if you know what I mean. Shola unzipped the dress and dropped it to the floor, she was wearing nothing underneath and as she revealed that silky black body of hers, I looked at her breasts and they were firm and pointed with perfectly formed nipples which stood out straight in front of her. Her stomach was flat and smooth and she was truly a black beauty in every way.

"Do you intend to stay in the room while I do this?" she said to me.

I replied, "No, I will leave if you want me to."

"No," she emphatically replied. "I would like you to stay and watch me take him."

I heard only one statement 'take him', it sounded very odd in the way she said that and it had a strong feeling of a woman trying to take a man from another woman. Shola knew I was having Hugh's baby and at first I thought she was being clever with me but somehow I realised that this was not the case at all.

Shola looked at me and smiled and I smiled back at her. She did not seem shy, nor did she appear to be ashamed or upset at the prospect of what she was going to do, as some of the other women had been. Shola stood beside the bed and her black skin shone in the low light of the room. She opened her legs a little and started to masturbate herself, her long slender fingers rubbed the outside of her pussy and occasionally they slid inside her fanny disappearing all the way up and then she pulled them out again and she rubbed the outside of the vagina.

Again this feminine activity was getting the right response from me and as for Shola, she started to moan lightly as she brought herself to what I thought was near to climax. Just as I thought she was going to come she stopped the masturbation and eased herself onto Hugh's bed, she kneeled over him and sat astride his body. She took his cock in her hand, leaned forward and put it straight in her mouth and she started to give him a slow blow job. Shola's head and her right hand moved up and down his cock slowly and deliberately. Shola licked the cock end like a huge ice cream using her tongue around the tip of the erection and from time to time revealing the throbbing purple cock end that was held firmly in her hand. Shola sat up a little and started to wank him off. She put her left hand around the base of the shaft to keep the skin tight and fully revealing the bulbous end of his knob she then used her other hand to rub over the sensitive area of a man's penis and I watched as the penis responded to Shola's womanly touches. Shola was enjoying every minute of this and I began to feel as if she were here for reasons other than to try to conceive a baby. Shola was having sex and she was determined to make the most of her time here, and that became quite obvious to me.

Shola rose up above Hugh G and positioned her cunt over his cock, she took hold of the erection in her right hand and impaled herself on the huge cock below her. As she pushed it all the way up her fanny she groaned as she sat down on Hugh and his massive cock was lost inside of her dripping vagina.

Shola sat upright, then arched her spine as she leaned backwards. As she leaned she pushed herself down hard onto his cock and took it as far up her as she could and as she did this she let out a moan of satisfaction. Hugh's cock obviously hit the spot and it showed on Shola's face, it was also obvious in her actions too. Shola ran her fingers through her long silky black hair, she then pulled and tugged at it in a passionate writhing motion, she weaved backwards and forwards and she moaned gently again and again. Shola kept her eyes shut and as she moved on top of this man she started to lift herself up and down in a slow and very deliberate fucking motion. Each time she moved on the downward stroke she sighed and after the eighth or tenth thrust on Hugh G's cock she started to masturbate herself. Using her left hand she started to rub the outside of her pussy and what a difference it made to the way she reacted. Shola was now fucking Hugh in one of the most passionate and erotic ways that I have ever seen and she kept on riding that giant cock harder and harder. Shola leaned forward over Hugh's face and spat on him twice. I was shocked and angered by this and yet I did not stop her or intervene. Shola was going harder and harder and with each fucking motion a moan or a sigh came from her mouth.

Shola was going as hard as I thought any woman could, she was now pounding Hugh and the big hospital bed was shaking beneath the two of them as she fucked Hugh and fucked to a fever pitch. Shola once again leaned forward and stopped using her left hand for masturbating. Instead she put her hand across Hugh's throat. I watched Shola as she started to prepare for a major orgasm. I was watching her hand across Hugh's airway and I was about to move it when Shola started to shake violently. At first I thought it was a seizure of some sort but she continued on as she had been doing, still fucking Hugh, and I realised it was part of her climax. Shola started to shake and her body stiffened as she hit a massive orgasm. It was clear to see what the orgasm was doing to her and for a moment I wished that I could feel what she was experiencing now.

Shola clearly had a major orgasm but she wasn't done. She climaxed again and again and again. I counted what I thought was four orgasms but I could not be sure, but whatever happened to her was a powerful expression of passion and eroticism and I had never witnessed in my life something like this ever.

Shola was now calming down but her hand was still over Hugh G's throat. I moved forward closer to the bed and got hold of Shola's hand and pulled it away from Hugh's airway. Shola jumped with a start, she did not know what I was going to do and she reacted with surprise. She looked at me, she looked at what I was doing and she realised why I was doing it. Shola released her grip and relaxed as I let go of her hand and she just sat impaled on Hugh's giant-sized cock which was still buried deep up inside her. Shola was a passionate thing but what I had just witnessed was not the actions of a woman wanting a baby, more like the actions of a woman just wanting a fuck and by Christ she has just had one. Shola lifted herself off Hugh's cock and it was clear his load had been shot as spunk dripped from her wet cunt and as his cock became visible, although still large, it flopped on his belly as clearly the erection was coming down after he had spunked in her.

Shola looked at Hugh as she climbed off the bed and as she did this she turned fully towards him and put his limp cock in her right hand and then into her mouth and she swallowed all the sperm and cleaned his cock end with her mouth and tongue. This was clearly not the responses I was expecting and it was obvious that she was wanting this and enjoying this connection very much indeed.

Shola stood back and let Hugh's cock fall onto his stomach. I watched her as she moved away from him and started to put on her clothes. "We need to talk," she said to me. My answer was, "Whatever you want Shola, will have to wait until we are away from here."

She nodded in agreement and dressed quickly and once again she became the smartly dressed and well heeled lady that I expected to see in front of me. I cleaned Hugh up and wiped his penis free of any bits and pieces from his encounter with Shola the vixen.

Hugh lay silent on his bed. I rolled him on his side to try and make him as comfortable as I could. Hugh seemed at peace, or at least that is how he looked to me. I kissed him on the cheek and as I walked towards the door to leave, Shola went to him and kissed him first on the cheek and then on the lips. I was a little surprised at this behaviour but not totally shocked. We both left the ward together and that was the end of that particular situation.

I walked over to Karen and thanked her, she asked if we'd had any other problems and I said to her, "No not really, but we can talk later when it's not in a public place like this." Karen winked at me and patted me on the back supportively.

Shola was stood beside me and I watched as she made eye contact with Karen. They looked directly at each other and the gaze between them became a stare, a deep and longing look at each other. Neither of them looked away and it was clear to me something was happening between them.

I spoke and said to the both of them, "We need to leave now please."

Shola turned and looked at me, she glanced briefly in my direction then she turned back to look at Karen. She stepped forward one pace, put her right hand on Karen's cheek and kissed her on the lips. I watched the both of them look into each other's eyes again and they just stood there. Suddenly Shola turned away and walked towards the exit doors. I extended my arm to Karen and touched her on the shoulder, I then also turned and left the ward and finally walked out of the hospital with Shola. We got into the car and drove to my home.

Linda was sat in the back seat of the jaguar waiting for the two of us to get there. Shola and I got into the car and we all set off for my home. As we went along in the car I said to Shola, "What was that all about in the hospital?"

"What was what about?" she said.

"You know what I mean, the kiss with Karen and the display you put on with Hugh?"

Shola looked at me, then looked away. It was the look of a woman who was not telling the truth.

"What are you up to?" I asked her again. "Do you want a baby or not?" I asked her directly. "And why did you kiss Karen in that way? What is the deal with you?" I could feel myself getting angry and that is not what I wanted. This anger inside was no good for me or the baby, I told myself to calm down. I said to Shola, "Tell me what is going on here."

Shola said to me, "I married an older man and he gives me everything I want, well almost everything. We have a sort of deal and part of that deal is he gets a baby, the only trouble is I don't want a baby. When I came to your clinic I thought I could fake the infertility thing and when I went through the testing process and they found nothing wrong with me they then tested Stan my husband and he was found to be OK too, so I paid one of the nurses to falsify the results."

"You did *what*?" I barked back at her. "Who did you pay?" I shouted at Shola hard.

"I don't want to say, it will cause a problem for her."

"You bloody well better believe it," I said. "When I find out who it is, she will be dismissed."

"You will be dismissed too."

I asked her what she meant by this statement.

"Well, the girl who helped me lied on some paperwork. Look what you are doing. Which is worse, your involvement in this situation or her small indiscretion? This girl did something to help me and the thing she did has hurt no one."

I stopped speaking and thought hard about what Shola said and she was right. I went very quiet and thought hard about what had been said to me and I realised how deep I was now into this situation. In a lot of ways I had flowed along this tidal wave of excitement and opportunity, but with what Shola had just said to me I was starting to feel that I was over my head, way over my head.

Shola drove us all back to my place to allow Linda to pick up her car and to drop me off at my home. Neither of us spoke at all for the rest of the 20-minute journey. It was a cold silence in the car but in some way I did not want to hear anyone's voice. I was once again going through an evaluation process in my mind and I was starting to think about calling the whole thing off. I went over the whole scenario from the day Sue told me about Hugh G and all the things that had happened, right up to the point where Shola said the things she did earlier. I was tired, confused, angry and afraid, all at the same time. I really do not know what to do but I feel that right now everything should stop and I should quit while I am ahead. As I was driving along I turned to look at Shola. I glanced a look at her but she did not look back at me. I put my eyes back on the road ahead and continued to go through things in my mind.

We arrived outside my home and we all got out of the car; Linda then left and drove away quickly. Shola handed me a small business card and she said to me, "Can you please give this to Karen and ask her to give me a call please, and before you ask me Leigh, it *is* very important to me that you do this *PLEASE!*"

I took the card from her, it had the business name Graphics Services and Supplies. I didn't ask what the business was, although it seemed very obvious. I looked at Shola and said, "Karen will get the card but it is up to her what she does with it, I am not going to try to influence her decision on calling you."

Shola said, "Thank you for all that you have done and I really mean that. Whatever you think of me please know that I am extremely grateful and I feel that all of the ladies involved in this are truly grateful for what you have done too. What you are doing and what you will have to do to complete this project successfully is such a big sacrifice that you are making and the girls and I have talked about this situation and the overwhelming feeling from them and me is gratitude."

Shola stepped forward, put her arms around me and embraced me. She whispered "thanks" in my left ear, she stepped back, turned around and went to her car and left.

I went into my home, opened the door, walked in, locked the door behind me, took off my coat, sat on the floor and cried and cried and cried. Was I in too deep with all of this? Honestly I did not know what to do but right now I was feeling the pressure and my main fear was the effect on my baby. The stress was high and that was bound to have implications on the baby and me. A night in bed (and I did actually sleep) was just what I wanted and needed. I awoke early in the morning and I just lay in my bed and tried to go through things with a little more objectivity.

I realised the night before how vulnerable I was in my current situation but I now still feel that I also have an obligation to Sue my friend who is in great difficulty financially. I also feel that the ladies that I have brought together who are in need of having children need my continued support and help to achieve their target of getting pregnant. My emotions were still high but I had to continue through to the very end and complete the task in hand. I got up and had a good breakfast with coffee, toast and cereal and yes, I was very hungry so my breakfast did hit the spot. I got dressed cleaned round such as my home needed it and sat down with a pen and paper to finalise the rest of the ladies going through the girls' night out project. I was going to finish it whatever happened.

The remaining ladies waiting to sleep with Hugh G were Julie, Helen, Christine, Grace and lastly Ruth.

I made the now usual arrangements with Karen and put the remaining girls into a sequence and I contacted them all in advance to give them plenty of time to prepare. The next girls' night out was the following Tuesday. Julie and Helen turned up at my home, I took them both to the hospital and without any issues really they both slept with Hugh and it all went very well. The ladies were as you would expect a little apprehensive, but the process went through without any problems and for me it was a huge relief. The following night it was Christine and Grace who were to be the next in line. Once again they both turned up and I took them through the routine as all the others before had done, and apart from Grace having what she said was an 'unexpected climax', the night was once again a successful endeavour.

The last participant was Ruth. She would be the final lady to share the experience of Hugh G. Ruth arrived at my home, she knocked at the door and I opened it to see a shy and sheepish lady stood there. I invited her in and told her to make herself comfortable.

Ruth was obviously very nervous but I tried to calm her down and she seemed a little easier. The time arrived where we had to go. We both left my home, got into my car and set off for the hospital. I was feeling good because this would be the last time and I could relax myself knowing that I would not be putting myself at risk anymore so tonight was going to be a good night.

We arrived at the hospital and Ruth seemed to get more agitated. I once again reassured her but it made little or no difference. We both got out of the car and we walked towards the hospital entrance when a man approached the two of us. He walked straight at us and I thought the worst and I was about to scream when Ruth said, "No it's alright, this is my husband Ray. The man in front of us embraced Ruth, giving me a little peace of mind about who he was but I am now uncertain why he is here. I waited a second or two and said, "Why is Ray here?"

"I need him to be there when I go with Hugh."

"What for?" I asked her.

"Because," she said, "I have never been with another man and this process has been killing both of us so we talked at length about things and decided that this may make the whole thing better for the both of us, well not better but hopefully easier. Please Leigh, let Ray go in with us, it is very important to us and we really need to be together. This is a difficult thing I have to do and it is painful for both of us."

I looked at the two of them stood there holding hands and I said, "Alright, let's just get this thing done and we can all move on with our lives."

They both acknowledged me and we went inside the hospital

together. This was another bloody problem that I didn't need right now but I felt that there was nothing I could do about it. As far as I was concerned this was the last time this was going to happen so I just decided to go with it and complete the mission so to speak. I had enough strength left to battle through one more crazy session and this was it as far as I was concerned, here and now was the last.

The three of us walked onto the main ward. I could not see Karen but that was a normal thing, she could have been anywhere this is a busy place. I wasn't going to look for her so I walked straight into Hugh G's side ward, followed closely by Ruth and her husband Ray.

I felt very strange and I could not work out what it was but anyhow I did the usual introductions, which I think Ruth and Ray found strange, but that is what I do and I just followed my usual ritual. I looked outside and the ward was clearing, it was just around 8 o'clock so our timing was perfect. I looked at Ruth and I tried very hard not to look at Ray. I asked them both if they were ready and they both replied "yes" in very soft tones. It was obvious this was going to be difficult for both of them and it was now starting to become a little difficult for me too.

I pulled back the bedclothes to reveal Hugh's naked body and all eyes fell on his erection. I saw Ruth gulp as she saw what she had to take inside her. I also saw Ray's face and he just looked sick and I could feel his pain; this man was in agony and it showed. Ray undressed his wife and as her clothes dropped to the floor he took hold of his wife in his arms and said, "I love you darling, I always have and I always will."

Ruth held onto her husband for a while and then moved away from him and climbed onto the bed. She positioned herself above Hugh's erection and slid down onto the full length, at one point I heard her wince as if it was hurting her but she continued on and started to ride up and down. Ruth looked straight forward towards the wall behind Hugh's head and she seemed to stare at one point on the wall, focused intensely on something I think just to take her mind away from where she was and what she was doing.

I turned to look at Ray and all I saw were tears falling down his face, this poor man was distraught and in pain of the worst kind. I moved close to him, put my arms around him and turned him away from seeing what his wife was doing and I held him tight. Ray extended his arms around me and held me too, however his grip was gentle but strong. Then I realised he was taking into consideration my baby; this was a good man suffering a massive pain. Ray and I stood there holding each other and Ruth continued riding on Hugh; she did not see her husband's face, nor did she see him crying.

I was looking over Ray's shoulder when suddenly I saw a nurse in the main ward. At first I thought it was Karen but as I looked harder at this woman I could see it was not her.

Shit, I thought, *what the hell am I going to do?* I let go of Ray and turned to look at Ruth who was still moving up and down on top of Hugh and this now felt like a long time. I was about to speak to Ruth when suddenly she slowed down and turned her head towards Ray and I. She just looked at the both of us and then she said, "That's it, we're done."

She lifted herself up and Hugh's limp penis fell from her vagina. It was clear she had felt the erection soften so she knew the act was over. I quickly assisted her from the bed and I cleaned things up and put everything straight while Ray and his wife sorted themselves out.

In a short while Ruth was dressed and ready to go. I had sorted out Hugh and cleaned him down and all was set and we were ready to leave. Suddenly the nurse that was in the main ward started walking towards the side ward where we were and I started to panic. I was filled with fear. As she came closer the three of us just stood in Hugh's room and I waited for the worst to happen.

The nurse walked in and she was surprised to see us. She looked shocked and took a gasp of air as she came through the door, we all stood looking at each other. The nurse said, "Who are you?"

I stepped forward and I spoke to her. "I am senior nurse Leigh Stratton, I brought this couple here to see Hugh. They had heard about him and thought they may have known him. Obviously his identity is still unclear and it was by chance they found out about him. A friend of theirs went missing a few months ago, a close friend, and they hoped that Hugh might be the friend they lost."

There were still tears in Ray's eyes and the nurse stood looking at him. She took it that Ray was upset at the disappointment of this patient not being who they thought he might be. There was an eerie silence, then I asked where Karen was. The still unknown nurse said, "She took ill earlier today and called in sick. I am a bank nurse and I was brought in to cover until the regular nurse comes back."

"Sorry," I said to her. "What is your name?"

"My name is Lucy Wood," she said.

I extended my hand out to her to shake hands with her. She put her hand forward and we took hold of each other with a firm handshake.

"I hope you don't mind Lucy, but this has been a difficult situation. I was hoping to ask you can we keep this quiet as I feel enough distress has been suffered here tonight?"

Lucy looked at me and quietly and politely said, "I have not seen anyone here tonight."

I looked at her and simply said, "Thank you very much."

"No need to thank me," was her reply.

We all left the ward and I turned back to see Hugh. I had one last glance and closed his door. The three of us left the ward as quickly as we could. As we left I said to Lucy, "I hope Karen gets better soon."

She laughed and said, "I hope she doesn't."

I looked puzzled and felt a little annoyed at her response. She saw the look on my face and she said, "Don't worry it's a joke, I need the extra work."

I should have known better, Lucy is a nurse and the nurse sense of humour is always there. I looked straight back at her and laughed with her. "Don't we all," I said. "Don't we all."

"Money makes the world go round, ain't that the truth?" she said to me. "Nice meeting you Leigh."

"Nice meeting you too," I replied. "Maybe we will work together one day."

"Maybe," she said. "Maybe."

"Good night Lucy," I said and she responded back "Good night to you". We left the ward and then out of the hospital.

Outside the hospital Ray and Ruth took hold of each other and I could see the love they have for each other. They embraced for quite a while, they kissed each other and they both burst into tears and cried together. I felt a tear roll down my cheek, I felt good for them and bad for them at the same time. I hope they get a baby if that is what they really want.

Things calmed down and I coughed to get their attention. A glance from Ray and he realised I was still there. I said to the both of them, "I wish you both the very best of luck for now and in the future." I hugged them both they thanked me and I turned and walked away.

I arrived home around 22.30, went into my home, locked the door, took off my shoes and coat and settled down to a nice bottle of red wine. My work was done and my tasks were completed, I had managed to pull it off. There were definitely a few problems but I was through to the other side and I felt satisfied and content.

The sad arrival of Hugh G into the hospital where I worked had created a massive impact on so many lives including mine and although it was a strange situation in many ways it was as though he was meant to be there. The very fact that he was there has changed so many people's lives and hopefully for the better. Were there some things I wish I had not done with him? Well, yes of course there are and some of the things that took place I certainly wish that they had not. I was now feeling that I had been on a short adventure and this adventure was full of risk, pain, sadness and a strong sense of hope. I have the belief that whatever had been done was helping to put some of the people, if not all of the people who had been touched by Hugh, in a better place in their lives for now and the foreseeable future.

Tonight had been a rough night with more than a shock to the system with the arrival of Lucy and the non show of Karen at work earlier this evening. I decided to call Karen and give her a piece of my mind for not calling me and warning me before I got to the hospital. I took out my mobile and searched for Karen's number. I scrolled down and found her number, a press of the button and the call was being made. It took seconds for Karen to answer and my first words were "What the hell are you playing at?"

Karen croaked back at me with a sore throat type sound, "I tried to call you earlier but there was no answer."

As Karen spoke to me I glanced at my phone to see it was still set on silent. I quickly apologised to her and said I could see the problem and continued to explain what I had just seen on my phone. I apologised again and went on to say that I had put my phone on silent earlier today to get a bit of peace before tonight's last girls' night out event and I had forgotten to turn the speaker back on. It took a few moments of humble apology when I said to Karen, "Look girl, no harm done, get yourself better and we can talk later." I also said, "Before I go I need to tell you I have a card from Shola to give you."

"Why?" said Karen.

"I don't know, when you get the card you had better ask her?"

We ended the call on a goodbye and see you later and Karen was gone.

THE PAYOUT

It was time I had a rest. I needed a break from work and from everything else. I have decided to take time off from work, at least for a short while, just to give me time to get my own life back in order so I will put in a few weeks holiday and just relax. That was a decision made so next day that is what I did. I went to work and booked two weeks of *me* time. One other thing I needed to do was get hold of Sue and give her the money. I still had it and I wanted her to have it all asap. I called Sue and asked her to come to my place. I met her on a Friday night, we ordered a Chinese meal delivered to my door, we had a small amount of wine, and I do mean small, and we chatted all night.

I eventually stood up and went to my bedroom where the cash had been hidden. I brought it downstairs and presented it to Sue. All told eleven ladies had contributed to this project, financially I mean, and as a result in the bag in front of Sue was a large sum of money. All told around £88,000. Of the money £22,000 was to go to Karen leaving £66,000 for Sue. I gave her the cash and I was relieved it was done and off my hands. The bundles were in £8,000 stacks and Sue put her hand inside and gave me two of them. She said, "Please Leigh, take two of these bundles – you have earned them." I was very surprised and grateful but I told her no. Sue pushed them into my hand and said, "Yes, you *will!*"

Sue was determined and I could tell by her tone that she was serious.

"I can easily put my life on track with what is left," said Sue, "and I am sure you could use £16,000 cash right now."

I looked at her and said, "Yes I could." I also became a little emotional and started to cry. My friend Sue leaned forward and put her arms around me and comforted me. I was now fully relieved that my task was finally complete and this was the end of this particular chapter of my life. Sue stayed until around 11pm and then left. In a way I was glad when she went, it was good to spend time with her but

I felt a sort of relief when she went. Being alone allows you time to think and gives you the time you need to clear your mind, and right now I needed to clear my mind.

*

I spent a week of my time doing not much at all really. I shopped, I went out walking and I read a couple of books. I also started to get back into my hypnotherapy. Although I had never used it before the night in the hospital, it had sparked my interest again and I felt that now was a good time to re-visit it. I looked at all of the training material that I had received and the videos that came with the course and I began to study the whole programme once again, and I actually enjoyed it all. Revisiting this hypnotherapy training was a form of therapy in itself; I allowed myself the time to enjoy something that I really enjoyed.

I was sat one afternoon when the phone rang and it was Karen. We had spoken a few days earlier; I had called her to ask how she was, she was embarrassed about the night when she wasn't at work and she was also sorry about it. I told Karen if you are ill you cannot do much about it. Apparently, she had tried to call me but couldn't get through and, well, the rest is history as they say. I told her not to worry about anything, it was all over and done. I had also not given Karen all the money she was owed, so I told her to come round for a coffee or a glass of wine, it would be nice to get together. Friday was the best day for her as she was off work so that would be fine and good for me too. It was the Friday of my second week so I would be back at work on the Monday morning, it would be a nice way to end the week seeing Karen and just chatting about things.

Karen arrived at around 6pm and she brought a couple of bottles of red wine, my favourite. We sat down together and we talked about everything, even the sex that we had shared together. I was not ashamed or embarrassed about all that we had done and, to be honest, it had been a nice experience and I told Karen this.

Karen suddenly said that she had called Shola and talked with her. I was curious because when we were at the hospital I had seen the connection between them and I knew that something had drawn them together. Karen said that she was on the phone for over an hour and that since then they had texted each other on the phone many times.

This communication led them both to go out for a meal at a local Italian restaurant and they had got on very well with each other, the night out was a success and after the meal they walked and talked for about an hour and a half. Shola told Karen about her life and her relationship with her husband and Karen gave Shola chapter and verse on her life too. At the end of that night out they had kissed, but no more. They both said good night to each other and went their separate ways. Karen said that she was sure they would have gone to bed together that night but neither of them said this to the other one that they wanted this to happen.

Karen talked some more about Shola and told me some of the things that they had discussed. However, Karen said to me that there were some things that were private and she did not want to break any confidences with Shola. I listened and said her privacy is hers and I totally understand what she was saying, a good friend would not tell the world about such things and that she was right to keep secrets a secret. Karen talked a little more when her mobile phone bleeped and it was a text message. She picked up the phone and Karen said it was from Shola.

"What does she want?" I asked.

"She wants to come round here – now."

"Why?" I asked.

"She wants to talk to you about something important and I want to be here when she asks you."

I looked at Karen and I said, "You *knew* she wanted to come here?"

"Yes," Karen replied.

"Do you know what she wants to ask me?" I asked.

"Yes," replied Karen, "I know what she wants to ask you."

I felt at a bit of a disadvantage and I was a little disappointed with Karen with the fact that she and Shola were involved in some sort of scheme made me feel a little uneasy. Nevertheless, I told Karen to call Shola and tell her to come round now. Karen made the call and 20 minutes later Shola was here.

Karen had told her to come straight in once she arrived and sure enough a small knock at the door and in she walked. Shola always seemed very confident but as she came into the house she looked very sheepish and her head was slightly down. She walked over to Karen and gave her a hug and a kiss on the cheek and she then turned to me and lightly shook my hand. I offered her a glass of wine but she declined. "I am driving," she said, "and I won't take the risk, but a coffee would be nice if I can have one."

I told Shola to make herself comfortable and I would go and make her a coffee, I asked her how she liked her coffee. "Black no sugar please," she replied. I was in the kitchen making her drink and I could hear both Karen and Shola talking, they were whispering so I could not get the drift of the conversation. I returned into the front room and gave Shola the coffee. By now Karen and Shola were sat together on the settee and this made me feel a little uncomfortable in my own home.

"Alright," I said to Shola, "what is on your mind?"

Shola and Karen both looked at me and said nothing for a moment.

"Come on then," I said, "spit it out. What is it you want to ask me?"

I said this in an almost aggressive tone and my voice was slightly raised, it made both of them jump.

Shola looked at me and said, "I have a proposition to put to you but it is a little complicated and a bit off the wall."

"Go on," I said to her, but this time my tone was lighter and my voice a bit softer.

"You introduced the group of ladies that you pulled together to Hugh G and what you did was an amazing thing. Whatever happens to them, whether they get pregnant or not, it was a good thing that you did. However, I see a potential for this to go on for longer, but not for women to get pregnant but to use Hugh as a *love machine*, for want of a better way of putting it."

I looked at her and I said, "You have got to be fucking joking! What do you think this was all about? My intention was to help women in need, not set the poor sod up as some sort of sex toy."

I do not normally swear but her request made me feel angry. "No bloody chance and no bloody way am I doing that!" I growled back at Shola and I glared harshly at Karen.

"Wait," said Shola. "Please listen, you *will* be helping women."

"How?" I replied.

Shola came back at me with:

"These friends of mine are all wealthy or well off, money is not really an issue for them but their sex lives are a problem. Some of these women are relatively young, with older partners or husbands, and although there may be some love there the passion is not and these women are craving safe liaisons without complications and this could be the perfect solution, at least for now.

Look, all I am asking is the opportunity for you to consider my proposals. Please think about it and consider this, in your thoughts the needs of the first group of women were maternal i.e. they needed a baby to complete their lives. The ladies I know need some type of male stimulation to help complete their lives but in safety and without a major risk to them or their marriages.

Please consider my request Leigh, and don't rush your decision, it means a great deal to my friends more than you can imagine."

I looked at Shola square in the eyes and then I turned my gaze at Karen. I sat and thought for a moment and I told the both of them I would consider it but no guarantees, none at all.

"I don't want to talk about this anymore tonight, I need a break from all of this talk so leave it with me and I will let you both know."

"I want to thank you," said Karen, and as she stood up she touched my hand as a supportive gesture. I received a hesitant thank you from Shola, although to be honest the gesture did not go very far with me, friend or no friend.

It appeared that they were both going to leave together when Shola said, "Can I have a glass of wine please?"

"I thought you don't drink and drive," was my reply to her.

"I won't," she said. "I can get a taxi and leave the car here for tomorrow."

"Alright, that sounds like a sensible move. What would you like, red or white wine?"

Shola looked at Karen and said, "The same as her please."

I suppose this was a diversion on Shola's part, but I went with the idea to see what else was on her mind. I started to stand up to get the wine when Karen said, "Stay there Leigh, I will get it. Just relax woman and take it easy."

I started to laugh and they both looked at me like I was crazy.

"What is so funny?" said Karen. I replied, "How the hell can I relax with you two around me?"

This comment broke the ice and we all started to laugh. It did change the mood and the atmosphere became lighter much lighter. We all had some wine and we started to talk and chat and the three of us began to enjoy the evening together. In the background the TV was playing and as we all talked I began to get involved in a film that was on, although I didn't know what the film was about. I just kept watching. I sat for a long time looking at the television and completely forgot about Karen and Shola sitting there.

An advertisement break came on and I turned to talk to the two girls and as I did I saw them both heavily petting each other. Neither of them saw me looking and to be honest I don't think they would have cared as they were full on with each other. Shola had her top pulled up and her bra pulled above her breasts, her skirt was around her waist and her legs were spread wide. Karen had taken her skirt off she had no pants on, they were next to her on the floor, and they both had fingers in each other's holes and tongues down each other's throats. I can't say I was shocked but I was certainly surprised at what I was seeing. There were no holds barred here and they were both very passionate and sexy with each other, if that is the right expression.

The TV movie came back on but I completely forgot about it and I sat watching the live action show in my front room, and with the blink of an eye the two of them ripped off each other's clothes and started to fuck each other in very womanly ways. Karen saw me looking and she did not stop, in fact she became more vigorous with Shola and they went hard at it.

I myself had experienced the feelings that Karen created in me when we had shared each other and I could only imagine what was happening to the two of them in front of me now, it was an expression of pure passion and it was an exciting thing to watch. The two women were all over each other, the two of them were both fit and active ladies and as they explored each other's bodies both inside and out it took my breath away. It was quite clear that Shola was going to orgasm first and Karen worked hard fingering Shola's fanny to ensure the climax was brought to a full and powerful conclusion. As I watched I could feel the anticipation as Shola screamed out loud as she exploded into the most powerful climax that I had ever seen. As she came she rolled on the floor and as the climax reached what appeared to be the height of ecstasy she pulled at her own tits, rubbing her huge black nipples and caressing them as she had a multiple orgasm. As Shola continued to move around the floor Karen fought hard to keep her fingers in Shola's cunt to help continue the masturbation of her fanny until she completed the full sexual experience.

Within two or three minutes Shola had clearly had a most outstanding orgasm and she fell back on the floor and became still. She was sweating heavily and panting with heavy breaths and moaning in what was clearly the end result of a most extreme sexual act. Shola was lying on her back and her black body shone; her skin was like a black mirrored glass and the beads of sweat rolled down her body from every position, her breasts stood upright and although she was lying with her back on the floor her tits and her huge black nipples were standing high and proud from her chest.

Shola's legs were apart and you could see a black vagina, but the lips around the inside where white. I stared between her legs and as she was moving gently, still obviously experiencing some aftershocks from the orgasm, I could clearly see a white milky fluid flowing from her fanny. I experienced this sometimes as a lubricant during sexual intercourse but nothing in the quantity that I was seeing from Shola's fanny.

My gaze went from Shola to Karen, who was by now starting to masturbate herself so that she too could continue her own orgasm to a full conclusion. Karen looked at Shola and I could tell that she wanted Shola to do this act for her. Sadly for Karen I think Shola was too deep into her own sexual experience and she had not finished. Both Karen and I watched as Shola was still in the throes of some sort of orgasmic state and it was clear to both of us she was not yet ready to assist Karen.

Karen looked at me and I knew exactly what she wanted. Throughout the whole session I watched the two of them perform heavy sexual acts on each other and it was erotic and sexually stimulating to me. At one point I had put my hands between my own legs to feel a flood of female fluids running out of my vagina. I had quickly pulled my hand out and not done anything about it. Right now Karen needed me to continue what Shola had previously started. I looked at Karen to get her attention and she saw me and winked at me in a most provocative way. It was very obvious that she had seen me finger myself and I knew she wanted me to help her climax.

I looked at Shola and she was still out of it so I moved across the floor and positioned myself close to Karen. I extended my hands forward between her legs with my left hand I tightened her fanny, stretching it so that I could rub the interior edge of her pussy lips where I knew it would stimulate her. I knew how to get her the orgasm she so desperately needed, and as I pulled the top of her vagina tight I used two fingers on my right hand rubbing the vaginal lips as hard as I could.

After the sexual contact that Karen and I had felt between us I knew what she wanted and how she liked things to be done. I was aware of what turned her on and I had also experienced her orgasm for myself so I knew what was needed. Shola fell quiet and I glanced towards her and for a moment our eyes met and then I turned away and continued my work on Karen. It was obvious that Shola did not expect to see this from me and I could also sense a feeling of jealousy towards me and what I was doing to Karen and her pussy. I turned my attention back to Karen's fanny and I began to rub it with my fingers again. It was already moist and lubricated but to make it easier to stimulate I bent my head forward and down and I spat on her cunt. Karen jumped a little with the force that came out of my mouth but she did not move away, she just allowed me to carry on with the masturbation of her vagina.

Karen began to respond as I knew she would and before long she was pushing her hips up and down in a fucking motion as she started to climb the orgasm steps to pleasure.

Karen pushed harder and harder and faster and faster heading towards one of her fantastic climaxes. Passionate noises came from her mouth as she started to scream and as I rubbed her pussy as hard as I could, moving my fingers as fast as was possible, she exploded into a fantastic orgasm. I felt her body shake next to me as she arched her back in response to this fantastic feeling she had just been able to achieve at my now very tired hands.

I was well aware of Shola watching the two of us together and although she had said nothing throughout the previous minutes I could feel that something was coming my way. Shola looked at Karen with a judging eye and Karen looked at her and said, "What's wrong?"

"I did not know you two were an item," said Shola.

"We are not," I barked at her, "we are just good friends."

"Good friends don't do that to each other."

"*We* do," I said, "and that's it."

Karen spoke to Shola with a very stern tone in her voice. "Please Shola, do not presume to know about my life. We have talked about many things, but not everything is for public discussion and that goes for things in your life too. What is secret stays secret and don't lose sight of that fact."

"I get the message," said Shola, "I get the message."

There was a little bit of an atmosphere in the room but nothing too bad. It felt like a schoolyard tussle that had quickly blown over. I stood up and poured some more wine for the three of us, Shola sat on the floor naked, and so was Karen.

The room was warm and the mood began to change, it was quite clear these two ladies were comfortable with their nudity but being pregnant, I was not so comfortable with my body. I had gone topless on a beach before some years earlier in Spain, but that was as far as I had gone. Under normal circumstances I would sit here naked in my house on my own, but this felt a little awkward. We all sat talking and we discussed each other's lives and things in general.

Shola talked about the life she had and it sounded good but inside her you could also feel a sadness and that was a shame because how could someone so good looking and attractive be so unhappy?

Or that is what I thought anyway.

We talked, we laughed and we joked. Shola looked at me and said a strange thing. "Leigh," she asked, "what does it feel like to be pregnant?"

I did not speak to her but I decided that she needed to feel and see what pregnancy was all about. "How does it feel to be pregnant?" I said, "well watch and see." At that point I lifted up my dress over my head, I took off my bra to reveal my now much larger than normal nipples and I took down my pants and stood before her naked. I moved closer to Shola and I took hold of her left hand and placed it on my tummy and said, "Here you can feel pregnancy." Shola left her hand there for a while and then I moved it towards my naked breasts, I eased her hand over my firm breasts and across my nipples. Her hands were warm and soft and her touch was nice but not sexual. Shola looked me in the eyes and smiled at me in a really nice and pleasant way.

Karen sat on the floor smiling at the both of us too. Karen knew what I was doing and I think I made my point very well. I went to sit on the floor and getting down was a bit of a struggle but Shola held me until I could sit down and get comfortable. I said to Shola and Karen that I was self-conscious about my situation having a baby and no father, well not officially anyway, and that I too had had a good figure and it was gone now.

"No it is not," said Shola. "Once the baby is born," she said, "Karen and I will get you back into a nice sexy shape, but to be honest I really like the shape you're in now." Shola went on to say, "Your nipples and tits look fantastic."

I began to blush but I still liked the compliment and it did lift me a little bit. Karen said to me, "This is just a phase and before long, and once the baby is born, you can get back to normal."

I looked at the two of them and I said, "I wonder what 'normal' will be, a single mother with a new baby and no job."

We were all sat on the floor naked and it seemed so natural and although I was the odd shape between the three of us, I felt at home and at ease the way the three of us were. I was happy and almost contented. There was a great deal ahead of me but I really did feel good.

Time was passing by quickly and Shola said she had to go soon. I asked if anybody wanted a final drink but Karen and Shola declined. We chatted for a while longer and Shola said, "I really need to go now." As she stood up I watched her and she was a gorgeous woman in every respect and although I did not say it out loud I still thought this in my mind. I also could see why Karen was attracted to her. I myself was not gay. Even though I had experienced sexual acts with Karen, I still felt that this was just something I had done and it was not my way of life and yet Shola did impress me in the way she walked, the way she talked and her black body was amazing in every conceivable way. As Shola got dressed I called a taxi for her, although earlier she had not wanted to have a glass or two of wine she had eventually taken some and now it was not good for her to drive. Shola made the right choice and it proved to me how sensible she was.

The taxi promptly arrived 15 minutes later. As the car pulled up she came over to me and put her arms around me. She whispered in my ear, "We will become good friends Leigh and I promise to be here for you and your baby now and in the future. You are not alone, you are definitely not alone." Shola kissed me on the cheek then walked over to Karen, kissed her on the lips and left my house to go back to her own home and her husband.

Karen and I were still sat naked on the floor. It was a little bit strange as I did not know what to do. Karen patted the floor beside of her and beckoned me to come over and sit down next to her. I went to her and eased myself onto the floor and sat down beside her. "You will be alright," said Karen. "I know things have been difficult for you over the past few months, but between Shola and me you will be alright. We will look after you believe me."

The words coming from Karen echoed those from Shola earlier and the confidence and strength that came from them was an amazing feeling. I now knew I really was not alone and that I would be alright both now and in the future.

Karen eventually stood up to get herself dressed but as she stood there I said to her, "Don't go home, I do not want to be alone tonight. Please stay with me, stay the night will you?"

Karen looked at me, she had already started to put on her skirt. Without a single word she let the skirt fall to the floor. Karen was once again naked and stood next to me. I was still sitting on the floor. Karen leaned forward and put her left hand out towards me, she took hold of my right hand and said, "Let's go to bed then." Karen helped me to my feet and without another word we went to my bedroom together.

Shola came back to my house the next day. She picked up her car but did not knock on my door. I was so grateful she did not come to my front door because if I had answered the knock she would have seen Karen in my home. Shola would have known that Karen had spent the night. With this in mind I neither wanted, nor needed, to explain myself to anyone, least of all Shola. I imagined Shola was busy as always and in a hurry to get somewhere else and today I was very happy this was the case.

It has been a year since Hugh G first arrived in my life and because of him a great deal had taken place. Not much had changed for him, but the fact that Hugh had a large penis meant that he had made many changes to many people's lives, including mine. Sadly, however, poor Hugh was not conscious or aware of what had taken place and that situation really pained me. I had spent the whole of my time involved in this type of situation evaluating and questioning what I was doing and why. It seemed that in such a short space of time I had thrown away all of my ethics and values, but in their place I had helped people and hopefully made their lives much better for the experience.

Because of Hugh and the giant erection I have been party to a strange set of events, my life has been touched in such a special and unique way that I cannot begin to explain how I feel or indeed how I felt. Throughout the whole situation I was going through I feel that now I am through the storm. I now also feel that I have achieved some really good things and that overall the effort was worth the pain and the general outcomes were good in most cases.

As an update: out of the ladies who slept with Hugh six got pregnant, four of them delivered healthy babies, one of the girls who was pregnant lost that baby and finally, one conceived with twins and delivered a little girl but lost the other. I don't want to go into details about this but for those who delivered it was a blessing and for those who did not it was a tragic loss and an awful experience to endure.

I do believe that some of them keep in touch and I also know for sure that those who still do not have children have joined together with those who were successful and now share in the experience of being part of a family with children. Some of the girls and their husbands even became godparents, so there is some good for them coming out of this situation too.

Just to let you know the gay couple Alison and Jade, they had a baby boy and they called him Hugh. I don't want to say which one of them was the delivering mother but regardless they are now a very happy family.

As for me, I delivered a son. His name is James and we are both doing fine. He is now three months old and true to their word Shola and Karen are a very big part of both mine and my son's lives. I still visit Hugh and I have taken his son to him and sat James on his father's chest, and for me it was the most painful experience of my life because in my heart Hugh can never be told of his son and James cannot know about his father. I also have a firm agreement from all the women who were involved that no disclosure of any kind will be made, so secrecy will be maintained. My life is not too bad now. I have not yet returned to work because I am still on maternity leave and to be honest there is no pressure to return yet either.

You may recall that Shola asked me if I would let her and a few of her wealthy friends use Hugh G as some sort of sex toy. Although at the time when she asked me to do this I was not agreeable on the matter, I have had time to reflect on this and my thoughts have changed. I am not quite sure how I would let this thing happen but my mind is now more open to the prospect of this happening. When, or indeed, *if* Hugh comes out of his coma, he will need nursing care and rehabilitation and help if his family cannot be found or even if he has no family. The recovery after a long stay in hospital, especially for coma casualties, is long. They need time to re-adjust to normal life again and at this point in time I think I am the only person who can do this and possibly I am the only person available to do this for him.

Since the birth of my son James I have slept with his father three times; the first time was four weeks after James was born. It was not the sex that I had wanted before with Hugh, but a closeness that I needed with the father of my son. I needed to be close to him in a physical way. However, the following two times it was passion and erotic sex that I needed, and I got exactly that. Nothing has changed with Hugh G. His penis is still large and almost permanently erect, and yes, it still excites me every time I see it. From time to time Shola comes to visit me and James, as does Karen. it is nice to see them both and I have to say that Shola does bring me cash to help with bills and other things.

I have tried to refuse the money but Shola was very firm with me and told me this is what she wanted to do for both me and my son. I now accept the help and I am very grateful for the support she and Karen both give me.

This is I suppose an exciting time in my life, many big changes have taken place and many things are still happening which will give me hope for the future. I am optimistic about my life and I have high hopes for my son James as well. I believe that the two of us are moving forward in a positive way and that we will both be happy as things move us both into our new future. I now have the makings of a good family: a healthy son and a healthy and positive me.

When Hugh G arrived at the hospital and, as is sometimes said, from a tragedy sometimes new beginnings can begin, although his original condition was not so good it has now come to pass that his health and general condition have dramatically improved. Although still in a coma he has shown signs of change for the better. Physically he is in good shape, he has regular physiotherapy, he is fed via a drip and medically his physiology is also good. The hospital has reached a point where they can do no more for him other than wait to see if his coma clears and he regains consciousness.

*

I was at home one day when the phone rang. I answered the call and it was my friend Sue. We exchanged the usual pleasantries and then she said she had some news for me about Hugh. I was a little bit surprised. "Tell me more," I said.

"There has been a patient review this morning here at the hospital and one of the topics raised was that of Hugh G. As part of the process a representative from the police was present to give an update on the investigation regarding Hugh and to date there has been no more information on what happened to Hugh, either about the attack on him or indeed his identity. Also the hospital position now is that they need Hugh's bed for more urgent cases and although Hugh is in a coma, he is not a critical care patient any longer and the hospital senior management are looking for a solution to this problem. Private care is out of the question because of the high cost and the hospital need the bed space, so I suggested that you take him as a home care patient."

My jaw dropped wide open at the thought of this happening. Sue continued to say that after the meeting was finished it had been agreed to consider the option of me working from home, looking after my son and having Hugh here as a home care patient. It was an unbelievable opportunity and one I would gladly accept. Sue went on to say I would receive full support from the hospital and instead of coming back to work to resume my old job I would be paid to work from home as a nurse carer. Sue was very optimistic about the whole process and she told me that the suggestion had been received very well and that she really believed there was a good chance it was going to happen – if I wanted it to that is. The news that Sue brought me was exciting, very exciting, it was like a dream come true to me.

I could not imagine a better surprise or a more bizarre thing happening to me. At this time it was like a ray of sunshine hitting me and lighting up my life. I have had a rough ride over the past few months with some high points and low times too, but right now Sue had brought me a big life-changing moment once again and I really feel that I want this to happen. If the opportunity presents itself and the hospital management agree, I will accept the chance to do this for Hugh and I will be very happy having my son's father in my home.

*

A few weeks went by and not much information came my way. Although I called Sue a couple of times she could not give me any more information, so I was really no further forward in knowing what was to happen with Hugh G. It was now getting near the time for me to return to work and I was very apprehensive about this. I was now at the point where I had resigned myself to the fact that I was indeed going to go back to work and resume my old job. I really did not want to leave my son James with anyone else and I was beginning to feel the tension this would cause me if I had to do this.

I was at home one day and both Shola and Karen had come to visit. This was now a regular thing and it was a normal part of my life, I even let them take James out for shopping trips with them. The girls would call me to say they were coming round and more often than not they would take James out with them for an hour or two. They enjoyed playing mother and I got a welcome break, so it worked well for the three of us, well actually the four of us because James also seemed to love the extra attention so it was a good thing all round.

This particular day the ladies came to visit we had a coffee and of course as usual they wanted to go out with James. I wasn't sure if Shola and Karen were becoming an item, it looked to me to be a very obvious thing because they were always together and I could feel a strong bond between them. Now I knew Shola was married but I was also aware of the relationship with her husband and the flexible nature of this relationship that was between them.

Anyway, I was at home alone and the phone rang. I answered it and Sue was on the line. She said, "Hello Leigh, how are you?"

"I am fine. How are you?"

"Good, I am good. Listen, I have some news for you."

I opened my ears, "I am listening, what do you have for me?"

"Well, the hospital has provisionally agreed to let Hugh come home with you. Social care will be involved and nursing support too, but essentially it will be up to you to take care and look after him. There are a few things to put in place but by what was said this morning I believe this can happen very quickly."

My heart was pounding and I was very excited because I did not think this would happen. It was also a bit of a shock hearing the news from Sue. We both talked for a few moments longer then Sue said she had to go and would call round to see me later. And with that the call was ended.

I sat alone for quite some time pondering on what Sue had said on the phone. I still could not believe what was about to happen, it felt like a year long struggle was finally coming to an end and the prize for me was Hugh. I started to get excited again, in fact very excited indeed. Suddenly a click and the front door opened. I looked to see Karen, Shola and my son James coming through the doorway. The two girls looked at me as if I was crazy because I had a smile like a Cheshire cat on my face. I looked at them and just kept smiling and then I burst out laughing.

"He's coming home!" I shouted to the two of them. "He is coming *home*!"

Karen and Shola moved James and the pushchair to the middle of the room and rushed towards me, grabbed hold of me and the two of them held me tight and all three of us started to cry. It was a fantastic moment and one to be savoured for as long as I could.

We eventually sat down and still teary eyed I popped open a bottle of wine while the girls organised James from his pushchair to his baby seat. James just sat in his chair watching three crazy women laugh and giggle and the house felt as if it was full of joy, something that had been missing from this home for a very long time.

The celebrations slowed down and baby duties kicked in. James had to be fed and watered and of course the statutory nappy change too. As I was going through the motions I did think briefly about the extra work that was heading my way with Hugh G. Although I had not given this a great deal of attention I did wonder what things would be like with the baby and Hugh here at the same time, it was going to be a very busy time. One other thing hit me too; what if Hugh does not come out of his coma?

Where does that leave things because I'm sure Hugh G could not stay here forever. For one thing I don't think social care would allow this to continue indefinitely. Suddenly I was full of questions, and some answers I probably would not be able to get because nobody would be in a position to answer them at this point in time.

The girls had left by now and I was left alone with James. The sad thing is that I was having a taste of being alone even though James was here. It was also a fact of life that when Hugh arrives he will also not be able to talk with me and, although I am happy that I will get the chance to look after Hugh in my home, I have just had a reality check of how the future might be – a single mother at home with her baby son, looking after a man who fathered the child and who is still in a long term coma-like state. Shit, I thought, is this my destiny and can this and will this situation of mine improve? Christ I hope so, I really do hope so. I was back in the deep thinker mode again, analysing everything. This was becoming a part of my everyday life. I used to brush things off but now I keep hold of things too tightly and it creates un-needed pressures. I must stop doing this and start to be a bit more free thinking and get back to the old Leigh. If things are to get better I need to stay positive and get my head back into gear and that thought process starts NOW!

*

It's been two weeks since Sue called me and things have moved along; documents have been signed and a great deal of the official stuff has been done. Social care have been to visit me several times and the questions were asked: can you cope with a young baby and a patient in a coma in your home at the same time?

I answered honestly about how I thought things would be and the people asking the questions seemed happy with my answers. Equipment was delivered to my home and the hospital-style bed was delivered. The bed was set up downstairs for ease and convenience. Everything looked good and as far as I knew all was organised and we were ready to go. Even though I thought I was prepared for what was coming at me I still had some apprehensions about what would happen. That said, I am still optimistic about how it was to be.

Early one morning I received a call from hospital administration; they were contacting me to let me know that they had chosen a provisional date for Hugh to be brought to me. I began to shake with excitement at the thought of what was about to happen. The administrator asked me once again was I sure about what I was about to undertake and I said firmly, "Yes I am".

The lady on the phone, Jan Mayer, said: "Well if that is the case Hugh will be brought to you on Friday 18th of this month."

That was four days from now!

I knew Jan from work and she let the official voice go and she talked as a colleague and a friend. Jan said, "Leigh, this is a big thing you are undertaking here, are you ready for it to happen especially so close to the birth of your son?" I said to her, "Jan, since it was mentioned to me I have thought about little else and after all the talk and considerations that have been put into this idea I feel as ready as I will ever be." I went further and said that I had good help around me from friends and the hospital and I really believed that between all of the support I could do a good thing here for this poor man and hopefully help him to recover from his long sleep and get him back on the road to recovery.

"I admire you Leigh," said Jan, "I really do. You are doing a wonderful thing, but quite frankly it is something I could not do."

"Jan," I said, "I am a nurse and I have nursed all of my adult life. It is a normal thing for me and to be truthful I have always enjoyed my work, so for me this is just an extension from the hospital to my home, in short no big deal." In actual fact it *was* a big deal but I was not going to tell her that. Jan wished me good luck and we both said goodbye and she was gone.

With all of the talk there were only a few people who really knew the full story of Hugh and I and although my motives were not known to the public, what I was doing still seemed to be a strong topic of conversation. To be honest I don't care, I just want to get on with things and see where it all goes.

Later that day I called Karen and told her the news, she was over the moon for me. She said that she would call Shola and let her know what had been agreed with the hospital. Karen also asked if I wanted her to be there when Hugh arrives. I wasn't sure about this and I said that I would let her know. I thanked Karen for the offer and I asked her to let me think on what she had said to me. Karen was fine with this and said, "You know where I am if you need me."

I told her to take care and I would see her soon.

Things appeared to be moving at a faster pace now and it was as if it was outside of my control. All of a sudden people were at my home checking things and re-assessing and generally it appeared everything that had already been done was now being covered again. The senior social worker who was my main point of contact was a lady called Mavis Green; she was a woman in her late forties, pleasant enough and easy to talk to.

I asked her why everything was being checked again, I actually thought that there was a problem or that things were not going to go ahead as planned. Her response was that this was a semi unusual case and that it was a standard practice by social services to re-check all the information, just to make sure everything that should be covered had indeed been covered, just in case of any come-back in the future from either family or friends of the patient.

This explanation made sense now as, to be honest, I had forgotten about the potential of family or anyone else for that matter taking legal action on Hugh's behalf – it just didn't enter my head.

After the comings and goings of people at my home things did start to settle down again and once all of the disturbance to my life had subsided things went back to normal. I had gone through two days of stress and pressure and now I had only two days to go and Hugh G would be here. I was starting to get really excited now and it was a great feeling to have. Boy did I feel *good*!

*

The day Hugh arrived was a little bit crazy. Both Shola and Karen were on hand to help with James and of course the whole medical team from the hospital and social services were there too. It felt like the house was full of a hundred people. I know it was not but it just felt like that. The ambulance arrived at 10.30; there were one or two of the neighbours looking on as things appeared to be a bit of a spectacle, my life on display so to speak. Hugh was taken from the ambulance and quickly moved into my home. I had the strangest feeling, as if my husband was being brought back from hospital, as if he had been in an accident.

I know this was not true but it just felt almost correct and normal even though I knew my life was far from normal and was probably not going to have normality for a long time to come. I felt as if I was under the spotlight. Different people were asking am I alright?, do I need anything?, do I have any questions? and so on. Before long people started to drift away. I was shown all of the care plans again, as if I didn't bloody know how that worked; years in senior nursing roles should have covered that tick in the box. However, I went through it all. I did not complain and I did what was asked, all in the name of conformity.

At around 11.30am the house was nearly mine again, Shola was still here, as was Karen, and 12ish Sue came round too. I was pleased she could find the time to come to see me, it made me feel good. Sue was the one person I felt would help cement things for me and when she arrived it was unannounced and most definitely appreciated. The five of us sat together for a cup of coffee: Shola, Karen, Sue, James and I. James was not drinking coffee, just milk, but anyway it was a really good feeling and I was actually happy and everyone said it showed and I really felt very happy indeed.

I looked across the room to see Hugh on the bed in the corner and you know I had forgotten about him being there, all the fuss and upheaval and it was all because of him. I felt a bit guilty but then I started to laugh. When I told the girls what I had been thinking they laughed too. Sue stayed for a while, then she had to leave. It was around 1 o'clock by now. She said her goodbyes and she left. Sue did, however, take the time to go to Hugh. I heard her whisper something but it was not clear what she said to him, she did not tell anyone what she had whispered to Hugh and we did not ask, private is private.

Karen was the last to leave. Shola left about half an hour after Sue, she had appointments to go to so she went on her way. Shola had also gone to see Hugh and she too spoke softly to him. This man did have an effect on people, mainly women, and he did not even know what he was doing to people.

Karen and I sat for a while when she said to me, "Leigh, I have a confession to make."

"What about?" I asked her. She replied, "Please don't be angry, but I have had sex with Hugh."

I looked at her with a deep stare. "When?" I said to her.

"The night I saw you fuck him it drove me crazy watching you and Hugh together, so after you left and when all was quiet I went to him and screwed him hard."

I was shocked but then I thought to myself I was not surprised and I told Karen this. It was strange but I had actually thought she might have done this but I had dismissed it in my mind because I thought it was a crazy thing to think.

Karen apologised again and I said to just forget it.

"You are angry," said Karen.

"No I am not," was my reply, "I'm just a bit mixed up and confused about everything."

"Does this have an effect on us?"

"No it does not. He has been with a few other paying customers, you had a free ride. Although it is not what I wanted to hear right now, I can live with what you have just said and done so no, I don't mind, honestly I don't."

"Thank you," said Karen. "Thank you Leigh, I never thought we could become such good friends and I have wanted to tell you for a long time. When you first slept with Hugh I thought it was just a bit of fun, I never believed it would have gone this far and become this complicated. Leigh you are my friend and I need you to know that from the bottom of my heart."

I looked at Karen and then I stood up, moved towards her, put my arms around her and kissed on the cheek and held her gently. It's alright Karen, I really understand. Just forget it and let's move on."

I felt a strong cup of coffee coming on so I went to the kitchen to put the kettle on. When I came back to the front room I saw Karen's reflection in the mirror. She had gone over to Hugh's bed and she was stood looking at him. At first I thought she was just checking him to see if he was alright, so I looked around the door to get a better look and she was holding his left hand and I sensed something more than a one-off screwing session had taken place between them.

I said nothing and went back to the kitchen to make two cups of coffee. I returned as if I had not seen her. When I walked through the door to the living room Karen was sat in the same chair she had been sat in when I went into the kitchen. It was obvious she did not want me to see what she had done because she acted as if she had not moved from the chair. I said to Karen, "Do you want to see Hugh?" "No" was her reply. "Let him rest, I will see him when I leave." And that was the end of that.

We had our coffee together and she said that it was time to get going. For me it had been a long day and I was very tired, I still had things to do: feed James and put him properly to bed, and now of course I need to tend to the needs of my new house guest.

Karen made moves to leave. We stood at the front door together and embraced. She apologised to me again about Hugh and I dismissed it, she seemed to need a little more reassurance and I gave her that. Karen asked if I needed any help before she left and I said, "No, I am fine, tonight is the first night so I need to see how I manage", but I thanked her for the offer and I said if I needed her could I call her or Shola anytime. She replied positively to me and said, "YES YOU CAN!"

With that Karen left. She did go to Hugh and kissed him on the forehead, a natural gesture with no obvious hidden meanings. It was actually nice to see and I was not bothered by this action whatsoever. Karen left and I said goodbye and closed the door and locked it.

I was now alone with my new family so to speak, and my thoughts. My world was now complete and it seemed that everything I had wanted had dropped on my doorstep.

THE SEXUAL FRUSTRATION

Although originally I did not need a man to be part of my life it felt as if I actually wanted this man in my home to remain with me for the rest of my life. It was a strange twist but it was a nice feeling and although the circumstances were not perfect it was better than I had thought it was going to be.

The next few weeks trickled along, people called, social workers came, friends called and it became a regular routine of visitors which I gradually got used to. The social worker Mavis Green was a big help. Quite often she would call in and it did not feel like she was snooping on me, more like a bit of moral support. She was impartial and it made a difference to talk to someone who was not emotionally connected. In actual fact we sort of became friends too and it was a nice open sort of relationship, comfortable and easy going. All in all now was a nice time for me and even though my days and sometimes my nights were quite hectic, life was not too bad at all. The issue with Hugh and the erection was still clearly there and from time to time the girls came round and we talked about the giant cock syndrome as they called it and of course the jokes were thrown backwards and forwards too. It did not seem to matter, although from time to time I asked Karen and Shola to not be so loud as Hugh may be able to hear us and I don't want him to be upset. Both the girls understood and obliged me by being quieter, but sometimes they did forget and became a little more vocal from time to time, after all girls will be girls.

There are many times now where I simply forget Hugh is in my home and there are other times when I just continually talk to him about everything and nothing. I put on the radio and sing as I work round the house and quite often the TV is on too. It benefits both James and Hugh and, to be honest, me as well because the television is sometimes the only adult company I have to listen to.

Some days things are very good and like the balance offered by the Yin and the Yan some days are not so good too. I have now got used to a routine and each day has become very repetitious, not that this is a bad thing, but routine also kills the spirit. Although I do try to vary things from time to time, it is difficult to make changes in what I do and when I do it.

It has now been some time since I had any sexual contact, either male or female, and I really suppose I was becoming frustrated and I think it is starting to tell on my mood. On a number of occasions I have snapped at James and I put it down to being tired and the frustrated feelings I was having.

One day I was watching the television and a romantic movie was on but somewhere in the middle of the film there was a semi passionate scene between the two main characters and although it wasn't much to watch it turned me on. As I watched the two of them making love in the film, and even though I knew it was just a TV movie, I started to sweat and I wanted some of what was happening on the television. Now I know I can't be the first person in the world this has happened to but this feeling I was getting was extreme and it took a hold of me in a crazy way.

I remembered James was upstairs asleep. It was mid-afternoon and he always slept around this time so he was not a problem. The next thing is, what was I going to do about these feelings? I sat down and pulled up my skirt and started to finger myself. My fanny was soaking wet so it was a nice soft feeling as I rubbed myself. I had not masturbated for some time and god did I need that feeling. I did this for a while but it was not enough. Then I remembered the vibrator Karen and I had used a while back. She had brought it to my home a few times and she had used it herself or we had shared it together. The last time she left it here and I thanked god for that.

I went to the draw where it was and pulled it out, I took off my skirt and my panties and switched the beast on. There was no gradual start today it was full power all the way and fuck me it was fantastic. I pushed the vibrator hard up into my cunt and it was amazing. I pulled it out and used it around the lips of my pussy, in fact I put it everywhere. I even stuck it up my arse and that felt good too. I started to feel my first orgasm come and I nearly passed out, it was a fucking beauty. I had been denied these feelings for some time now and it was good to just let myself go and not have to worry about anything else and just enjoy what I was feeling.

My first orgasm has come and gone but the second one is rapidly approaching again, with the vibrator still on full power I pushed it up inside my fanny as far as it would go. I twisted it around and around and then withdrew it from inside my cunt and used the head of the vibro on the lips of my pussy, this was an extraordinary feeling. I still had on my blouse and I could feel my nipples standing out proud from my breasts. I kept working the vibrator with my left hand while playing with my tits using my right hand. Sure enough, orgasm number two hit me like a steam train and then it was there, fully and complete, and it was equal to the first climax in every way possible.

I sat back on the floor and relaxed briefly for a moment, I was sweating very hard indeed.

Before the pregnancy I had a good figure and as all things of this nature once you have a baby you need to work hard to get the figure back. Since James had been born I had been exercising regularly at home and with a bit of dietary control I was starting to return back to where my body used to be. It was not exactly as it was but my figure was coming back slowly and surely. These thoughts were going on in my head when I started to feel horny again; it was strange but I wasn't done yet.

I was about to start to masturbate when I looked across the room and saw Hugh G and his cock. It was almost a reflex reaction that I stood up and went across the room to him. I could see clearly the bulge under the sheets and I wanted it here and now. I pulled back the bedclothes and there it was, as large as it always was and it looked magnificent. I went over to the baby box where I kept all of James' baby items such as powders and cream as well as other items and I pulled out a bottle of baby oil. I went back to Hugh and put the oil in my hand and then covered his cock in oil.

I pulled back the foreskin and slid my hand up and down his huge shaft. It felt fantastic in my hands so I started to wank him, I decided to bring him off. I sucked his cock end for a while, I could taste the baby oil but I did not mind that. I rubbed his cock and licked the end and eventually I took it far into my mouth and down my throat, I felt like Linda Lovelace from Deep Throat fame and that is going back a few years now. Anyway, I worked Hugh's cock hard and eventually it gushed spunk like a fountain, it shot off everywhere. It seemed like it would never stop, it was thick and creamy and very hot indeed. His erection gradually went down and I licked his limp penis and some of his spunk for a while but that was not all I wanted. I rubbed the rest of the oil on his body and dried my hands on my own skin and I waited for the cock to grow again and it was not long before it came back up.

I got onto the bed and sat astride Hugh. He lay still under me as I plunged onto his cock with full force and I started to ride him like a mad woman. I started to fuck him and banged my body down on top of him over and over again. A couple of times I felt him push back in some sort of automatic response but I was doing the work and I was enjoying every fucking minute of it. I turned around and put my back towards Hugh but I was still sat on his cock and I worked my fanny up and down on his cock. This was a good position for me and it touched different parts inside my cunt and it made me climax a different way. I started with a steady rhythm and gradually picked up speed until I was bringing myself to a third orgasm, and this was the best of all.

I felt my body getting tighter and tighter until I erupted in an amazing and exploding orgasm. *Fuck me* it was fantastic and God was it good. I collapsed onto Hugh's legs with my back towards him and I just lay still. I was sweating like crazy but I had just worked very hard for my pleasure.

I had read somewhere once that having sex vigorously was the equivalent of walking four miles. Well if that was the case I must have just run 20 miles! With that thought I started to laugh. It was nice to have felt this powerful sexual feeling and a good laugh too. It was a good day and to combine laughter and passion together was something I had not done for a long time. And as for today I won't forget this moment for a long while. I turned around and lay on Hugh's chest and I kissed him and as I did this I felt his cock grow again inside of me, what a wonderful feeling indeed.

While lying on top of Hugh I noticed a curious thing. Although Hugh had been inside a hospital for a long time his skin was still tanned, almost as he was the day he arrived at the hospital. In my mind I had naturally assumed it was a suntan, but looking at him now it was more obvious to me that he had a natural skin colour, like that of a foreign person, maybe European or something like that. It is strange how you don't always see the obvious in front of you and this skin colour thing had been staring me in the face for months. It only became clearer because I was spending a lot more time with Hugh. I realised I was seeing many things about this man in a different way, just like a new marriage I suppose, but not, if you know what I mean.

Anyway, I was now more relaxed and feeling much better about myself. My sexual tension was gone and with three good orgasms under my belt so to speak I felt good. I kissed Hugh and thanked him for letting me make love to him; it was a silly thing to say really because he had no choice at the moment as he could not really say no. I climbed off the bed and cleaned Hugh down with baby wet wipes and then I cleaned myself down too. I did feel the usual guilt about what I had done but those feeling were getting less and less.

I suddenly heard James cry. I went upstairs and put on my bedrobe, then went in to see my little boy. I looked at my watch and it was feeding time for him. I lifted him from his cot and took him downstairs to feed him. It took about ten minutes to prepare his food and when I came back into the front room I looked at James and then looked at Hugh and I could see the resemblance, they looked like father and son. With this thought I had a tear in my eye as I realised that they may both never know this fact simply because I was not sure, if or when Hugh comes out of his coma, would I be able to tell him the truth about his son, or indeed tell James the truth about his father? What a hell of a dilemma to be in. That said I created this situation that means I have to live with it, and I will!

It is a strange feeling but when Hugh arrived here and even before he came home to me I thought that it would be the perfect end to everything that has gone on, but now as I reflect on all that has happened I feel a different sensation. I am not as clear in my belief about what I want anymore. Things feel cloudy and my vision seems impaired so at this point in time I feel very unclear about exactly what I really want from my life right now. I don't know what I want and that includes Hugh G the father of my son. I held my son James in my arms and stood next to his father who was as usual lying in a coma-like state in a hospital bed in my home. Hugh G had been here six weeks now and my routine was firmly fixed and nothing much changed. I looked at James and I looked at Hugh and thought... what is your name? Who are you? Where do you come from? I still had so many questions with no answers but to be honest there was nothing I could really do so I guess I just have to wait to see what turns up or to hang on and wait for what the future is going to show me. Some choices need to be made; I have fate and providence as my friends right now that makes me feel really good inside; what a comforting thought – NOT!

I got a call one Friday and it was Shola. We exchanged the usual pleasantries then she said to me, "Are you busy tonight?" I replied with a sarcastic tone, "What do you think?" I then quickly apologised to her. Shola quickly jumped in, "I know how things must be so don't worry, I can imagine life gets tense from time to time." I thanked her for being understanding and I really appreciated her sympathetic response. "Anyway," said Shola, "I need to talk with you and I want to see you tonight, if that is OK with you." I said yes and Shola said she would be with me at around 6.30 if that was good for me. I said yes it was and that was it. "Oh," said Shola, "one other thing. I don't want Karen to know that I am coming to see you, well not just yet anyway." I said that was fine by me. "See you later," said Shola, and that was it.

I was very curious but that was all my life was right now. Things were so strange at the moment that even odd situations seemed quite normal to me. To be honest, as the day went on I almost forgot about Shola calling round. I had so many things to do that it completely slipped my mind. Anyway, around six o'clock I did remember and Shola was coming round so very quickly I cleaned up and made the place presentable.

Honestly, the house was actually alright. I spent so much time at home that I was on top of all the jobs, so it took me five minutes and the place looked clean and smelled clean to.

Before long a knock on the door and there was Shola. She walked into my house with a confident stride. Shola was always upright and straight and she was an elegant and beautiful woman and I can imagine wherever she goes both men and women admire her.

As she walked into the living room she turned to me, put her arms around me and gave me a hug. It was a nice gesture of friendship and it made me feel good, something I needed to feel right now. She took off her coat and as she did this Shola asked "How is he today?" referring to Hugh. "Just the same healthwise. He is good, in fact, in all respects. He is good apart from his sleeping state." I offered Shola a coffee and she said yes please, then she jumped up and said to me, "Sit there, I will make them. Are you going to have a cup?" "Yes please," I said. "Good," said Shola, "then you have a rest girl."

On her way to the kitchen she went across the living room near Hugh and put her hand on his forehead, just for a brief moment, it was a way of saying hello. Well that was what I thought. Anyway, a few moments go by and Shola came back from the kitchen with two cups of coffee. She put them on the table in front of my chair and then sat opposite me and looked at me.

Shola sat facing me and sat looking directly at me. I asked her if there was something wrong. Shola smiled and said, "No, there is nothing wrong as such, but I have a couple of things to say which have been on my mind for a while now." Shola paused as if she was about to speak, then she stopped.

I said, "If you have something to say then just say it."

Shola sat up straight and said, "I asked you a while ago about Hugh and when he comes to live here would the possibility of using him for sex be possible. Since he has been here you have not mentioned our previous conversation and I was wanting to know what your thoughts were on this subject."

I looked back at Shola and said, "To be truly honest I haven't given it much thought. In fact I have forgotten about it until now."

Shola said, "Well now the subject is back up for discussion what do you think?"

I asked her why it was so important and Shola replied, "I have women who will pay £600 to a £1000 for a fuck with Hugh, maybe even more. It's good money, it's regular and invisible as well. You also take fifty per cent of everything we get. One other thing, if you agree I want to use him too."

I looked back at Shola and really I did not know what to say. I of course remember the discussion we had about this and I recall saying something like 'alright we will look at the possibility' but I can't remember any more than that. Shola wanted an answer and I didn't have an answer to give her. I took a drink from my coffee cup and sat back in my chair to think this thing over in my mind. I recalled Shola had said she had things to ask me.

"What were the other things you were going to talk about?"

Shola leaned forward towards me and spoke softly. "You do not miss much."

"No," I replied, "I do not."

"Listen," said Shola. "I am heavily attracted to you and I want to make love to you."

I sat looking at Shola straight in the eyes. It may sound crazy but I was not surprised by this statement. Shola kept on looking at me, waiting for a response. I sat up straight in my chair and my first thought was to say to her, what about Karen? So I asked Shola the very question, "What about Karen?"

"I have already told Karen what I want and she is OK with the idea of this. Karen knew I was coming here today."

"You said to me on the phone not to tell her."

"I know what I said to you, it was a small test to see if you would call her and tell her."

"The games people play," I said to Shola. "The games people play."

Shola did not reply to that statement, she just sat back in her own chair and took a drink of coffee. We both sat looking at each other, neither of us spoke for quite a while. For my part I had a lot to think about and I wanted time to get my head around what Shola had just said to me. Another glorious day in paradise was what was going through my head at that point, although I did not say it out loud.

"You know how to stir up a quiet day," I said to Shola.

"Are you angry?" she said to me.

"No, it's not anger I am feeling," I replied to her, "just a bit surprised as this conversation was not what I was expecting today."

Shola always sat there with an air of confidence; it was a thing that emanated from her in the way she walked, the way she looked and even the way she sat in a chair. At this point I thought to myself, is it confidence or arrogance? And right now I wasn't sure which it was.

Shola sat back in the armchair and just waited for me to respond to what she had said, and I was waiting to see how I felt about things, a Mexican standoff was the first thought in my mind. I glanced away from Shola for a moment and then I took a sip of coffee from my cup. I returned my eyes to Shola and she was now looking at Hugh and she was focused intensely on him and I knew exactly what was on her mind.

Before I knew it I said, "You want to fuck him don't you?"

Without a thought she replied, "Yes I do!"

Her response was positive and firm so I said, "Go on then, fuck him."

Shola never even looked at me, she just stood up and turned her back fully towards me. Shola was wearing a midi dress in blue silk type material. It had a zip down the back. She put her hands behind herself, took hold of the zip and pulled it down. Once the zip was undone she let the dress fall to the floor, it slipped effortlessly down her silky brown skin and she revealed a naked body – no pants, no bra and absolutely no fear whatsoever. She looked fantastic as always. I could not believe I was thinking this of another woman, but it was a strong thought in my mind.

She walked over to Hugh's bed and pulled back the bed sheets to reveal the fully erect cock that was waiting there for her. Shola took hold of Hugh's erect penis and pulled back the foreskin all the way until it was tight; the end of the cock was purple and bulging. Shola leaned forward over Hugh and put his cock in her mouth. She moved her head up and down the shaft nearly taking the whole thing deep inside her. She started to suck his cock faster and faster, then she slowed down and revealed the bulging head of the cock only to start running her tongue around it and sucking on it hard. Shola was making slurping noises almost as if it were on purpose and wanting to draw attention to herself.

I had a strong feeling that Shola was an exhibitionist and this display of sexuality sort of confirmed my thoughts. I watched Shola and the way in which she touched Hugh it was like a dance, very well planned and very deliberate and very obvious. I could imagine what Hugh would be like if he were conscious and awake. I am sure she would drive him crazy. Right now, just me watching her was starting to drive me crazy, but I suspect that was part of the reason she was doing these things to him, or maybe she just wanted to fuck him. To be honest I don't really know what this was all about.

As I sat back it was nice to watch this all going on. I wondered if I should go over and get involved and then I thought no. Before long Shola did the inevitable and climbed onto the bed and hovered over the immense cock, stood it up in her hand and slid herself down onto the fuck machine and, sure enough, she started to ride Hugh very hard and rough.

I thought she was being very aggressive and Shola banged Hugh very hard and very fast and before long Shola was having a powerful climax and with a slight moan and a shudder of her body she came. I think she had two or three orgasms. Before long, Shola lay down on top of Hugh and held him. Shola was done and she eventually climbed off the bed and stood besides Hugh. Shola has a hell of a body but she knew it and she was proud of it.

Shola said to me, "Look, no spunk. Hugh didn't come so I think I will wank him off, it only seems fair for the poor old boy", and she started to laugh. Then she took hold of the erect penis and started to move her hand up and down his shaft in the customary wanking motion. Shola now seemed in a playful mood and outwardly and openly enjoying what she was doing to Hugh G. Shola stood naked next to Hugh and her right hand was moving up and down the erect penis and as she did this she increased the speed, gradually getting quicker and quicker. Shola put her left hand onto Hugh's balls and squeezed them gently, she then looked at me and said, "He is about to come, I can feel it." A few more motions with her hand would bring him off.

Shola once again looked at me, smiled then put her mouth around the end of Hugh's penis then wanked him very quickly, it was very clear to me what happened next, it was obvious he came in Shola's mouth.

I wasn't shocked at this but maybe a little surprised. Shola stood up removing her mouth from Hugh's penis and she started to walk towards me. She stood beside me, bent forward and kissed me. She then released some of the sperm in her mouth and put it into mine. At first I resisted but then I just let it happen, I could taste the salty warm fluid and I became excited at what Shola was doing to me. Shola stopped kissing me, she then stood up and in a swallowing motion gulped and I knew she was taking the spunk into her. She looked at me and said, "Swallow it", and without hesitation I swallowed the sperm just as she had done. I looked Shola straight in the eyes and she just stared back at me. I wondered what was going on inside her mind and then I asked her: "What do you want?" She moved towards me and leaned over towards my left ear and she said to me, "I don't want anything," she paused and then said, "YET!"

I moved slightly back away from Shola and I said to her, "Well, we will see won't we?" She spoke back to me and said, "Yes, we will", and then she smiled at me and I gently smiled back at her.

Shola started to get dressed and she even managed to do that in a sexy way too. I watched her intently and I could see was also taking a sly glance back at me as well. Shola was ready to go. She now looked her usual regal self, smartly dressed and confident.

"Before I go I need to give you this."

She opened her bag and pulled out an envelope. "Take it," she said. I reached out with my left hand and took the envelope from her. "Open it," she said. The envelope was A5 size. I opened the lip of the envelope with my fingers and pulled out the contents; it was money, a lot of money.

I asked Shola how much was there and why she had given it to me. Shola replied, "There is ten thousand pounds and it is the start of

the payments you will receive for my friends having sex with Hugh."
I looked at the money and I have to say the amount of cash in my
hand shocked me. Shola could see the surprise on my face and she just
smiled. "That money in your hand is just the start of it, there could be
a lot more to come your way."

I looked over at Hugh and then looked at the money and finally
my gaze turned to Shola. Before I could speak Shola said, "Do not feel
guilty, I can see the look on your face and it is not about guilt Leigh,
it's about building a future. No one is being hurt here, so do not feel
guilty, feel proud that you are helping people in a very special way."

I smiled back at Shola and thanked her for her words. It did help
and it gave me a small piece of comfort. However, the guilt she had
seen on my face was still there and I could still feel it inside of me
too.

Shola gave me a kiss on the cheek and with that she was gone
and Hugh, James and I were alone together again once again. I
looked around and I feel alone and my solitude is really of my own
choosing, although I feel alone I know I am not but tonight feels
especially difficult because I want to be able to talk to my man and
sadly I cannot.

A great deal of thought is in my mind and I feel distressed, I want a
human conversation and even though I can talk to him he is not able
to talk back and converse with me. Here I go again, the tears are falling
down my cheeks once more and my heart is heavy. What the hell am I
doing with my life? I feel like I have lost control and everyone around
me is making changes to my life and I can't seem to get a grip on things.
It seems crazy to me that Shola has just put £10,000 cash in my hand
and I don't have to do anything for it except let her and her friends have
sex with the father of my son who by the way is in a long term coma-
like state and he does not know what the hell is happening to him. The
whole situation is bloody crazy and at times I feel guilty, but the more
I think of things I keep saying to myself, what the hell, let's do it – take
a chance. After all, Hugh, or whatever the guy's real name is, might
be lying there thinking '*Wow*! This is great bring it on, I am loving
this, all these women shagging me. Christ this is fantastic.' The other

side of the coin is that he may be in pure misery and fully aware of his surroundings and in agony and pain because he has a real wife and kids somewhere else in the world. Jesus Christ give me a break and let me make some sense of all of this shit. What the fucking hell am I going to do, my mind is in turmoil?

In the foreseeable future there was no chance of me going back to work and as it is now all plans I might have had were on hold. I had always wanted to travel and right now that seemed a distant prospect at best. Strange as it may seem I now have more money than I ever had but I was trapped in my home life and this was of course of my own choosing; I had just never really considered the consequences. I really needed to explore my options and start to get some sort of plan in place, the trouble is I am not sure what I really want, I need to give this some serious thought and hopefully get some direction back in my life and I need to start doing this now!

I got myself a pen and a writing pad and started to write down some basics, in fact the usual positives and negatives and this is to be the basis for my life directional planning. I wrote down holidays, cars, clothes, furniture and things like this. However, it all seemed materialistic and that was not all that I wanted. I thought about Shola and how she seemed to have her life together and maybe if we sat and talked together about this plan of mine she might be able to give me some pointers on a direction to take. One thing on my mind right now was that I have started feeling the need to let Hugh go back to the hospital because truthfully I feel that I am putting the blame on him and really it's not his fault. It is only through a chance encounter through Sue my friend did this current situation come to be. I know I have to accept the blame for how things are right now but also circumstance and fate have played a part here too, and although in the scheme of things there is a down side to all of this, there is also an upside as well. Let me put them on my list: I met this poor man in hospital in a coma and from that situation I have helped some people to have children who at that time could not have done so. I helped my friend Sue out of financial difficulty, I have made some very good new friends, I have now got cash in my hand for the first time in years and I also have access to a huge cock anytime I want it.

Fuck me, I have completely forgotten about the cock, the very thing that started all of this – that huge enormous *cock*.

I looked across my living room to see Hugh lying there alone in that bed and all I want right now is to fuck the brains out of him. I don't care if he knows it or not I am going to mount him and fuck myself as hard as I physically can using that massive erection. And with that I went to him, took off my clothes, pulled back the bed sheets, jumped onto Hugh's long thick cock, rammed it into myself and I fucked him and fucked him and fucked him.

My sex session lasted around ten minutes, I climaxed twice, I got very hot and very sweaty and I felt as if I had released a lot of tension and I really did feel much better. As usual, Hugh made no motion. He did ejaculate and there was sperm dripping from me, actually quite a lot of sperm was flowing out of me. I put some of his juice on my fingers and I brought my hand near my nose to smell it. There was a strange sensation and a flooding of emotions and although I did not cry, I felt unusually euphoric and very lightheaded, not in a bad way you understand, but I think the smell of Hugh's sperm took me back to the first time I was with him and I could feel how it was with me and him in the early days. At that point in history it was uncomplicated and easier to deal with, whereas now it was a situation that was fraught with so many pressures, decisions, lies and sadly, deceit.

I cleaned Hugh down and myself too, I got dressed, made myself a cup of tea and sat in my favourite chair and thought about how I was going to move forward. I reflected on the sex I just had and it was almost insignificant. I needed it, I wanted it and I had it, I felt as if I had just been through an emotionless event to release the sexual tension within me and the frustration I was feeling as well. That said, it did have the desired effect and I did feel better now than I did before I screwed him and believe me I did screw him!

I picked up my mobile and called Karen and then Shola. Once again I invited them round for a chat, I did not tell them why but I simply said I needed some advice and they were the ladies to help me with my dilemma.

*

Karen was first to arrive. She just walked straight into my house now there was no longer any formality; she was becoming more like a sister. Equally Shola was the same. No longer a knock at the door, she too just arrived and let herself in. This familiarity was almost comforting to me and seemed to add to the strength in our friendship and it was actually a nice thing for me to know that these two friends felt that comfortable with me.

They both came in and sat down. I was about to put the kettle on when Shola produced two bottles of champagne from a bag she had brought with her. "Get some glasses," she said, "Let's have a nice drink for a change."

I brought the glasses for the three of us as Shola had asked and I watched as she popped the cork like a professional. I actually felt a little excited and a bit girly and it was really a very nice yet simple feeling that I was having.

We all sat together in the living room, I was sat in my usual favourite chair and the girls were sat on the sofa, the conversation was light-hearted and jovial, we had a few laughs and all seemed good. The mood generally was pleasant and I was actually enjoying myself and the two ladies appeared to be happy too. We had been talking for around half an hour when Karen said, "What was the reason for calling us here tonight?" I went very quiet and just put my head down and stared at the floor. "Have I said something to upset you?" said Karen. I replied no it was me and how I felt and it was nothing either of them had done.

"What is wrong?" said Shola.

"I am not absolutely sure," I said, "but I think that I am hitting some sort of crisis and I don't really know what to do or what I really want anymore."

"What has brought this on?" said Karen. "Everything seemed fine, has something happened that we don't know about?"

"No not really," I replied. "I just feel as if something is not quite right at the moment, I feel that right now I need a break and to just pick up and go and get away from everything."

Karen looked at Shola then she turned towards me and said, "It sounds like a touch of post-natal depression to me."

I felt shocked at what Karen was saying and I must have given her a bit of a start because I snapped back at her saying, "That is bloody rubbish!" My tone to her was harsh, my voice was raised and I felt anger inside.

Karen went quiet and I suddenly realised what I had done and the next thing I started to cry and I even began to sob, I spilled a little of my champagne on the floor too. Shola came to me and held me as Karen went to the kitchen for a cloth to mop the carpet. I held onto Shola with a vice like grip and she held me as tight back. Things started to calm down and I began by apologising to Karen. She smiled at me and said, "Forget it Leigh, I have seen this coming for a while now." In fact Karen said to me that both she and Shola had been talking about this exact situation only a few days earlier.

I asked them both was it very obvious how things looked and they both said yes. I had been talking to my social worker on a number of occasions and she clearly had not picked this up. Karen responded by saying that when the social workers visited I probably hid my feelings very well and I knew she was absolutely correct, I was masking my emotions in public and I knew that now. It seemed that the way I was feeling had crept up on me and although my close friends could see it, obviously I did not. The three of us talked a little more and I did feel better, it was like some sort of therapy session talking to the girls but it was making a huge difference to let out my emotions. We talked some more and from the conversation we were having it became clear that I needed a break from everything and the idea of a holiday was brought up by Karen. It sounded like a good idea – I have some money now and it was much easier with cash in your pocket. We began to talk about the possibility of somewhere to go and the dynamics of how to do this, especially having James and Hugh to consider.

I went very quiet and the two girls looked at me.

"What's wrong?" said Shola.

"It is all well and good making plans, but I have my obligations here to consider."

Karen started to smile, then she laughed. "You silly woman Leigh," she said to me, "I am a nurse and I am sure we can get it cleared for me to stay here with James and Hugh, and if we ask her nicely I am sure Shola will help too."

Shola started laughing as well. "What a stupid bloody question! Of course I will help, we can do this together no problem at all." Shola smiled at me then looked at Karen then she turned back to me. Shola said, "I want to start by helping you right now."

"What do you mean?" I said.

"Well listen girl and I will tell you," said Shola. "My husband and I have a place in the Caribbean, to be precise in the island of the Grand Bahamas. We have a beach front house and I want you to go there for free."

I looked at Shola and said, "I can't accept that."

"Yes you can and you *will*," she said, "unless you have objections to the Caribbean."

"Not at all, I have always wanted to go there. I just never thought it would happen."

Shola stood up and came across the room to me and said, "It's going to happen and it starts now!" Shola put her arms around me and held me tight. "You deserve this," she said. "Let me make this happen for you Leigh please."

I looked at her then I glanced at Karen. By the look on her face I could see she was excited for me and I simply said, "Yes, do it please."

A great deal of emotion followed and the night was an unbelievable relief. The girls left about an hour or so later and once they were gone there was a strange calm about the house, not in a bad way just a feeling of change and you know what, it felt good. While the girls had been here they had pushed me to get things going so I agreed to contact the hospital administration and social services the following day to see what has to be done to make this happen. It was agreed and I feel good about this opportunity and I am going to give it a good try.

The next morning my first call was to social services and Mavis Green. I asked her if she could come and see me and she replied, "Of course, is there a problem?" I told her no, I just wanted some advice and guidance on a few things. Mavis checked her diary and she asked whether 10:30 that morning would be OK for me.

"Perfect," I replied, "I will see you then."

Mavis, as usual, was prompt and at the appointed time she knocked on my door. I opened the door and in she came. Mavis always gave me a friendly hug. She was a larger type lady, not fat you understand, just a bit round and cuddly. Mavis had always been helpful, pleasant and very supportive to me. However, I could imagine that if you upset her in any way she could be a vicious enemy if provoked.

Mavis took off her coat and sat down. She always went to the same chair and she positioned herself in a certain way, almost like she was assuming a position of authority, I suppose this posture was part of the job she did. I made us both something to drink, I had tea and Mavis liked coffee, white and two sugars, and she liked chocolate biscuits too.

We settled down and she said to me, "Alright Leigh, talk to me, how can I help you?"

"Well," I said, "I am thinking about taking a holiday and I need to know what I have to do to make this happen." Mavis looked at me and smiled she then said, "I was hoping you would do this."

I was a little surprised at her statement. "How so?"

"The past few times I came to see you it was obvious that you were looking tired with all the work you were doing. If you hadn't suggested, it I would have said something to you soon."

I was a little taken aback by this. "Was it that obvious to you?" I said to her.

"Yes it was," she said. "Don't forget Leigh, it is my job to look for things like this and I could clearly see that fatigue was setting in with you." She carried on by saying, "It is very common in situations like this for people to be worn down by circumstance and to be honest you have done better than most by lasting as long as you have, you need to be proud of yourself, you are doing very well indeed."

"I appreciate your words Mavis and it does make a difference to me. I cannot see how good or bad I am doing in this situation, I can only be aware of how I feel and right now I need a break."

"No problem," Mavis said. "Let us look at what you need to do and let us make it happen."

With those few words from Mavis I was lifted, she made things sound so easy that I knew I was doing the right thing. After talking with Karen and Shola I felt a lot better, but now talking to Mavis I feel great and I mean fantastic. Mavis and I talked and we discussed what we had to do to make my holiday break happen. I told Mavis that I had spoken to Shola and Karen and in fact Mavis had met both the girls on an earlier occasion so she knew them already and this seemed to make a difference too. Mavis went on to say that we needed to contact the hospital and inform them about the changes needed and request support from them too. I asked Mavis if Hugh could stay here in my home and be cared for in familiar surroundings and Mavis said she would need to look into it further to see. Mavis asked me if I would be comfortable having a stranger in my home looking after Hugh and I said to her immediately, "Karen is no stranger." Mavis asked me if I had asked Karen about this and I replied that when we had spoken she told me whatever I needed she would do, so I suppose this means staying here with Hugh fits into that category. "That's good," said Mavis. "That will help us a lot." We talked some more, we had another coffee and we drew up a plan.

This plan is actually an official document which has to be signed by all parties involved which are: any carer change, the hospital, social services and, of course, me. Now feeling much better I told Mavis of the house Shola and her husband own in the Bahamas and I told her that was where I was going to spend my break. Mavis replied, "Good for you Leigh, very good for you indeed" and she gave me an uplifting big cheesy grin. I am now feeling great, it looks as if things are finally moving along in a really positive way and life feels like its back on track.

Mavis and I wrapped things up and we agreed that I would call her once my side of things was in place such as dates I want to go and also confirmation from Karen. I have also decided to leave James here and although it hurts me I need a break from him also. I told Mavis what my thoughts were regarding James and she was quite happy and very supportive. My intention is to ask one of the girls to take James in. There should be no problems because he knows Karen, Shola and Sue. Whoever I ask will be OK with it, my only thoughts on this are, do I try to keep him at home with Karen, or is it too much to ask of her?

Anyway, one step at a time. I will ask the girls to see what will be best all round. I feel such a relief inside that the decision has been made that I cannot express myself – I really do feel good.

Mavis and I said our goodbyes but before she went I signed a few forms of consent and releases for a temporary leave, all normal stuff apparently and nothing to worry about according to Mavis, so I put my name on the dotted lines and that was it done.

Mavis left an hour after arriving and that left me with some things to do and some phone calls to make. My first call was to Karen and I explained what had taken place. I told her about what Mavis and I had discussed and she was very confident we could make things happen. I mentioned to Karen about leaving James at home with her and she said that as far as she was concerned it was not a problem at all. I did ask her if it was going to be too much for her to cope with and she laughed and replied, "I am a nurse for Christ's sake, this will be a walk in the park Leigh, a walk in the park!" Karen also reminded me that she had the support of Shola if she needed it and I then said I would ask Sue as well. "Whatever you want," said Karen, "just stop worrying girl and do it."

*

A lot was happening right now and all very quickly, and even though it was all good things there is still a strain on me. The work with Hugh was often tedious and difficult and although I did have the support of a district nurse three or four times a week, which helped a lot, I still carry a heavy burden, together with James and Hugh it was at times difficult and things were very pressured and today is one of those days.

I was noticing a change in me and this change was having an effect on the way I was doing things and indeed how I felt too. I love my son James and I had thought that I had loved Hugh as well. However, I am gradually beginning to feel differently towards him. My thoughts often stray to his giant erection and the more I thought about Hugh the more my mind went to *it*.

When Sue had first told me about the stranger in the hospital with the big cock it seemed very funny, but as time went on and I met and then got to know Hugh, my feelings did change both for him and about him too. But that was then and this is now and I have definitely changed in many ways since meeting Hugh.

Having sex with him and then having a son by him, sometimes it was all just too much to contemplate. I am in a state of complete change with many confusing thoughts inside my head, some I can talk about and some I cannot discuss with anyone. I feel vulnerable and that is something I do not want to be right now. I need to feel stronger than I do and that needs both physical effort and emotional thought to achieve; this needs to be supported by the mental belief that I can do what I want to do to make my life better. My goal at this time is to have a break and to go away and have a holiday where I can be left alone to think clearly without being interrupted or having to care for someone else.

I don't think I am being selfish, I just feel I need the time to evaluate and to get myself back on track once more. Right now I have a list of things to do and I am gradually working through this list to achieve something tangible for me, and this is important right now. There also seems to be an urgency about what I have to do and I am not really sure why I feel this, but I do. I have spoken to social services and Mavis and that is moving along nicely, I have discussed things with Shola and Karen too and that discussion has also produced positive things, so that makes me feel good. My next call needs to be Sue.

I have known Sue for many years but lately we have not been in touch too often. There is no particular reason why, just a bit too much on my plate and I suppose she is busy with her own life too. Although I do have new friends in my life, I still consider Sue to be my best friend. I decided to call her and ask if she would come over to visit me.

I made the call to Sue and it really was nice to hear her voice again, it seemed like such a long time since we spoke last. As we talked I asked how she was and she did the same. Sue of course asked about James and Hugh and I gave her the low-down on the two of them, all in all a pleasant chat. Sue suddenly said, "Are you alright Leigh?"

I hesitated and then said to her, "Truthfully, I don't know how I feel Sue." I went on to tell her some of what was going on but what I really needed was to see her as soon as she could make the time.

"Give me an hour and I will be there," Sue said, without hesitation.

"Thank you Sue," I said. "I really need to talk with you and I am looking forward to seeing you so much I cannot begin to explain it to you over the phone."

"See you in a short while," she said. "Bye" was her last word and the phone went dead.

Over the years Sue and I had been very close but over recent months things seemed to get in the way and we did not get together as often as we maybe should have. I was really pleased she was coming to see me and in a way I was a little excited to see her.

It was not long before I heard a gentle knock on my front door. I waited for a second or two and in Sue walked; I had left the front door unlocked for her. Sue bounced in and came straight towards me. As usual she had a nice bottle of red wine with her. She put the wine on the coffee table and then gave me a big hug.

"It is good to see you," I said to her.

"It is good to see you too," said Sue.

She took off her woolly cardigan and placed it on the back of her chair then sat down, took off her shoes and made herself comfortable. I sat opposite her and just looked at her. "Is anything wrong?" she said. "Not at all," I replied, "it's just good to see you and I am just enjoying the moment."

I looked at the wine on the table and said, "Do you want the red stuff open now?" She replied, "Is the pope catholic?" and then we both laughed. I went to the kitchen to get a cork screw and two glasses, I came back in and sat back in my usual chair facing Sue. I opened the wine and poured out two glasses full, I gave one glass to Sue and the other for me. "Cheers," she said. "Good health" was my reply to her. We touched the glasses together in a toasting motion then we both sat back in our respective chairs and relaxed into a more comfortable position.

"I don't know where to start with everything," I said. "There is so much to say."

"Start at the beginning," said Sue, "and just take your time. But before we go on I want to thank you again for the help with the money. My life is now back on track and it's all down to you Leigh."

"I do not want any thanks. If you had not introduced me to Hugh G laid over there, none of this would have been possible. Please Sue, just enjoy what you have from one friend to another."

We toasted each other again and that was that.

"Well, the reason why I called you is that I am going away for a small holiday – the Caribbean."

"Wow," said Sue. "That sounds great, are you going with anyone?"

I shook my head. I looked over towards Hugh and said, "It should have been Hugh, but that is never going to happen and, to be honest, I can't wait forever."

Sue detected a stern note in my voice and said, "What is wrong here?"

I paused for a moment and looked her straight in the eye and then I said to her, "So many things are wrong but also a lot of things are right, I am just having a hard time separating one from the other. People around me don't know what it feels like."

"What do you mean?" said Sue.

"Well, if you can imagine being in a room full of people and yet feeling as if you are the only one there, that is exactly how I am feeling at this moment in time. I have good friends around me but I still feel as if I am alone."

Sue went on to say that she understood a little bit, or at least she thought she did. When she and Steve separated it was not as clear cut as people thought and not as amicable either. Sue stopped talking and started to cry.

"What's wrong?" I said.

Sue hesitated and gulped, then said: "Steve had an affair at work and I found out. He said it was just a fling but I saw them together once and it did not look like a fling to me. I waited until he got home later that day and I confronted him. I told him I had seen them both together holding hands and kissing and cuddling. At that point he broke down and confessed his love for her there and then. I exploded, we argued and the marriage was done at that point. What I am trying to say to you Leigh is that I felt so desperately alone and although I too had good friends around me, I was desperately and absolutely alone, and the worst thing was I still loved him and I think I still do."

I looked at Sue and said, "I never knew any of this."

"No one did," said Sue. "It was my life and private and I could not talk to anyone about it, not even you. Anyway, it's done now but the point I am making is I think I know what you are going through and believe me when I say this Leigh, you are not alone, not at all."

Sue leaned forward and took hold of my hands and squeezed them and at that point I think I knew that she knew some of the emotions I was feeling, it did help me to feel a little better. Solitude is a sad place to be but the fact that a friend reached out to me and talked to me about her own life made my situation feel a little better, well at least for a short while.

I realised that you can't always see things clearly, even though they are in front of you. People get wrapped up in their own world and do not always see the obvious. I never imagined the pain Sue had gone through or by what she is saying now she is still going through. I always thought when Steve went out of her life she had moved on pain free, obviously now she was still suffering in silence. Ironically, I was suffering in my own way from what was happening to me and my dear friend Sue was suffering from her own life pains too. We both sat quietly for some time; we really had nothing to say. I was full of my own thoughts and I could see that Sue was now reflecting on her own life as well.

Suddenly Sue spoke and said: "I should have fought harder to keep him but I just gave up. On reflection I should have done more and could have done more to preserve what we had. It is only now talking with you Leigh that I realise I did not do enough and that I wasted a chance on a lifetime of happiness with a man I loved and a husband who loved me. It is that old tool hindsight, if we could all go back and do better or change things it would be great, but sadly life does not give you that option, once a thing is done it is almost impossible to change things back and that is my life regret with the man that I loved and married. I loved him then and I love him now. What a wasted time and what a painful experience to have what you always wanted and to let it slip away because of an affair. That said, it is a feeling I can't change. I hate him for what he did to me and that will never change, no matter how I felt both then or now.

Changing the tack of the conversation I asked Sue what Steve was doing now.

"I don't know," said Sue.

"Do you still see him?" I asked.

"Sometimes, now and again we bump into each other but not often."

"When was the last time you spoke to him?" I said to her.

"About six months ago," she replied.

I jumped in quickly. "Give him a call."

"Give who a call?" said Sue.

"You know who stupid, just give Steve a call just to say hello."

"I can't do that," said Sue.

"Yes you can. Yes you bloody well can!" I said in a positive voice.

Sue looked at me and said, "Ok I will." She picked up her phone and scrolled through the phone directory until she found her ex-husband's number. Sue looked at me one more time, I winked at her and she pressed the number, and Steve answered.

I could tell by the conversation they both had a lot to say to each other. The conversation went on for nearly half an hour, the gist of the phone call was covering old times and current events, my name was mentioned once or twice and from time to time Sue said to Steve that she was doing well. At the end of the call I heard Sue say 'I love and miss you' and I am sure Steve's response was the same. They agreed to meet for lunch the following week and the phone call ended on a high point. Sue ended the call and she had the biggest grin on her face and both she and I knew she had done the right thing.

Sue and I stood up together and embraced each other and I was over the moon for my good friend, she really looked happy and I felt happy for her too. Sue had drunk a couple of glasses of wine and it would have been unwise to drive so I called her a taxi and told her to leave her car here until tomorrow. Sue agreed, she was the sensible type and knew it was the right thing to do. The taxi arrived 15 minutes later, Sue and I embraced again and she said, "Thanks Leigh, for everything."

"No," was my reply. "Thank you my oldest and best friend."

Sue had tears in her eyes, I wiped them away with my hand and I said jokingly, "Be off with you woman and sort out your life."

With that she left and got into the taxi. As the car pulled away she wound down the window and said, "I will call you later."

I waved back at her and said, "Bye, talk soon."

GOODBYE SUE

About two hours later I received a call on the house phone, the number on the display was from the hospital where I worked. I answered the phone and a distraught voice on the other end of the line said, "Is that you Leigh?"

"Yes it is, who is this?"

"It is Sally Wroe" was the answer; sally was an A&E nurse from where I work. "I have some really bad news."

"What news?" I replied.

"It's Sue," she answered.

"Sue who?" was my reply.

"Sue Parker."

"What about her?"

Sally answered that Sue had been brought into the hospital around 20 minutes ago; she was brought in by ambulance after a serious car accident.

"How is she?" I yelled.

Sally replied, "I am so sorry Leigh but Sue was pronounced dead on arrival. She is gone Leigh, she is gone!"

*

I woke up with someone shaking me and saying, "Come on Leigh, wake up." I looked up to see Karen and Shola stood over me. "You passed out," said Karen. I was not sure what she was talking about, then I realised my phone call had been the cause of my collapse.

"Is it true?" I said.

Karen confirmed and replied to me, "If you mean Sue then yes it is."

"How did you get in here and how did you know to come round?"

"Firstly I have a key remember, for emergencies, and secondly, while you were on the phone to Sally one minute you were talking the next the phone went silent. It was then Sally called me and told me to get here quickly and I did. As I was on my way I called Shola and asked her to meet me here ASAP just in case I needed her. When I got here Shola was sat outside waiting for me. We both came in together and found you on the floor with the phone next to you. The phone line was dead and you looked in a bad way. You were clearly unconscious, it took a few minutes to pull you round; it was obvious that the shock of the phone call from Sally had caused you to pass out. Do you want a drink of water?"

I replied, "Yes I do please."

Shola quickly went to the kitchen to bring me the water. She arrived back as quick as a flash. The water was cool and sharp and just what I needed. I put the half glass of water down onto the table and I thought about standing up. I felt as if my legs had pins and needles which was probably the case as I had been sat in the same position for quite a while. I was still in a state of shock and as I tried to stand up, my legs gave way again. Shola and Karen quickly grabbed me and held me until I managed to compose myself. I had tears in my eyes and I said to the girls, "Sue was just here not a few hours ago, I cannot believe she is gone. Is she really dead?"

Karen's eyes filled with tears as she confirmed to me she was dead.

It took a good half an hour for me to compose myself and although I was not good I was a little better. The three of us sat together and just kept looking at each other. To be honest, there was not much to say. I did begin to tell Karen and Shola about Sue's conversation with Steve her ex-husband. I suddenly realised no one would have told him and he simply would not be aware of the loss of his ex-wife and her sudden death. I thought I should maybe call him and let him know, I did have Steve's old phone number and I was hoping it was still the number he used now. I scrolled through my phone's memory and up came Steve's number. I hesitated and then pressed the button and the call began. Karen and Shola sat beside me and they both held hands as the call was answered.

"Hello," I said. "Is that Steve?"

A man's voice replied, "Yes it is."

I spoke slowly and softly as I said, "Hello Steve, this is Leigh."

"Hello babe," was his reply. "Nice to hear from you, this is a nice surprise. That has been two lovely phone calls in one day, the first from Sue and now you, it must be my lucky day."

"Steve, please listen to me, I have something to tell you."

"What's that babe?" he said back to me.

"It's Sue."

"What about her?" Steve replied.

I paused and then said to him, "I am so sorry but Sue was in a car crash a couple of hours ago and she was killed. She is dead Steve, she is *dead*."

I heard Steve start to cry and he said, "I will call you back" and he cancelled our call. On hearing Steve cry, I started to cry again myself too, I was in pieces.

Shola and Karen held me tight and we just sat together and cried, it was the worst time ever and I felt sick and drained of all emotion. Tonight was going to be a bad night and I still had my son to look after and of course my house guest Hugh G. By the look on my face Karen and Shola could see what I was going through and without any hesitation the two girls offered to stay with me and help me through the coming night. It was a nice gesture and I accepted it gratefully. To be honest, the way I was I don't think I could have coped on my own and the girls knew this.

As I thought, the night was the worst it could have been. No matter what I tried to do it was impossible to sleep. The two girls managed to get a little sleep but not enough and they too had a rough night. I was lucky that my son James slept soundly and of course Hugh, well, he was no bother at all so we were grateful for that.

The night passed and daylight came around as it always does, the morning woke the world and it was a bright and clear start to the day. I was so sad because it was a lovely morning filled with so much sadness and God do I miss my best friend Sue!

It was about 8 o'clock in the morning when I suddenly remembered about Sue's cat Bimbo. Who was going to deal with her? I decided to call Steve again. I was a bit nervous about this but it had to be done. I dialled the number and a moment or two went by and the call was answered. "Hi Steve, it's Leigh. How are you?"

Steve's reply was, "I am not the best, how are you Leigh?"

"Same as you, I could be better a lot better."

Steve sounded rough and it was obvious he had been through a rough night; sadly I wasn't much better myself.

"Steve, I called you about Bimbo. When Sue had the accident she was heading home and I assume that no one has thought about the cat."

Steve said, "It's alright, I went to Sue's house my old home and brought Bimbo to my house so she is back with Zac her Alsatian pal. It was nice to see them together again."

I heard the hesitation and pain in his voice and it nearly broke my heart. As I sat talking to Steve my thoughts went to Pat and Bill Parker, Sue's Mam and Dad. I asked Steve if anyone had told Sue's parents. Steve replied, "It was the first call I made after talking to you last night, I had composed myself enough to call them. It was the worst phone call I have ever had to make in my life."

"How did they take it?" I asked Steve.

He replied in a quiet voice, "They were destroyed, but what can you expect?"

Although Steve could not see me, I was nodding my head in an acknowledging motion. "My heart aches for them, I need to call them," I said to Steve, "but I will do it later in the day." I still could not believe all of this was happening and I still could not come to terms with the loss of my best friend Sue.

Karen and Shola were staying with me until I could manage things better, although the loss of Sue was having a major affect on me I still had to look after my son and his father Hugh G. I did feel bad about Shola and Karen staying with me but I was also ever so grateful. I felt as if my life had slammed into a brick wall and although I had lost my lifelong friend in tragic circumstances, my two latest friends were helping me get through this terrible time.

I had other things I needed to do, the first was to go and see Mr and Mrs Parker Sue's parents and then I must go and see Sue herself. Both of these things were going to be possibly the hardest things I have ever had to do in my life. I prepared myself for the tasks ahead, I felt sick and also I think a little afraid. This was going to be a horrible and painful experience.

Shola, Karen and I were sat having coffees and I was talking to them about my apprehensions and fears, both the girls were full of reassurance and support and while this was nice of them it was me that had to do it. Sadly for me I do not do death very well and I was also very aware of the affects this situation was having on me, I just hoped that my tension would not transfer to my young son James. I kept telling myself I needed to get ready and go and do what had to be done, Sue's parents and indeed Sue herself were weighing heavy on my mind and I was having a hard time getting my head into gear. Oh God, what the hell am I going to say to Mr and Mrs Parker? I have known these people most of my life and I am still having difficulty going to talk with them. I eventually mustered the courage to go and see Pat and Bill; I did not call them, I had decided just to turn up unannounced.

Sue's parents lived in a nice house in a popular upmarket part of town. As I pulled up outside the house I felt terrified. I had been here many times before but this has to be the most difficult visit I have ever made to Pat and Bill's home. I knocked on the door and Pat answered. She looked at me for a moment and just reached out and grabbed me and held me tightly. We seemed to embrace for a long time when over Pat's shoulder I saw Bill, he looked in bad shape and not good at all. Bill came towards us and put his arms around Pat and myself. We stood together and said nothing.

We eventually released our grip on each other and went into the living room, although it had only been a day since Sue had died the house was full of sympathy cards. Bad news travels fast I thought.

"Coffee?" Pat asked.

"Yes please," I replied. "How are you both?" A stupid question I know, but it was the obvious one to ask them both.

Bill spoke and said, "I can't begin to express how we feel, it sounds so stupid but the pain we are feeling is like a knife through the heart."

"I think I understand how you feel," I said. "As Sue's best friend the pain is destroying me, but what you must be feeling as her parents I cannot begin to imagine." I hesitated before asking my next question but eventually the words came out, "Have you been to see Sue yet?"

The room fell silent as Pat said, "Yes, we saw Susan yesterday."

I had forgotten that Pat and Bill always called their daughter by her full name Susan and I never heard them shorten it to Sue.

"We were called to identify her as her closest relatives. It was a formality as everyone at the hospital knew our daughter but legal is legal and it had to be done.

Bill then said, "It broke us both in two, when we saw our little girl in the hospital and lying there without life in her. Christ why her and why us?"

I felt the emotion in his voice and I started to cry, I did not mean to become so soppy but I had no control over how I was feeling and it was a natural reaction in response to such a tragic situation.

Bill put his hand on my head and said, "It's alright Leigh, let it out girl, it will do you some good. To be honest, all Pat and I have done is cry; sometimes it helps and sometimes it does not."

The three of us kept on talking about Sue, sorry Susan, and we even found time to laugh a little about some of the fun times we all had shared together, these shared memories lightened the mood a little and for a short while masked some of the sadness we were all feeling. Eventually, I reached the point where I felt that I needed to go and leave these poor people alone to grieve in peace. I can imagine many more people would visit before the week was through and they needed some time alone, or at least that is what I thought and felt was right for them.

As I was about to leave Pat said to me, "I know Steve has been to Sue's home to get the cat but there are things that will need to be done and I don't think I can do it, so I want to ask you a favour."

I replied, "Name it, anything Pat, you know that."

"Well," she said to me, "I want you to clear out Susan's house when you can face up to it."

I must admit I was a little taken aback with this request but on thinking about it I suppose it made sense. Without a second thought I agreed to the request Pat had made. I told her I would give her a call or she could let me know when it was the best time and I would get it done for her. With that final statement I kissed both Pat and Bill and with tears in their eyes I left them both stood in the doorway of their home. I turned and looked back at them and as I did so they both waved goodbye and then went into the house and closed the door behind them.

One thing that I had not realised is that I must have reminded them of Sue. For many years Sue and I spent so much time together that we were almost inseparable and of course I can imagine seeing me alone without Sue at my side must have also brought back memories for her grieving parents. I still cannot believe she is gone, what a painful thing to have to come to terms with. One other thing has just hit me too and that is I would need to go to the hospital and see Sue for myself. I am talking about her and yet I have not been to see her. I need to go to the hospital sooner rather than later, if nothing else for the respect and high esteem in which I hold my dear friend and also the fact that I love her so much. What the hell am I going to do now she is gone? Jesus Christ this is a shit time. Why Sue and why now?

I went back to my place and Shola and Karen were holding the fort so to speak. As I walked in Karen greeted me and said, "The bloody phone has not stopped ringing!"

"That's normal," I replied. "What else would you expect? People want information."

"I suppose you are right," replied Karen. Shola just nodded her head in agreement and carried on doing whatever it was she was doing when I walked in. Shola then spoke out and said, "All is well here though, no problems, the boys have been fine."

The words she said hit me hard, *the boys are fine*. It almost felt to me as if they were her boys. Was I being too sensitive at this difficult time or was I feeling something else?

Don't be bloody stupid Leigh, I said to myself and I dismissed the thought and let it go; I was being silly and I knew it. I started to tell the girls of my visit to Sue's parents.

"It can't have been easy," said Karen.

"It wasn't," I replied. "It definitely was not." I also said that I had to go to see Sue at the hospital. Karen looked at me and asked if I wanted some company.

My eyes filled with tears again and I looked at Karen and said, "Yes please, I would like that very much."

Karen smiled at me and said, "Consider it a done deal then." She passed me a tissue to wipe my tears away and as I wiped my cheeks I smiled at Karen and she just nodded back to me. Shola once again chipped in, this time with, "Anyone for a glass of wine?"

Karen and I started to laugh.

"What's funny?" said Shola.

"It's you and wine," I said. "It cures all ailments." And Shola too started to laugh.

The mood changed and lightened a little enough to forget things, well, at least for a while. Shola had popped open a good bottle of red wine from her husband's collection which she had brought from home. As she did so she said, "He doesn't know and what he don't know won't hurt him." She was laughing as she said this and it made Karen and I laugh to.

It almost felt a bit naughty, not in a bad way, just a sense that we maybe should not be drinking this lovely wine. However, we drank it anyway and it was lovely, obviously not bought from Asda or Sainsbury's.

"Cheers girls," I said and Shola and Karen replied, "Cheers"; it was a friends' gesture and it had a warming feeling, something I felt I really needed right now. I had lost my best friend but I have good friends around me to help me carry the weight of loss at this very sad time in my life. A thought suddenly struck me and that was I would not have these two good friends if it had not been for Sue. I realised that had it not been for Sue and her bringing together of Hugh and myself, these two ladies would not be in my life. It was a strange feeling that in this room here and now Shola, Karen, Hugh and my son James would not be here together had it not been for her. Isn't life and indeed fate a strange thing? I had a shiver over my back as if someone was walking over my grave. Sue I miss you my good friend was the thought in my mind!

A touch of reality as I heard my son James make a noise and I guess it was feeding time at the zoo. As I stood up to see to him Karen said,

"Sit girl, we will do it, you take it easy at least for a while longer."

I sat back into my chair with my glass of wine in my hand and took a sip of the red stuff. Good friends I thought, good friends indeed.

*

The next day approached too fast and I had made my commitment to go and see Sue. It was around 11 o'clock on this Thursday morning and both Karen and I were now ready to go together and see our friend. We left my home at around 11.15 and headed to the undertakers, Sue's parents had used Smithson's funeral parlour. There were only two funeral homes in the town, the other was the Co-op. Because Sue had died in an accident the cause of death had been determined by autopsy, Sue had died of a major head injury with internal bleeding. Karen and I arrived at Smithson's and entered the main door, there was a small reception area and a young woman was sat there in attendance.

"Can I help you both?" she asked us. I replied that we'd come to see Susan Parker.

The young woman stood up from behind the counter and said, "Please wait here a moment. Oh, by the way, are you family or friends?"

I replied, "Friends." With that the young lady went through a brown door only to arrive back 10 or 20 seconds later. "Please follow me," she said. The young woman pushed open the brown door again and both Karen and I followed her through to the chapel where Sue was laid at rest. The young lady asked if we wanted her to stay or whether we were both alright. I politely thanked her and said we would both be fine. The woman nodded her head at me and gently smiled and walked out of the chapel and back to reception.

I tilted my head down towards the coffin where Sue was lying. As I did so I felt a tear roll down my cheek, Karen too had looked towards Sue and she also had tears in her eyes. Neither of us spoke but we were both feeling the same things I think and as we stood there I put my left hand across to Karen and she put her right hand out to mine, we connected our hands together and just stood there in silence together holding hands and feeling the pain and sadness together.

All told we were there about 15 minutes and as we stood there I reflected on how attractive Sue had been in life and how peaceful she looked in death; it was a strange thought but it was what went through my mind. As Karen and I were about to go I leaned forward and kissed Sue on the forehead. As my lips made contact with her skin, I could feel the cold harsh sensation of death and it brought a stark reality back to me of what I was here for.

My best friend in the whole world was dead and a large part of me has just died with her.

I turned to look back at her one more time and for me this would be the last time as I did not want to see her in that box again without it being covered up. As I walked away, still holding Karen's hand, I said in my mind: Goodbye Sue, I love you and I will miss you forever.

Karen and I walked out of the chapel and through the brown door. As we came back into the reception we saw the young woman sat back behind the desk, she looked up and said, "Are you alright?" We both replied, "Yes we are." I then said, "Thank you for your help." Karen said the same and without another word from the two of us we both left the Smithson's funeral home and away we went.

When we got back to my place Sue's mother had called and left a message with Shola. She had left information about the funeral and also to say there was a piece in the local newspaper about Sue's death. Sue was well known in the community and it will obviously be a big shock to all those that know her. She had a great deal of family, friends and colleagues who will all miss her terribly, it is a real tragedy for everyone, especially me!

The funeral had been planned for the following Tuesday. There was to be a service at Sue's parents' local church and then Sue was to be cremated. I was not looking forward to any of this but as usual Karen and Shola will be with me to support and help as best they could. In the past year I feel that I have been on a turbulent journey, some of my path has been filled with joy and some elements scattered with pain. Sadly, right now I firmly believe that I would trade all of the happiness found if I could bring back my best friend Sue. My heart has never felt so much sadness and never have I hurt as much as I do right now.

Tuesday came around all too quickly and the time of the funeral drew near. I felt physically sick in the pit of my stomach and I think Karen did too. Shola was to stay with the boys and also a bank nurse was going to help out as well. I asked the hospital and social services for the extra help through this difficult time, there were no objections from any party. In actual fact I was commended for asking for the help. I was told I had used good sense and sound judgement. It made no difference to me, all the extra praise meant nothing; all I needed was some support for Shola right now and for me after the funeral and beyond. I could not expect Karen and Shola to devote all their time to me and the boys, I would need to take hold of things sooner rather than later so I was preparing for this as well.

Karen and I were ready to go; Shola gave both of us a hug and then I went to kiss my son James and Hugh G too. Karen also gave the boys a kiss on the cheek and then we were ready to go on our way. We left the house and set off for the church where Sue would be taken to, then onwards to the crematorium. We arrived at the church a little early I thought, but when we got insight of the church there were a lot of people there. I was shocked. I did not expect so many people to turn up, although I knew Sue was very popular and well known for her work this turn out of people has literally taken my breath away. It is indeed a moving tribute to see so many people turn up to pay their respects to a lovely and well respected woman.

We pulled up away from the church and parked the car, we got out and made our way towards the church and the crowd who had gathered there to say farewell to Sue Parker. As I looked around I could see people I knew from work. There were quite a few nurses there, some in uniform and some dressed in dark or black clothing appropriate for the occasion. The nurses in uniform I believe had been released from work for a short while to attend Sue's funeral, then they would return back to the hospital afterwards and carry on with their shifts.

As I looked around I caught sight of Sue's parents Pat and Bill Parker, they were in a really bad way as you would expect. I walked over to them and hugged them both, Karen followed me and as she stood beside me I introduced Pat and Bill to Karen. There was not much that could be said, we just seemed to stand together the four of us and wait to be called into the church. Pat did mention the amount of people who had turned out. She said it warmed her heart to see so many people present for her daughter. Karen said it was a fitting tribute for a wonderful person. This comment brought a tear to Pat's eye. Karen quickly said she hadn't meant to upset her and Pat replied she hadn't. "You are only saying what everyone else must be feeling." As we continued to stand there a man came out of the crowd, it was Steve, Sue's ex-husband. He looked at Pat and Bill and he stood in front of Karen and me. Steve paused a moment and then shook hands will Bill and he then took hold of Pat, he put his arms around her and just held her tightly in his arms. Eventually, he let go of Pat and he then turned to me and put his arms around me too, he gave me a kiss on the left cheek and stepped back. I think Karen felt a little uneasy so I introduced her to Steve. They shook hands politely and for a moment or two we stood there in an eerie silence. Steve spoke and said, "There is a good turn out" and Bill laughed. We all looked at him and we laughed too. "What's funny?" said Steve. "We've all said the same thing," I replied. "Got you," said Steve. "I understand."

We stood a little while longer when the vicar of the church came to the doorway and asked everyone if they would please come inside as the service for Sue was about to start. It was a bit strange because people normally go inside the church and wait but I think those present had waited outside as a courtesy because Pat and Bill had not gone into the church first, a nice gesture I thought. As we walked into the church I went to sit behind the front seats but as I did so Bill took hold of my hand and said, "Please sit here in the front with us, you are family Leigh." I looked at Pat and she nodded for me to come to the front, I turned to Karen and she just smiled and nodded at me to go. "I will sit behind you," she said.

The church filled quickly and very quietly, with a few standing at the back of the church this was indeed a full house.

The Vicar stood at the front of the church and began to speak. As he spoke I remember hearing him say, "We are gathered here today to say farewell to a beautiful young woman Susan Parker ... " and that was as much as I can remember. From that point onwards my mind was a blank and all I could think of was Sue and I discussing a man that had been brought into the hospital a year or so ago – that man was Hugh G. My thoughts and memories flooded back into my mind and they were vivid.

My thought process was broken when I felt someone move next to me and it was Bill. He stood up to go to the front of the church and say a few words. Bill stood next to the vicar and he looked like a little lost boy, Bill paused for a moment to compose himself and he began to speak of his daughter. As Bill addressed the congregation my eyes were grabbed by the sight next to him and that was the coffin that Sue was in. I had not noticed it when I arrived but I could definitely see it now. I once again felt sick inside as the stark reality hit me again as this was truly goodbye to my best friend Sue. As I sat there my head fell forward and I thought I was going to pass out when suddenly a hand on my shoulder brought me back to the here and now. Karen had leaned forward and said to me in a whispered voice, "Keep breathing slow and steady, in through the nose and out through the mouth and keep doing it." Without a word I just nodded my head once and did as she asked, within a moment or two I started to feel a little better.

The next thing I remember Bill was now sat beside me once again and he had finished his eulogy, and for me I can't remember a word, not one word! Before I knew it we were all leaving the church and heading for the crematorium. Sue's coffin was brought out and put into the back of the hearse. The hearse then moved off and the convoy of vehicles fell in line behind it. Pat and Bill asked if I wanted to travel with them but I declined saying that I had brought my own car. Within ten minutes of travel we were at the crematorium.

The hearse drew up outside the main door way of the crematorium. Sue's coffin was taken out of the vehicle by the bearers and everyone followed behind as the coffin was carried through the door and into the crematorium itself.

It was not possible for everyone to get in and although a number of people from the church service had not come to the cremation, there was still quite a number of people attending the cremation itself.

I was stood about half way into the building with Karen at my side, we both held hands as I heard the vicar say a few short words and as he did this the coffin was drawn into the furnace and Sue was now gone forever. This was almost a final statement of non return. It seems almost strange to say but it was as if Sue may still have come back, up to that point, even though I knew she would not. The deed was done and the funeral of my best friend was over. However, I felt that a time of mourning was about to start and not just for me but for many other friends and family members too. As I looked around I saw Pat and Bill. I made my way towards them, hastily followed by Karen. "Are you coming back to the house?" said Pat. "No," I replied. "Thank you, but I need to get home to my son James."

"I understand," said Pat. Karen and I gave Bill and Pat a hug and I told them I would come round and see them soon. With that final statement I was on my way to leave the grieving parents to see to the rest of the mourners, a task I did not envy them at all.

As I went towards my car I saw a man walking my way. I looked closely and it was Steve, Sue's ex husband. He put his arms out to greet me and I did the same, we moved close together and embraced each other. Steve had tears in his eyes and I was crying too. We exchanged a few words and Steve was about to go into a longer conversation when I said, "Steve please listen, I need to get away from here. When things settle down I will give you a call, I promise." Steve smiled at me then kissed me on the cheek and said, "See you later alligator." He squeezed my hand and walked away. He turned briefly and gave me a short wave of the hand and he was gone, disappearing into a group of mourners.

As we drove back in the car Karen said, "You could have gone with them you know, it was not a problem."

"Not a problem for you," I replied. "But I feel it would have been a big problem for me, I could not have gone with them Karen. All I wanted was to get away and go home. Things got worse when I saw Steve, I was not too bad until then, but seeing him sent me over the edge." Karen replied by saying that she understood completely what I was feeling and that maybe discretion was the better part of valour. We arrived back at my house around 20 minutes later and I was hoping I could begin to get my life back into some sort of order. Sadly for me I was not sure how the hell I was going to do that!

Three weeks have now gone by and there is some sort of normality back in my life. I was thinking about Sue all the time and I was constantly reviewing the life we had shared together. I was going about my daily duties when the phone rang. I answered the call and it was Pat, Sue's mother, on the line. "How are you?" I asked.

"Not too bad," Pat replied. We exchanged a few words when Pat said, "Do you remember me asking you to help me clear out Sue's home?"

"Of course I do," I said.

"Well, I need to do it as soon as possible please." I could hear a tension in Pat's voice and I asked her when she wanted it done.

"Today please, if you can," said Pat.

"Give me an hour to get ready and I will come and pick you up."

"No," said Pat in a very firm voice. "You can come to my house but only for the key, I cannot come with you." Pat started to cry and put the phone down.

Pat was upset and that made me upset too. I called Karen to see if she could come round to look after James and Hugh but she was at work. "Give Shola a call," said Karen. "She will be able to help."

I cancelled the call to Karen and rang Shola immediately, I asked for her help to look after the boys.

"Give me 20 minutes and I will be there."

Sure enough, true to her word, Shola arrived about 15 or 16 minutes later. She came in and said as brisk as you like, "Off you go then, I know where everything is, go and do whatever you have to do."

Shola's attitude made me laugh and I simply picked up my coat and car keys and off I went to see Pat.

I arrived at Pat's house around twenty minutes later. As I pulled up outside I could see Pat in the window looking out, obviously for my arrival. As I stepped out of the car Pat came rushing out, she put a key into my hand and said, "Please go and do this for me and Bill."

I asked Pat what was wrong and she simply said, "If it's not done now, it will never get done."

I think I understood what she was meaning. I asked Pat what exactly she wanted to be done with Susan's things and Pat said, "Use your best judgement and let me know. After you are done we can sort the rest out later."

I went to Sue's home. I had not been here for quite a while. I parked my car in the small driveway and went to the front door of her home. I hesitated before putting the key in the lock. As I turned the key and opened the door I looked inside to see an empty and unlived in little house, I say 'little' but it was not exactly little, it just seemed smaller because there was no one living there. By no one I mean Sue. I entered the house and closed the door behind me, the house felt cold and lifeless and it did not feel right me being there on my own. I do not think anyone had been here since Steve took the cat away with him. There was a lot of post on the floor where it fell through the letter box and that in itself was a giveaway sign.

I eventually started to move around the house evaluating as I went and looking at the large and the small items to be dealt with. It was clear at some point I was going to need help from somebody but that would be after I had taken stock of things. I moved upstairs and started to look into the drawers and the cupboards. It felt as though I was invading my friend's privacy and although I knew she was dead it did not make me feel any easier in my task. As I walked down the side of Sue's bed I saw a light blue box underneath the middle of the bed. It looked unusual so I pulled it out and opened the lid. As I lifted the lid up I found a small pink towel inside, I unwrapped it and found a vibrator within. I started to laugh quietly. I have one of these, I thought to myself. However, mine is considerably bigger.

My laughter stopped and I wrapped the item back up in the towel I had found it in. As I was about to place the vibrator back in the box I noticed a small lump in the bottom of the blue box. The lump had a green cloth covering it so I pulled at the cloth and found money, four large bundles of money. I put the vibrator on the floor and took out the cash; the bundles were in ten, twenty and fifty pound notes. I suddenly realised where the money was from – this was the cash I had given Sue from the girls who were trying to get pregnant. I started to count the money and all told there was just over forty-five thousand pounds. I was shocked as I did not expect this money to be here, I thought it may have been put in the bank but quite obviously it was not.

I was not sure what to do when suddenly I did an insane thing. I put the vibro back in the blue box and closed the lid, I then pushed the box back under the bed, wrapped the money in the green cloth and took it downstairs. I looked for a carrier bag and found one under the kitchen sink, I put the cloth and the money in the bag and went outside and put all of this in the boot of my car. I went back into the house and spent a further 20 minutes organising things and then I left.

I rushed home and arrived back at my place in a panic, Shola just thought it was the experience of going to Sue's on my own. Little did she know about what I had done. It took a little time but I managed to get Shola out of the house, I told her I was tired and needed some time alone. She got the hint and left. I did thank her as usual but I was also clear I needed time alone with the boys.

Once Shola had pulled away in her car I went out of the house and opened the boot of my car, the carrier bag was still there and I picked it up quickly and took it back into the house. I was shaking and a little excited too. I knew what I was doing was wrong but I had other thoughts too, which were: 1) no one else knew about the money, 2) who would it hurt? Sue was gone and finally, 3) I had helped to earn this money, maybe it was meant to be there for me and the boys. I also had a strange feeling of fate, after all it had taken Pat three weeks to get me to go to Sue's house, she could have asked anyone else or she could have gone herself, so maybe I was meant to have this money drop in my lap. God does work in mysterious ways and maybe this is his work or is it Sue's way of saying goodbye and thank you to her oldest best friend?

I stood with all of this cash sat in front of me and my mind was running wild, but the guilt I had been feeling was gradually melting away and I had a sort of acceptance about what I had done. One other thing I did was to say out openly, "If you can hear me Sue thank you for this gift and also believe me when I say I am truly sorry. If you disapprove, I love and miss you Sue, I really do!"

I eventually managed to sort the house for Pat and Bill; I had put things into sections and packed many boxes. I eventually managed to get Pat to go into her daughter's house and I think it did her some good to do this, I think it closed a few doors for her. I contacted Steve, Sue's ex-husband, and asked him to help as I believed some of the things in the house would be his or at least he would have liked to have had some things to keep for himself, as a reminder so to speak. I did arrange also to meet up with Steve to talk things over. He had a few questions for me and I feel he thought I had the answers to give him.

Time had moved along and it was nearly six weeks after Sue's funeral, my life was still busy and I was devoting more time to the boys and life was steady once again.

Sue's house was now empty and up for sale and the insurances had been paid out from her life policy. I believe Steve, Pat and Bill shared the money as the policy had still been in joint names between Sue and Steve from their marriage and never been cancelled. It was a nice gesture from Steve to share the money with Pat and Bill; I think this made them feel closer to Steve, not for the sake of the money but the fact that he still was part of their lives as well. I always thought that Bill saw Steve as the son he never had and I think that was still true now, even though Sue was gone from their lives, but not I can assure you from their hearts.

Karen and Shola were regular guests at my home. They had their own keys and basically came and went as they pleased. I also feel it was an escape for Shola, it was a refuge and a sanctuary because she had a part-time family in my home and she seemed to enjoy the escapism of it all without the baggage attached to it.

We were sat one evening, Karen, Shola and I, having a light-hearted evening when Shola said out loud, "The offer of the holiday is still there for you Leigh."

I looked at Shola and said that I had forgotten all about it. The whole idea had genuinely slipped my mind with all that had gone on.

"Well, do you still want to go?"
"When?" I replied.
"Any time you like," said Shola.

THE BAHAMAS

My heart started to race as I felt that this was exactly what I needed right now. "How long will it take?" I asked her. "As long as it takes you to get the flights booked," she said.

Without wasting any more time I fired up the laptop and got on the internet to check out the flight schedule to the Bahamas. It took no time at all to get flight information and costs of the flights and journey dates and times; there were a number of different options either flying from Heathrow or Gatwick via Chicago, Florida or Miami with similar prices for all routes. The cost was not an issue as I knew I had enough cash put away from what I had made from the girls' night out project and also from what I managed to recover from Sue's house. I was making plans to go and it felt really good.

I was talking to Karen and Shola and as we talked I planned how I was going to get things in place. I was originally thinking a week away would be nice but Shola said, "Take two weeks, what is stopping you?"

I actually agreed with her and said, "Ok ladies, if you will help and social services agree I will aim for two weeks in the Bahamas."

It was agreed and the following day I made all the calls to social services and the hospital support line to see how to move forward and make my holiday happen. It took around three days and all was in place. I had support from Karen and Shola, nursing support from the district nurse and hospital back-up on a rota system too. I had all the documentation signed for, Karen to be the main carer in my absence. The good thing was that James and Hugh G could stay together and that made all the difference to how I felt about my having a break away in the Caribbean. As I see it my family stays together and I have the holiday break away I both need and deserve. The plan was set and the deal was done, I was to fly away from Heathrow airport in London on Friday 10th October.

The night before I flew the girls came around and got settled in. Although they had spent a great deal of time here at my home, tonight was a bit different. Karen would stay the whole of the time while I was away and Shola would be there now and then. My confidence was high and my comfort level was really good with everything. We were having a drink or two of the red stuff when Shola pulled out a piece of paper; I asked what this was and Shola said it was a list of things to do and places to go.

I took the piece of paper from Shola and on it was Rum Runners Bar in Lucaya; this is the heart of Grand Bahamas. The bar is situated in Count Basie Square, a famous place named after a renowned black jazz pianist, musician and bandleader. Other things to see were the dolphinarium, where you can swim with dolphins in an enclosed area, and the place named Paradise Cove – a Caribbean coral reef where you can swim in the sea with all different types of marine life. The whole list of places sounded fantastic including the casino with live music and karaoke too; the whole thing sounded magical and I said this to Shola. She replied to me, "It *is* magical and you will fall in love with the place."

The address of Shola's condominium was in King's Bay Apartments, Grand Bahamas. Shola had pictures and it was indeed a beautiful place. "You are so lucky," I said to Shola. "Yes," she replied, "I am, but there is a price to be paid for this lifestyle and it is not paid in money."

I think I know what she is talking about but I did not pursue the issue with her. I just let this one slip by as I imagine it would be a rough conversation to have with Shola – a discussion I did not want to have right now!

Friday morning arrived and I was ready to go. It was about two hours drive and Shola was going to take me in style in her jaguar. We loaded my bags into the car and were ready to go. I kissed and hugged James and I put my hands on Hugh G and kissed him on the cheek. A hug for Karen and a thank you and Shola and I were on our way to Heathrow airport, next stop the Grand Bahamas.

We arrived at the airport just over two hours later, we made good time and there was no pressure to rush or take chances on the roads. We parked in the short stay car park and Shola came with me to check in. The flight was with British airways and it would be a 747 jumbo jet. I was bubbling with excitement as I checked in my baggage, all was done and I turned to look at Shola. "Do you want me to wait?" she asked. "No," I replied, "I will be fine thank you." Shola stood looking at me then she stepped forward, put her arms around me and kissed me passionately on the lips; I let it happen and responded back as if we were two lovers.

We kissed for a short while then Shola just stepped back, tapped me on the shoulder and said, "Enjoy and see you here in two weeks." Without another word she walked away and left me in the check-in lounge. I was full of hope and expectation and all alone for the first time in I don't know how long. I felt absolutely fantastic and ready for an adventure.

The flight time on the first leg was roughly nine hours flying to Chicago, from there it was on to Miami International and finally Grand Bahamas islands in the Caribbean. Shola had suggested this route as she says you see a bit more and she always enjoys this flight path, I knew no better so I took her advice and booked the flight accordingly. I had a two-hour wait before boarding the flight and sure enough at 12.30 lunchtime the call was made to board the aircraft. It took around 30 minutes for everyone to get on board and we were ready to go. I had booked a window seat as I wanted to get the full experience, I wanted to see everything. This was only the third time I had flown in an aircraft, I had been twice before to Spain and that was it, those planes were nothing like the size of a Jumbo Jet.

I was seated next to a business man I think, he was dressed in a shirt and tie. As he sat down he did say hello but shortly after take-off he put on some headphones and plugged them into a laptop, obviously not the talking type. I had a Kindle to read my books and that was to be my task on the flight, to immerse myself in a good book and enjoy the peace undisturbed. I had so much I wanted to do when I got to the Bahamas that I did not know where I was going to start. However, first things first, read the book and start the holiday in the best frame of mind.

It had not been long before drinks were served, the hostesses came round and offered us a choice from the trolley. I had a gin and tonic, the guy next to me had a whiskey and water. Although he kept his headphones on, he raised his glass to me and said, "Cheers". I did the same back to him. Throughout the course of the flight we were served a couple of meals and, of course, a few more drinks. As each meal was ended I returned back to my book and my thoughts. Eventually a call came over the intercom system: all passengers be advised 30 minutes to landing. At this announcement I really got excited and I had to contain myself, it was not easy at all!

We arrived in Chicago around 21.30 UK time, around 3.30 their time, a bit confusing I know but I don't care. It was an hour and thirty minutes before the transfer flight to Miami International and a flight time of two hours forty-five minutes to get there. The flight from Miami to the Bahamas was around 20 minutes. By my reckoning I should arrive in the Bahamas in around six hours from now, give or take a few minutes.

I travelled across the airport on a shuttle train, this airport was huge. It was a bit frightening on my own but I managed to do it and find where I needed to be. I got to my gate in good time and I sat down with a cup of American coffee and my Kindle.

Before I knew it the flight was called and we boarded the plane, and in no time at all I was on my way. The second flight was a bit bumpy and I did not like some of the feelings I had. The woman sat next to me was a large American lady, she was the opposite of my previous companion, she never shut up and it was annoying me because I wanted to continue reading my book. I think for her it was nervous chatter as I don't think she was a good flyer, that said she was pleasant and that made a difference. I eventually gave up on the book and put the Kindle back in my bag. I can always read my book on the return journey back to the UK I thought to myself!

Arrival in Miami was fantastic, the view as we came in was spectacular and the flight seemed very quick indeed. Going through US customs was a bit strange but manageable, once through security it was a short wait and a quick hop on a very small plane to the Grand Bahamas. I was here at last and it was amazing.

As I got off the plane I could feel the heat and it felt wonderful. I picked up my baggage and found a taxi outside, I gave the driver the address and away we went. Less than 20 minutes and we were at King's

Bay Apartments. As we pulled up the driveway it looked like I had arrived at a palace, it was fantastic. The journey cost me $5 so I gave the guy a five dollar tip, he was over the moon and very appreciative. I got out of the taxi and the driver got out as well, he carried my suitcase to the door for me, thanked me again for the tip and away he went. I pulled out the key from my purse and put it into the lock, I turned the key and opened the door. As the door swung into the apartment I could not believe what I saw, the place was unbelievable.

I walked in dragging my case behind me and closed the door. As I moved further in I saw a huge bouquet of flowers on the dining table. I picked up a card and it said: *Welcome to the Bahamas have a great time, love Shola and Karen.* This lovely gesture brought a tear to my eyes and it gave the holiday and the arrival here a great start, and what a place to be starting in. The whole downstairs area was painted in a brilliant white, the floor was all marble tiles and the kitchen full of gadgetry.

I walked to the end of this very long room towards some lined heavy curtains, I pulled the curtains back to find a huge patio door, I unlocked it and then slid the door back to reveal a large veranda complete with dining table and chairs and in front of me was the marina. It was a magnificent view and I was now officially impressed. I came back inside and left the door open for a while; I looked at the huge bunch of flowers for a while and admired them, I then started to unpack my case. I put some things downstairs and then carried the case upstairs. I knew the main bedroom was at the top of the stairs but there were in fact three large bedrooms and a huge bathroom too. I put my case in the main bedroom and checked out the others.

Everything here was quality and it was more like a well maintained hotel than a home. I did know that the apartments were serviced by a team of specialist personnel and a manager too, so it showed that they worked very hard to keep this place in this type of condition and it was a credit to them all.

I eventually put my things away and went downstairs to make a cup of tea, sorry coffee. Everything had been laid on for me and as I looked around I found the fridge had been stocked with goodies including milk and a whole host of food stuffs, it was perfect. I was feeling a breeze blowing through the room and realised I had left the patio door open. I went to close it and then locked it as well, Shola had said it was safe here but I was taking no chances being here on my own.

I was feeling tired and so I made my way back upstairs, I quickly stripped off and left my clothes where they fell, I pulled back the silky white sheets and slid into this huge American-style king-size bed. I must have fallen asleep immediately as I can't remember my head hitting the pillow.

I woke up late in the morning to a bright blazing sun shining through the bedroom window, what a way to start the day. The bedroom was incredibly warm so I pulled back the sheets and just lay on my back and enjoyed the feelings I was having. I still could not believe I was here and all of the recent events seemed like a distant memory, this holiday really was the tonic I needed. I lay a while longer and eventually decided to get up and go downstairs for a coffee.

I put on a bathrobe that I presume is one of Shola's, it had been freshly washed and folded neatly and left in the bedroom I was staying in. The robe had a lovely fragrance and it smelled really sharp and sweet, just fitted well with the holiday theme as if I were staying in a hotel. I made myself a cuppa and decided to sit on the porch; I opened the patio door and went outside with my coffee and a couple of ginger biscuits at the ready. It was a truly glorious day full of possibilities and potential, I went back inside to find a pen and paper so that I could make a plan of what I wanted to do. My first thought was to go shopping to Lucaya, this was the main area of the island according to Shola and it was a good place to shop and get a feel for the place. I decided to stick with taxis as opposed to hiring a car; Shola had warned me that driving was risky here because they used both the UK and American road systems. With what Shola had told me it sounds like there is no system here at all but there were some crazy rules. In the Bahamas you are allowed to drink and drive even while at the wheel of the car, however, if you are drinking alcohol while driving without a seat belt on they arrest you and lock you up. This place does have some crazy rules. I had by now planned some things to do and one of the sights I wanted to see is the beach where they filmed the Pirates of the Caribbean, it was about five miles down the coast from where I was staying and I had been told by Shola it is a beautiful beach to visit.

My mind is now set and my plan is all mapped out, first stop Lucaya. I booked the taxi for half an hour from now, roughly elevenish, this gave me enough time to get ready and go. I had a quick wash and brush up and I was easily ready when the taxi arrived bang on 11 o'clock. I heard the horn beeping and out I went. The driver wished me a good morning and I got into the back of the car. "Where to Madam?" he said. "Lucaya please," I replied and off we went.

"Are you on holiday Madam?" he asked.

"Yes I am."

"First visit?" he asked.

I nodded.

"How do you like it Madam?" he said.

"My first impressions are it's a fantastic place to be." I looked in the driver's mirror and I could see a big cheesy grin with a row of bright white teeth smiling back at me, my words must have tickled him. It was not long before we arrived at Lucaya. There was a small car park to the side of the shopping area, the driver pulled up, I paid him and I got out.

"Do you need picking up?" the driver asked.

"Yes," I replied. "How about two hours from now right here?"

The driver smiled at me and said, "See you then, have a good day Madam." I thanked him and off he went.

I walked towards the shopping area and as I entered I saw an array of shops, market stalls, bars and restaurants. It was like a maze but so interesting and lively with so much colour and life, it seemed like such a happy place with many people from all over the world.

One of the main tourist trades here was the cruise liners; these huge ships brought many tourists here especially Americans. As I walked around I could hear the different accents and sounds coming from the tourist visitors from all around the globe, it was a truly international place and I was falling in love with it!

As I continued moving through this busy place I eventually came to Count Basie Square and this was the place Shola had said I would find Rum Runners bar. I looked around and sure enough there it was on the left hand side of the square. This bar did not look like I imagined it to be but apparently it was the place to be at night, it was a hub within the Bahamas and everyone knew about it. At this time of day it was closed but I made a point of telling myself I would be back tonight to check it out!

I decided to widen my walking circle to see what was around the outside of the shopping area. I had looked at many shops selling gold, watches and clothes, the usual stuff, but mixed in with this was a great deal of traditional Bahamas native types of items too. Things such as clothes and ornaments were on display with so much colour and a really wide choice of stuff too. It was both interesting and informative and generally all in all it was good to see these things. Once I had looked at the shops and I had eventually found my way to the outer edge of Lucaya I walked onto a large boulevard and here I found all the big hotels such as the Hilton and the like. These were impressive buildings as well and I imagine cost an arm and a leg to stay there. They did have the appearance of high class and style but to be honest I was happier where I was at King's Bay, that place just seemed to feel right to me.

As I looked around and took in all the sights and sounds I looked up and saw a clock and it was about the time to go back to meet the taxi at the pickup point. I looked along the roads left and right to orientate myself and I found a quick way back to the car park. I turned right and within a minute or two I was there and sure enough the taxi was waiting just where I had been dropped off. I walked up to the driver's side of the car and said "hello". The poor guy jumped with a start so I presume he had been there for a while and dozed off. Anyway, this guy did say "Hello Madam, are you OK?" I nodded and then opened the back door of the taxi and climbed in. I had with me a couple of bags with some things I had bought, not much but you always buy something on the first day and I was no different to anyone else. The driver said "Home Madam?" "Yes please," I replied and off we went.

As we travelled along I noticed both left hand and right hand drive cars mixed together and I realise why Shola had said the driving here was crazy and unsafe; it was obvious that the two road systems were mixed up.

I asked the driver how he managed to drive here and he said, "Makes no mind to me Madam, I am used to it." "I suppose you are," I replied. It was then I felt as if I made a stupid comment. I asked the driver his name and he replied Luther Madam.

"Hello Luther, my name is Leigh."

"Hello Madam Leigh."

I laughed to myself and said to just call me Leigh.

"OK Madam."

I laughed again.

Not long after I was picked up I was back at the apartment. We pulled up and Luther jumped out of the car and opened my door. He had not done this previously but it was nice he did it this time. As I got out I asked what hours a day he worked and he said, "Between 12 and 18 Madam Leigh." "Wow, that's a lot!" I said. Luther replied, "That's normal Madam Leigh."

I snapped at him a bit and said to him to just call me Leigh – I was a bit abrupt I think.

"Do you have a direct number and I can call you if I need you?"

He pulled out a card and said, "Here is my cell number, just call me anytime if you need me. I work for myself but through a cab company, so calling me direct saves me money, no charge to pay to them."

"OK," I said. "I can do that, I do have places I want to go if we can work out a deal I will use you all the time."

"OK Leigh," he said. "We can sort something out I am sure."

With that Luther asked me for the $5 fare and I gave him a ten. He went to give me change and I said, "No, that's for you, a bit extra." Luther's face widened into a big smile and he thanked me.

"I will have some lunch and plan what to do next, so I may call you later if that's alright?"

"Surely Madam," he replied.

With that we said our goodbyes and I went inside the apartment. It was a bit unfair to call Shola's place an apartment, it was bigger than that and much more lavish. I would call it a high-end American-style condominium – a condo, as they say on TV. Anyway, a meal and an hour or so later I was planning my next excursion. It was still exciting, almost an adventure you might say. One other thing I had not given another thought to was home, not once. Not the boys, nothing – and it felt *good*.

Looking at my list of things to do I decided to have a look at Paradise Cove, the day was still young and it sounded like a great place to go to. Shola was quite knowledgeable about the Bahamas and she had been very strong in her belief that I should go to Paradise Cove. I called Luther the taxi driver and asked if he could take me to Paradise Cove. He replied, "But of course I can, when do you want to go Madam?" I asked Luther to come round and pick me up straight away, I asked how far away it was and he told me it takes half an hour or so to get there. I replied, "Fine, that sounds good, see you shortly." It did not take long before Luther was at my door and we were on our way. I asked Luther if he had been here before and he said he had, many times.

Paradise Cove has become a small business which has grown to be a very popular tourist destination. The business is run by a family and although they make money from the tourists they also protect the reef and the marine life that live there.

We chatted some more about the cove and also the Grand Bahamas in general. As we went along the poverty of this place was also clear to see. We passed through some fairly desolate places and it did not look good. It was not a place I would like to break down in, God knows what would happen to a blonde white woman in a black man's world. Anyway, I dismissed that thought and we carried along on our way. It was not long before we arrived. We turned into a dusty dirt road and travelled through what looked like a plantation. We pulled up and parked in a sandy car park area, there were around eight other vehicles here but no one in sight. Luther could see I was puzzled. He just pointed and said, "You need to go over there and someone will take your payment and show you what to do. Do you want me to stay Leigh?" he asked me. At least he was calling me by my first name now, that was progress. I asked him how long it was normally for people to stay here.

"It depends on the affect the place has," Luther replied. "Some folks stay a few hours and others stay all day, it depends on you."

"If you stay here," I asked, "how much will you charge for your time?"

Luther pondered for a moment and then said, "Give me forty bucks and that will cover the journey here and to take you back."

I thought that was a great price as I was expecting more, and asked him if he wanted the money now. "No," he replied. "I trust you," he laughed. Luther pointed the way to go once again and said, "You are burning daylight Madam." He smiled. I nodded at him and smiled back. "See you in a while," I said and off I went.

I went in the direction he had pointed out to me and as I went over a sand dune type of thing I saw some wooden buildings. As I got closer I could see people and a reef and the beach, it all looked beautiful. A young and very attractive black woman came over to me and said, "Hello, do you want to stay a while?" "Yes please," I replied. "It's $20," she said. I paid her the cash and she showed me onto a wooden veranda. She told me to wait and that someone would be with me in a moment to explain things to me. I thanked her and pulled up a chair and waited.

I could see people swimming in the water and I could also clearly see the coral reef in the distance. It looked quite a way out and there were people swimming around that area and some others were snorkelling too. Whilst my focus was on the water and the reef my concentration was broken by a man's voice saying hello. I looked up to see a tall black man looking at me. "I am Ron the instructor," he said. "How are you today?"

"I am fine thank you," I replied. "My name is Leigh."

"You English?" Ron asked.

"Yes."

"Would you come over here please, I need to give you some information and to explain the rules to you."

This all sounded very official and not what I expected at all.

"This reef is a place of natural beauty and it is also protected. Although I run this as a business I need to protect the coral as it is in a state of decline." Ron showed me some pictures of fish in the area and also different types of coral present on the reef. He went through the names of the fish and the coral but Ron said very firmly, "Beware of this one. If you get your skin near this it causes you a big problem, it is known as fire coral and believe me madam, it will burn you and it is very painful too."

Ron went on to say that everything was easily recognised so I would not have a problem. "Also, one other thing, we have nurse sharks here too." As he said this I looked shocked and felt a little afraid. "These won't hurt you, they are more afraid of you than you are of them. Are you happy so far?" Ron asked me. "Yes," I replied. "Well," he said, "let's get you kitted out."

I followed him to a counter and behind it were masks, snorkels and flippers. I did use the word 'flippers' and Ron corrected me by saying these are fins not flippers. I stood corrected and thanked him for the information. I tried a couple of different sets on before settling with the ones that seemed to fit me the best. Ron then led me to a spot on the beach and said I'd be OK there. I had my bikini on under my sarong. I unfolded my towel and put it on the sand, I put my bag on the towel and then proceeded to take off my sarong. Ron stood there for a moment and, as I stripped off, I saw his eyes widen. It was clear he liked what was in front of him. I felt a little uncomfortable but it made me feel good too.

"Ron come here, I want you now."

I looked over and it was the young woman from earlier shouting him. "I had better go," he said. "That is the wife calling. Have a great day." And with that he was gone.

I sensed a bit of jealousy from his wife. I just smiled discreetly and got myself ready to enter the water.

There was a mixture of people around me, all shapes, all sizes and all ages. There was a number of nationalities there too, including blacks and whites, all mixed together with seemingly no issues at all. It was nice to see the interaction between all the different people here, it had a calming and relaxing affect on me – something I desperately needed. I made sure I knew where my beach towel and stuff was laid so I knew where to come back to once I'd been in the water.

I picked up the mask, snorkel and fins and went to the water's edge.

the day was blistering hot so I expected the water to be cool but as I stepped into the water it felt lovely and warm, it was not hot but it was not a shock to the system so I sat down into the water with confidence. The water was like a warm bath, just the right temperature for your body to be in; my first thought was that this snorkelling experience was going to be a really good one. As I looked towards the reef I saw about a dozen people swimming in that area. I was told by the instructor that this area was deep water and at the point these people were swimming there were all sorts of fish, including sharks, turtles and many other types of marine life. This was the best part of the snorkelling experience so at this point I decided I was going to swim out to the area where I could see all the marine life. I was here and I wanted the full Paradise Cove experience.

Before I started to swim I had put the full kit on: mask, snorkel and of course the fins. I was moving along on the surface of the water and I was looking at the coral below me. It was only a couple of feet deep at this point but it was gradually getting deeper and deeper. That said the visibility was absolutely perfect and I could see everything. As I moved along in around three feet of water I saw two sea rays swim below me very close to the sea bed moving across the white underwater sand. I continued out towards the large coral reefs and as I got to the half way point I took a rest at the floating buoys anchored midway between the shoreline and the large coral reefs that were in the deep water area.

The buoys were the same as the 'ringos' in Spain that they tow behind speedboats and give tourists rides on. These ringos had a large anchor weight on the bottom to keep them in place. As I took hold of the ringo I looked down to the sea bed below which was around ten feet deep. As I did this I could clearly see the anchor weight at the bottom which held the ringo in position. I took hold of the handle around the outside of the ringo and just rested myself there, it had been quite tiring so far and although I was quite a fit person the swim had taken it out of me. There was also a strong current running too which did not help matters either.

I was looking around and people were still swimming around the deep water area. Some others were resting like me, holding onto other ringos that were anchored about the place, there were around six to eight of them in total with people at most of them. As I waited there I looked to see where I was going to go next. There was a gap in the reef and most people seemed to head in that direction, so that is where I was going to go.

I spent about five minutes or so hanging onto the ringo and this gave me enough time to get my breath back and be ready to move on. I put the mask and snorkel back on and set off for the gap in the reef and the deeper water where the marine life would be. I had to swim about a further 200 hundred yards to reach the group of people swimming in the deep water area.

It took me a few minutes to reach the group and once I got there everyone was very welcoming and warming to me. I did not know anyone there but it was nice to feel part of this moment. A couple of the people pointed for me to look down into the water. I put my snorkel on and looked down towards the sea bed and as I did a new world opened up to me, it was truly unbelievable. There was an amazing amount of marine life moving around below me. I could clearly see shoals of fish of all types and all sizes. The colour was amazing and it was a fantastic sight to see. I could now appreciate why so many people stayed in that area for so long, it was very hard to go away from this place. I started to move around the deep water area and continued to look down. At one point I saw a turtle and a few more ray fish too.

As I swam further out I realised that I was out past the reef line, the instructor had told me not to go too far as the currents were stronger there and it was a bigger risk. As soon as I realised where I was I turned around to go back towards the inner line of the coral reef. As I started to swim towards the beach and still with my head down in the water and looking at the sea bed, I saw a shark. The water was about 20 or so feet deep and the shark came from nowhere. As it moved along the sea bottom I nearly panicked but I quickly remembered what I had been told from the instructor. He had told me that there were nurse sharks in the area and that they were safe. Although I believed and trusted what he said I was still feeling the adrenaline inside of me pumping and I decided to make for the shallow water and relative safety. As I swam back to shore I passed a few people who were just enjoying the scenery and the marine life picture show down below. A few people waved or just smiled at me and I just kept on going.

I eventually reached the shoreline and climbed out of the water. I was exhausted and I realised now how hard I had been swimming. I removed the fins from my feet and the mask and snorkel from my head. The sun was still beating down and the heat was great. I was almost dry before I reached the place on the beach where I had put my towel and things. I picked up a smaller towel I had with me and started to wipe myself down when I noticed a dark shadow coming from behind me, I turned around and found the instructor Ron from earlier stood close behind me.

"How is it lady?" he said to me in a strong Caribbean accent.

I looked at him and replied, "Everything is fine thank you."

"How is it you are alone here without a man with you?"

I replied that I was on holiday, that I needed a break from work and so a friend recommended here.

"Is you looking for some black man action baby?" he said to me.

I was a bit shocked. He is coming on to me in broad daylight with not a care in the world. I was about to answer him when he started to rub between his legs and it was obvious why. This guy had a hard on and it was clear to see through his tight shorts. He pulled the shorts tighter so I could see what he wanted me to see.

"Like it white lady?" he said with a big white-toothed grin.

"That's not why I am here."

"Sure it is lady, why would you come here alone unless you want some black man action?"

"This is not what I want, please go away," I said.

He moved closer.

"We can go around back and get it on no problem."

"There *is* a problem," I said. "I do not want to do this, not with you or any other black man."

"You must be a gay lady," he said to me. "Every woman wants a black man. Come on, try me. It might do ya some good."

I had a thought and said, "Does Mrs black lady approve and by that I mean your wife?"

"She has no say," he said. "I do as I want to do and that's the truth lady."

I was by now getting very afraid and it must have showed on my face when suddenly I saw someone moving towards us from the left. I thought this could have been an accomplice. As I was getting ready for the worst to happen and thinking I need to scream for help I heard a voice I knew. It was Luther.

"Hey man," said Luther. "Why you bothering the white woman?"

Ron the instructor guy looked at Luther and said, "Hey brother, just a bit of fun ya know."

"No fun here, man, on your way! Swim man, on your way *now*."

The instructor guy looked at me and looked once again at Luther and he then turned away and walked off.

I wanted to hug Luther and I said so to him. Luther looked at me and said, "No worries, Leigh, I saw him a long while ago and knew what he was wanting from you and it wasn't to give the swim lessons ya know. When do you want to go?"

"Now would be a good time for me please," I said.

We picked up my things and went back to the car. As we walked up the beach the instructor guy was stood on the wooden porch where I had first met him. He looked briefly and turned away. Luther said, "He is looking for his next target, some poor white girl again I expect."

I walked faster and got to the car quick sharp. Before long we were on our way back to Shola's condo/apartment. As we went back I saw once again the poverty of this beautiful place.

"Are you shocked at what you see?" said Luther.

"A little."

"I was born there, you just passed my parents' house on the left."

That statement did shock me.

"Not all you see is what you see, is it Leigh?"

"No," I replied. "Not at all."

We arrived back at the apartment around 6 o'clock. We pulled up outside the front door and as soon as we had stopped Luther jumped out of the driver's seat and opened the car door for me. I had made a deal with Luther for forty dollars for the day's hire of his taxi but I gave him $60 as a thank you.

"You don't need to do this Leigh." he said.

"But I want to, I appreciate what you did today for me."

"Thanks white lady," he said and laughed.

I looked at his smiling black face and just laughed with him.

"Is there anything else you need before I go?"

"I don't think so. I was going to go to Lucaya tonight and see the world famous Rum Runners bar but I am tired."

"No problem madam."

I asked if he knew the bar in question and he replied, "Sure I do, my best mates work there."

"Why does that not surprise me?" I just smiled at him. "I will call you if I need you, if that is OK with you."

"No problem," said Luther again. "Whenever you need me just yell."

"Thanks Luther, I will see how I feel later and if I am alright I will give you a call."

"Ok Leigh," and at that he was gone in a flash.

I waved goodbye as he pulled away and then went inside the apartment to get a shower and something to eat.

Twenty minutes later I was showered and ready to eat. I put a pizza in the oven and 15 minutes after that it was cooked and ready to eat. I was so relaxed and chilled out it was unbelievable and the feeling of freedom was fantastic. I sat down with my food and a glass of white wine, I normally drank red but I fancied a change. I was still going through the food and drink that had been put in the apartment when I arrived here. There was a great choice of food and drink available so I had no pressure to go out and food shop with the stock of stuff in here; the fridge and cupboards were full, as was the wine rack. I decided to go to the Rum Runners bar after my meal. I felt a bit fresher after my hectic day and a night at a lively bar might do me some good. I called Luther on the landline and asked him if he could call round in about forty-five minutes to take me to Rum Runners. Luther just laughed down the phone at me and said, "Madam Leigh, you just don't quit, I will be there for you. Bye white woman."

"Bye black man," I replied and put the phone down.

I was about to get ready and put on some gladrags when I remembered that I had not turned on my UK mobile phone since I had arrived in the Caribbean. I went into my bag and pulled out my iPhone and turned it on immediately. It took several moments for the phone to boot up but eventually it had picked up the local Bahamas network and I had a good signal strength. I did not expect much on the phone in the way of missed calls or messages, maybe only from Shola or Karen.

As I looked at the screen I could see many missed calls and messages on the screen. I opened the first message from Shola and it said: *call me urgent call me now!* Next message: *Karen call me or Shola now its important call us ASAP!* All the messages were the same and I panicked at the thought of what had happened. I dialled Shola's number as quick as I could and as soon as I dialled the number the call was picked up from Shola.

"Where the hell have you been, we have been trying to get hold of you for two days? What the hell have you been doing girl?"

"What's wrong, tell me what is wrong? Is it James, is he alright?"

Shola replied, "James is fine, it's not James, it's Hugh G."

"What about him?" I screamed. Shola screamed back at me, "Listen, Leigh, listen. Stay calm and listen to me very carefully. Are you calm?"

"Yes, sort of."

"Alright then, on Monday night we were here, that is Karen and me, when we heard a groaning and moaning sound coming from Hugh's direction in the front room. We looked over and his eyes were open."

"What do you mean *open*?" I asked.

"Listen Leigh, Hugh G has woken up. He is awake and you need to come home as soon as you can. Hugh G is awake and out of his coma, Leigh you need to come home *NOW!*"

To be continued...

ABOUT THE AUTHOR

I WAS BORN in the UK and have lived part of my life in the North East of England.

I have travelled and worked around the world, managing some of the largest engineering projects onshore and offshore in many different countries, including in Africa, Asia, the Bahamas and Europe.

In addition to having studied martial arts, I am a hypnotherapist and tarot card reader.

There are many facets to my life; those I have now and others yet to come.

Lightning Source UK Ltd.
Milton Keynes UK
UKOW04n0238130114

224405UK00001B/1/P